MY LOADED GUN,
MY LONELY
H E A R T

Also by Martin Rose

Bring Me Flesh, I'll Bring Hell

MY LOADED GUN, MY LONELY HEART

MARTIN ROSE

Talos Press

This is a work of fiction. Names, characters, places, and incidents are either the products of the author's imagination or used fictitiously.

Talos Press books may be purchased in bulk at special discounts for sales promotion, corporate gifts, fund-raising, or educational purposes. Special editions can also be created to specifications. For details, contact the Special Sales Department, Skyhorse Publishing, 307 West 36th Street, 11th Floor, New York, NY 10018 or info@ skyhorsepublishing.com.

Talos® and Talos Press® are registered trademarks of Skyhorse Publishing, Inc.®, a Delaware corporation.

Visit our website at www.skyhorsepublishing.com.

10 9 8 7 6 5 4 3 2 1

Library of Congress Cataloging-in-Publication Data is available on file.

Cover design by Anthony Morais

Print ISBN: 978-1-940456-40-9
Ebook ISBN: 978-1-940456-54-6

Printed in the United States of America

"The term *blowback*, which officials of the Central Intelligence Agency first invented for their own internal use, is starting to circulate among students of international relations. It refers to the unintended consequences of policies that were kept secret from the American people."

—Chalmers Johnson, *Blowback*

Prologue

HAPPILY EVER AFTER

I want to give you a happy ending.

I want to tell you that Niko and I piled into the Ford Thunderbird and drove off into the sunset. That we bought a house with a thirty-year mortgage on a sensible budget. Every year was a photo album of barbecue cookouts on the holidays. I'd squint into the sun with a spatula in my hand and Niko would stand in a square of green lawn in a yellow dress stretched over her swelling belly. We'd be surrounded by friends who reflected our good social standing with diverse stock portfolios that never crashed. We'd be so charmed, even the fierce coastal mosquitoes wouldn't sample us. Laughing and drinking beer. Life by glossy catalog, paint by numbers.

I'd flip steaks on the grill and laugh at politically correct jokes. I would never, ever let anyone know that in another life, I'd been a zombie. An honest-to-god, eat-your-brains zombie with a wicked prescription drug habit that kept my brain agile enough to master sarcasm and a bad attitude with psychopathic tendencies.

Blood would dribble out of the meat, sizzle on the red hot coals, and conjure a smell from the grave. I'd fall quiet while I contemplate the past. The sun would dim with a passing cloud. Niko would explain my quiet as unease from the time I spent in Bosnia, or that ill-fated trip to Sarajevo when I was sixteen. Any of these would be enough to forgive my stoned gaze as I remembered what it was like to be as bloody as that steak, as I remembered Jamie. The brother who authored my demise and made me a monster. Bending people to his will as one folds paper into origami.

I spent a decade as a rotting, decomposing, undead corpse until a twist of events gave me a second chance. Jamie's son gave me that second chance. He traded his life and sacrificed his body. Instead of sustaining my final years as a restive corpse, I now fret and strut in my nephew's skin.

I want to tell you my days and nights were filled with suburban idyll. I want to tell you that Niko and I got married and built a family from scratch, a family that didn't include my brother or my father, the wily gray fox. I said goodbye to the military life and all its subterranean machinations. I said goodbye to godforsaken New Jersey and the junkies and thieves and casinos and mob bosses and every crooked resident.

I want to tell you I kissed my brother on the cheek and I forgave him.

I want to tell you I honored my nephew's sacrifice.

I want to tell you things were good.

You and I, we both know better, don't we?

★

They sat me in a chair in the interrogation room and asked me what happened, the beginning of November 2010. I told them I didn't remember. There's a darkness in my memory like an empty space in a shark's grin.

Witnesses saw a young man tear out of my driveway in a Ford Thunderbird. On traffic surveillance, I'm pushing the car through intersection after intersection with my fingers tapping the wheel and a gun in my other hand.

I watched myself, this new version of me in my nephew's skin but wearing my fury in his eyes, grinding through red lights and lurching down side streets. The full-time guard at Ruby's Retreat gated community reported a young man he recognized as Amos Adamson blew past his window and rammed through the gate, breaking the automated arm into bits across the concrete.

Footage from Jamie Adamson's house showed a Thunderbird skid to a stop in front of the castle-sized McMansion on the waterfront. I watched myself exit the vehicle and leave the door swinging open. The resolution high-definition crisp. Dash light blinking. In my head, I imagined the automated *ping ping ping* accompanying the seat belt, clattered limp as a snake over the fabric. Keys dangling in the ignition. Fumes coiling from the exhaust pipe. Sand like lumpy cookie dough batter in the street gutter.

They told me the man in the footage is me. I looked angry enough to shake the ground through my walk, to crack pavement with my heels. The gun at my side pointed down. My old zombie corpse had been refunded and exchanged for this new one, but I could not reconcile my identity with the image on the screen. Me, Vitus Adamson. How like Amos he looked—but every twitch and idiosyncrasy is me down to my bone marrow. The way I held myself with my head down in the hot and unforgiving coastal sun. The evil northeast ocean wind punching ragged claws through my hair. A cigarette clamped in my teeth. I've got new skin and I'm already making a down payment on a set of smoker's wrinkles.

Exterior video showcased my brother's lawn, mowed in neat diagonal patterns. His mailbox in the shape of a lighthouse. A silhouette of a woman through a frilly white curtain. Megan, my brother's wife. I watched myself increase speed and make my body a battering ram, pushing my shoulder into it with the cigarette still throwing smoke up into my face. The lock broke and fell to the ground. The door opened. I disappeared inside.

Screams followed. Witnesses report several shots fired. An officer recovered spent shells and dug two bullets out of the studs later. They'll dig the other out of Jamie's dead heart. Minutes passed. In my head, I pictured the light on the car's dash blinking frenetically, on and on, calculating minutes into infinity.

While the surveillance footage played, they let me stew in the chair. But I didn't need footage. My memories filled in what the surveillance missed, expanding into Panovision technicolor.

On-screen, police cars arrived and screeched onto the roadway, one by one. They stacked themselves into every corner of the property with their weapons drawn. A man with a bullhorn. Neighbors peeked through their windows and stood in their door frames while officers waved at them to stay back and to get inside. They didn't listen.

Screaming and commands. Red-faced men in uniform and then a figure appeared in the doorway. A bystander reported his longtime neighbor Jamie Adamson screaming one thing over and over again before the gunshots silenced him: *Beware the echoes and specters! The echoes and specters! The echoes and specters!*

I watched myself drop the gun into the manicured lawn. My hands crimson to the wrists. Blood spattered all over my shirt. Blood on my mouth, forming a clown smile. Blood tracked through the entry way. I expected a river of it to spill out behind me.

Two steps forward and I fell to my knees. Cops rushed me. I leaned forward and vomited into my brother's green lawn. They repelled in disgust, and the last chunk was not even out of my mouth before they cuffed me, my face down in my own sick, and dragged me into the back of a police van.

After that, the screen faded to black.

If you don't know by now, we don't deal in happy endings here.

PART 1

BLOWBACK

I spat out blood onto the prison floor and caught the ox's fist on the second throw.

On the third, he flattened my lungs and settled in to tenderize me. Prisoners howled in a ring, hissed and clapped. Money and discreet packets of drugs changed hands. Like my old suburban neighborhood, but the scenery changed, this HOA run by tattooed men with daddy issues. I wheezed and French kissed concrete walls. The world deconstructed and put back together at random while I took punch after punch after punch.

Spend enough time dead, even the pain becomes something you miss. And you watch it from outside of yourself, like surgery on television. Turn the volume down. Rewind. Freeze the frame. Play it back, make it last longer.

After ten years as a corpse, pain plays a confidence game with pleasure. Every sensation overwhelming and intense. I was starved for it, and I grinned with each throw, moaned when he hit pay dirt and knocked my bones loose. The ox stared in horrified confusion long enough for me to rear back and spit blood into his face. Every cut sustained became a blissed-out high. "Fuckin' mook gets off on it!" I couldn't breathe, but didn't care. I spent ten years not breathing. Why pick up new habits?

I slumped a long bloody line until my ass hit the floor and guards arrived to beat back the congregation. The crowd dispersed. Unruly prisoners pulled away. Someone complaining about the money he lost betting on me. Prison guard, McSneer, snapped: *This ain't no fuckin' casino.*

A blurry silhouette blotted out the cool florescent light while I spiraled into memories of Niko's mortuary. Keys rattled on the chain as the screw held out a hand to help me up. I grinned through a film of blood and gave him a gentle suggestion for how to put his recreational time to good use and keep his hands occupied. Hint: It's not knitting.

He didn't like my suggestion and picked up where the ox left off. They sent me to my cell with a fractured rib and bruises pulping down the middle of me.

Ah, the joys of living.

Going from death to life is like walking backward into puberty. Just when you thought you were done with getting random boners or growing pains, here you are, a thirty-something bastard in twenty-something skin, waking up in the middle of the night slick with sweat and trying not to think too hard about the past.

So I don't think about it. I sleep at night, or pretend to sleep. Navigating a brand new body on fire with sensation and acclimating to the sound of my beating heart, keeping me up all night with the racket. Between bad meals and worse memories, I find a few minutes to myself between lights out and on. Jolted from my zombie consciousness and into this young flesh is like being drunk every hour of the day. In the hours and the days and the months since they threw me in the county slammer while they built my case and gathered evidence and waited for my turn in the clogged judiciary system, I spent time parsing through an avalanche of emotions, mood swings, and memories.

They buried Jamie in the rain while I languished in a cold prison cell.

I wondered if the old gray fox came to his funeral with his retinue of black-suited men in tow. Wondered if they buried my brother with a flag and a medal. Wondered if they left Megan to weep by herself, wondered if Niko was the one who prepared the body for burial and, if she was, did she think of me and remember those halcyon days when I had been dead?

Did she see what I had done to my brother?

"Did they go all Spartacus on you again?"

A hand dangled down from the top bunk, the thin arm of a kid offering me a lit cigarette balanced between his fingers. I took it.

"Not as bad as last time."

I inhaled. The kid's name was Lincoln Tanner, and the crime that got him sent into these lavish digs had something to do with smoking pot and shocking vending machines with tasers. I wasn't sure if shocking vending machines with tasers was the principal crime, or if he'd been put away for both, but he said he ate Reese's Peanut Butter Cups for free an entire year doing that—when he wasn't hacking game station accounts online to max out his player level into God mode. Mostly, he talked, I listened, he gave me free cigarettes, and I nodded in all the places I didn't understand.

A boot scraped the floor. The clank of the cell door. Then, a guard jerked me from the cot and up from the dank concrete flooring where the blood of convicts past lingered. The cigarette fell and scattered. Lincoln disappeared, sinking into his cot and becoming invisible.

A pair of handcuffs and ankle chains dangled from the guard's hands.

"I'll take five more just like it," I croaked as they threw them on and yanked my arms one over the other and locked me down. The hood came down over my eyes. I was in deep shit. These guys weren't the regular guards. They're too 1950s buzz-cut for prison fare. Military spooks.

They dragged me, stumbling, over the concrete floor and threw me into a room. Wind rushed in behind me and, with it, footfalls, labored breathing, the creak and groan of an iron door.

A smell coiled tight around me. A deluge of childhood memories rode in on its tail winds:

The old gray fox by the hearth with the roaring fire. My mother in her pearls and her Coco Chanel black dress handing my father a whiskey while he paged through Julius Caesar's *Gallic Conquest* and yes, *that smell.* His aftershave above the woodsmoke. Pinaud-Clubman. The scent formed an insidious meat hook into the room and pulled me up to my tip toes until I could taste it.

Had he come at last to see his prodigal son?

Someone yanked the hood off. Silhouettes before me resolved out of the shadows into bleached light.

Not my father.

An older gentleman—his spine hooked, trembling hands. As a young man, he might have once been tall, but infirmity shrank and diminished him. His eyes yellowing around the edges. White hair tonsured as a monk's.

Close your eyes and imagine the grandfather you wished you'd had instead of the angry drunk who used to beat your father. This is the guy you would picture. The guy who takes you fishing and puts together model ships.

"Astonishing," the older man whispered as he studied my face in the bald light. His eyes jittered and jumped as he committed to memory my every feature. His brown suit looked like it'd been exhumed from the 1970s. "I take it you are, indeed, Vitus himself. It took the good folks in the Pentagon a tick to figure it out, but we've straightened out the paperwork. We know who you are now."

"And who am I, exactly?"

"You? Shall I elucidate your resume? You were born as Vitus Adamson, the youngest child of a May-December marriage, and by all rights with a silver spoon seated firmly in your sulking mouth. Reports tell me you were a fractious one. You shed blood on the school ground, and most of it was yours. Violent, irascible. Your father offered you a political position in the hopes of calming your wrathful nature by a season spent learning the intricacies of diplomacy, but you enlisted for infantry instead. Your father's report surmises you did so hoping to die in service, a kind of vengeance-motivated death wish. Instead, you did well, suffered no major conflicts, and then, troubles began in the Balkans. You and your brother were sent; and this is where the worm turns. Need I tell you the rest?"

"Don't stop now. Why not give me the online dating profile version?"

"And then there's the posturing sarcasm you perhaps picked up from bad eighties action movies. You're known for deflecting. That's hardly unique. Rather tiresome, to be honest. What was unique was when your brother, Jamie, ran a test virus on you and a subset of soldiers."

The man clucked his tongue.

"That did not work to your benefit, I am led to understand. The side effects were what they now call a 'pre-deceased,' a condition during which you killed your wife and child in a fugue. Afterward, you made a kind of deal with the devil, eh?"

"Well, you hardly need me to fill in the blanks."

"Hmm. Jamie's son, Amos, was the lamb. The sacrifice. And now you occupy his body, no longer a 'pre-deceased' sufferer. I believe that brings us up to speed. Of course, your murder of Jamie has left us the trouble of legal wrangling, for what kind of civilization are we if we do not abide by the rule of law?"

A blade of shadow cracked the concrete floor into halves and pointed the way to a woman beyond him entering the room. Dark clothing. Dirty sweater and black jeans sideswiped with rust stains—or dried blood? She looked like she gutted sharks for a living. An unsmiling face. Beneath her attire, the form and fit of discreet body armor. If this were the movie version of my life, this would be the plucky, tough-as-nails heroine with perfect rock star eye shadow and dressed head to toe in leather. But this is reality and this bitch looks like she sets fire to rock stars. With an acetylene torch.

"I don't know who you are," I said.

"Once upon a time you could call me Agent, but those days have long been over for me. I was recently retired. Recalled for this special purpose. It would seem you are something special indeed, Vitus. Call me Lionel, Lionel Valens. The young lady over my shoulder, you may call her Elvedina Susic. Now I would say we've been properly introduced."

Lionel watched me, severe.

"Do I have to tell you that you are in quite a lot of trouble, Vitus?"

"You're not my dad. I know when I'm in trouble."

"I knew your father."

I forced my face into a stone, into a moonscape where all signs of life have dried up and left hard-packed desolation behind. Water sang through pipes buried in the walls. When he turned his head or scratched his neck with his rough and dry fingers, his mothball suit creased and rasped. Elvedina did her best impersonation of a grave marker.

"Couldn't be bothered to come down himself, could he?"

"We served together, after the war," Lionel said.

"He talk about me?"

"No, actually. He spoke of Jamie. Which is what unites us all here, at the moment. We have greater jurisdiction than the local police department, in your case."

"Who is we?"

"Come, Vitus. You know our policies."

"There's been so many of you from the alphabet soup agencies lately, it's getting hard to keep track."

Lionel sighed. A gust of breath. "Your unfortunate decision to kill your brother has resulted in a change of priorities. Your father has taken interest."

Lionel's voice lulled, tailor-made for Shakespearean theater. He orated as in a grand speech before a vast and unseen audience. I smelled his aftershave, particles of stink settling in my mucous membrane. Like swallowing pieces of my father. What a shame I'd never had the chance to do so when I'd been pre-deceased. Perhaps that's why my father had never visited.

"What happens now is both above and outside of the auspices of any agency. There is no 'alphabet soup' when it comes to you, Vitus."

"What's it like, knowing my father sent you on a mission to babysit his brat son?"

Lionel ignored this. "I have the greatest authority in the nation when it comes to making decisions in your case. The local police department are in the dark. They believe you are Amos Adamson, and you have just killed your own father. Your future, should you remain here, is one of endless incarceration. Your sanity in question, your past unknown, unrecorded, classified. You will die within these cell walls without our help, Vitus Adamson."

"I've been dead before—"

He cut me off with a hand. "Save your bravado for later. In your father's court, your swaggering sarcasm has no currency."

Sullen silence. He was right. I could throw out every cheesy two-bit line designed to bite, but the invocation of my father cut out the spine of my devil-may-care banter. He and I both knew I was no more than the smallest cog in the most ruthless machine. The high standing of my family was the only reason I was being offered an escape hatch.

"You can choose to wait out the rest of your life in this cell. I don't need to describe to you the interminable years ahead, do I, Vitus? You may be crude and vulgar, but if you think you will fool me, rest assured now, approaching eighty years old, it takes no great genius to see through you. Do you want to spend the rest of your life in an institution?"

"No."

He inclined his head. "That's good, for a change. Now we're getting somewhere. I'm a civilized man, Vitus, and not unreasonable or unsympathetic to your plight. Your decision to kill Jamie came at an inopportune time. Your brother had a number of ongoing projects. Those, we've been scrambling to reconfigure and replan as needed. That is not so much a catastrophe as it is an inconvenience."

"So what's the catastrophe?"

"Quick. Good. You'll need to be. The catastrophe is that Jamie was running projects he could not commit to paper."

"Black projects."

"So dark they could not be written. There is no record of them. We depended entirely on Jamie's resilient memory to keep them in line."

"And now Jamie's gone. What a shame."

"You are the author of that shame, Vitus. More than a shame, very wealthy investors expected results from those projects and experiments. How do you think you were funded all these years? You don't think New Jersey property taxes pay themselves, do you? Or your prescriptions?"

"What do you want from me, old man?"

Lionel smiled, revealed a line of teeth behind expanding wrinkles. His mouth looked like mine when I had been dead. But without the mold.

"You were a private investigator before this, yes?"

I nodded.

"We will give you freedom and a clean slate. In return, we need you to sniff out your late brother's hidden secrets. We will, in essence, hire you."

"Oh?"

The old man came forward from Elvedina's monolithic shadow to stand before me. His aftershave, an invisible python, constricted the air. He reached up with one shaking hand to take my cheek in his cool palm. The gesture unnerved me, forced me to lean forward so he could whisper into my ear.

"Your father wanted me to give you a message. He regrets he could not deliver it in person."

He withdrew a paper from his breast pocket with one tottering talon. I snatched it, rattling both chains and paper as my eyes adjusted. I ripped open the envelope and unfolded the single paper.

White House stationary. The sort they kept in the guest rooms on Pennsylvania Avenue. The eagle against the blue shield.

Beneath it, my father's scrawl, like squirming night crawlers burrowing into the paper:

I'm proud of you, my son.

And to my everlasting shame, I burst into tears.

★

Life has a way of drying you up inside. It becomes so you don't notice this missing part of yourself. And then it floods like the river Nile. Like the Ganges.

For years, I'd watched Jamie blaze the path before me. He did it in the warm afterglow of our father's pride and approval. Me, I was the crooked shadow stretching behind him. The sorry, second-born backup plan if anything happened to Jamie.

We knew it, even if we didn't talk about it. If it weren't for the genetic stamp of our features, we would have cast doubt on our own paternity. But for the same pattern of wrinkles at the corners of our muddy eyes. The odd-shaped nose that looked like it had been perfectly fashioned and then dropped on a sidewalk in all the wrong places. Our faces, wider in the cheeks and narrowing to an underdeveloped chin. We'd never be leading men material, but that was our charm—good looking enough to break hearts, ugly enough to mean business.

And people are at their ugliest when they spill their tears. I turned to face the wall and attempted to manfully suck it up while Lionel stepped aside, polite. I was grateful to him and his ancient manners. Elvedina's presence gave it a special agony as she continued to stare with rigid and granite control. Eyes as empty as automated camera lenses.

"What are you looking at?" I muttered.

She said nothing. I swallowed a mouthful of tears. At least the waterworks had stopped long enough for me to breathe like a human being instead of a gaping fish.

"Will you work for us, Vitus?" Lionel asked.

"You know I don't have any other choice."

The cell door opened. Lionel picked up his cane from where he'd left it against the wall. Its silver top shook a crescent of light out into the hall and then he was tapping his way down, past a thousand and one closed cell doors, leaving Elvedina and I alone.

Looking at her was like being in an empty theater when the film credits stop but the reel still runs an empty frame. Her eyes didn't flicker. Smoky eyelashes but no makeup on her face. Bulky clothes swallowing slender wrists, narrow neck hiding a thinner version of herself.

"Don't say much, do you."

Nothing.

"You got a father, Elvedina?"

Nothing.

"You're some hard case, huh?"

Her eyes remained fixed on me.

I wasn't ready for this. I was still trying to figure out how to get comfortable in my new skin and I hadn't even gone into Niko territory. If my arms weren't constrained to my belly, I would have been smoking like a chimney and pulling out my hair thinking about how, exactly, I was going to fix my fuck-up with Niko.

What do you get for the woman you handcuffed to plumbing and then left out in the cold after making hot monkey love with her on the kitchen counter?

★

A sneering guard bearing the charming scent of tobacco and halitosis unlocked the chain and then the ankle bracelets. Elvedina remained my ever-present shadow. Time and time again, I attempted to decipher her purpose and her meaning, but there was nothing there to interpret or figure.

Elvedina jammed a box of tissues in front of me on the table. I plucked one out and blew a pound of snot into it—and then another ten pounds of spite. In the days of being pre-deceased, my tear ducts had dried up like the canals on Mars; now that I was alive, it made my disappointment in this human body all the more bitter.

A kick to the chair jarred me. I flailed, stumbled, and rose to my feet.

McSneer.

Named by virtue of how his lips cut through his face to form his pirate's smile, leaning on his knee with his foot on the seat of my chair. Like my balls were under his heel and he was mashing them into the plastic.

Some people like the prison life. I should have taken to the structure and the discipline with my military background, but I never had been a good soldier. McSneer could smell it on me. Some people lived and breathed prison. I loathed it. Every day from sunup to sundown, I was taking mean-spirited sucker punches from convicts and crooked guards. Some prisons are more violent than others. I was in one of the better ones. But every prison makes an industry off neglect, and I'd watched while McSneer flirted with a female guard for a half hour while a man with a broken leg screamed and screamed for his medication. His pain increased, and McSneer just shook the bottle of pills and kept chatting.

Rumors circulated of "accidental" deaths. Heart patients whose medication was mysteriously never refilled. You don't need to put a shiv through a person's heart when bureaucracy sufficed.

Unfortunately for McSneer, my heart came straight out of the box still in its plastic wrap. And he'd been playing low-grade pranks for my benefit all through my miserable stay. Did my water taste like urine, or was that just a feature of the rusting pipes? McSneer had suspiciously zipped his pants up in the hall. . . . Was that the oily sheen of plastic wrap stretched across my toilet bowl? Did I dare relieve myself without indulging in my paranoia? I provided the watching guards with endless amusement as McSneer's favorite captive guest.

But now his prize weeble wobble had been handed his walking papers. I wasn't his most hated prisoner, I wasn't his favored target—I was just the shitty tetherball he played with at recess if all the other toys were taken. In his hungry eyes, I hadn't become his preferred thing to fantasize about dismembering until it was apparent I would no longer figure into his universe. That wasn't supposed to happen.

McSneer shoved a set of clothes into my chest. They smelled musty and I recognized them as my own. All my effects from the crime scene—wallet, watch, and even the mysterious skeleton key Jamie had bequeathed me before I killed him— that I thought were missing and taken into evidence were now returned to me.

This button-down shirt and a pair of jeans had been filched from somewhere else. The men in black had raided my wardrobe and been to my house. They had infiltrated and knew all my dirty secrets. Guns hidden behind loose panels. Secret hideaways. Magazines of ammo lodged in the underbelly of fake Raid cans. Maybe even the missing porn mag I didn't like. What else had they been nosing through while I'd been wasting away in county prison?

"Next door's a spare room before you get processed out," McSneer said.

"So sorry our time together had to be cut short. I'll send flowers."

He gave me the finger. He'd find someone new to hate and go on being the same schoolyard bully he'd probably been in his youth.

As I turned to follow his shadow into the hall, he stopped and jammed his boot back in one calculated step, grinding his heel into my toes. My face bled out white. A splinter of pain knifed up from my bones and into my gray matter.

Before I could finish my exhale, Elvedina crossed an impossible span of distance to stand beside me. Her speed gave the illusion that her shadow lagged seconds behind her. She reached ahead of McSneer in one arc and swept the door back into his face.

His nose broke—the sound a peanut makes when crushed by an eighteen wheeler.

His hands at his face, McSneer snuffled blood, but it sprayed down his chin. A tirade of curses erupted from him. Elvedina yanked me out of his path with her fist knuckled into my prison orange, pushed me into the hall. My cracked toes howled. She hadn't broken a sweat. Her lips parted, yet no breath moved through them.

While Lionel signed papers in the hall, I entered a new and more soulless concrete block room than the one before. Air-conditioning cranked high enough to see my breath. McSneer's yelling faded into a background din. Footsteps behind me. Elvedina filled the doorway.

"Whoa, you're not coming in with me."

Lionel's voice snaked around the corner.

"Perhaps in time, when you can prove you're both emotionally stable and trustworthy, it won't be necessary. I think if you can tolerate having your privacy stripped from you all these weeks at the prison, Elvedina poses you no threat. She's here for your protection."

Or to keep me prisoner?

"You afraid I'm gonna jump out the window?"

"Elvedina is here for many reasons. As am I. Your brother's death has left a mess of inconceivable size. You do, in fact, need a babysitter."

So I am still a prisoner.

I pulled out the packet of clothes. Underwear, socks, all the fun trivial things I didn't miss from being a zombie. Now I got to do the boring stuff again. Shower, shit, shave, eat, sleep. Rinse, repeat.

Maybe being a zombie hadn't been all that bad, after all.

I unbuttoned the prison jumper and did my best imitation of a surly stripper not being paid enough for Elvedina's one-woman bachelorette party.

"So, how you liking Jersey?"

No answer.

"That's what most people say," I said. "Got a boyfriend? Husband? Girlfriend?"

No answer.

Oh, fuck it, what's a little modesty these days, and I continued to shuck off my prison clothes, down to the last stitch. Bare skin in the stale air. The body might technically be mine but it was going to take some getting used to. Freckles not where I remembered them. Moles in different places. A whole different gravity. I missed my bowling ball belly in my center that used to hug my disintegrating guts inside me. Even my center of gravity shifted to suit Amos's compact frame, and it came with a surge of contradictory feelings—sorrow and guilt, unreality of trying to fit into a body that wasn't mine.

I couldn't shove my clothes on fast enough, yanking myself into sleeves and thrusting into uncomfortable underwear. One pant leg in, an object clattered to the floor along with a dime, a penny, and my tattered wallet—all the things I'd carried on my person and had to surrender when I got processed. I scrabbled after the spare change and shoved my wallet into my back pocket before bending down to retrieve the other object.

The skeleton key, on a chain.

I held it up and it swung in the impersonal light. The end of the key was still ringed in Jamie's blood, where he'd touched it, pressed it into my hand. My murder key. *Beware the echoes and specters.*

I slipped it over my head and stashed it out of sight beneath my shirt.

"How do I look? Ready for my close up?"

I snapped my fingers in front of her face an inch away from her nose. She blinked and looked at me like a spider crawling on her prized carpet. A faint whiff of disdain. Even she knew I was still a monster, deep down inside.

Elvedina, I thought. *That's a name I haven't heard since Sarajevo.*

But Sarajevo was long ago and far away, and I had bigger problems.

★

Home sweet home.

The place in which I decomposed and rotted away my hours for a decade while I solved petty crimes, tracked down missing people, and surveilled unfaithful spouses. Lionel parked the car in the blacktop driveway before the single car garage, and I stared from the window.

Formless hedges ran riot. The lawn, overgrown. My house stood out in the sleepy Levittown division like a rotting mushroom.

Paint peeling off the porch. Had I really lived in it all these years and not realized it was falling apart? Weeds sprang up from the gutter and the windows were layered in dust inches thick. Moths and insects smothered the lamp beside the door so only the tip of the bulb was visible.

Beside the door, a black shadow perched on the wooden railing—my resident turkey vulture haunting the premises.

It looked like the place Uncle Fester went to blow off steam with hookers and coke.

My car door jerked open. Elvedina stood behind it like the Devil's personal chauffeur. My own personal Jiminy Cricket, now that I was a real boy after all.

I lurched out of the vehicle.

Lionel dug his cane into the lawn and placed a shoe in a dandelion patch, a look on his face like he'd stepped into a dead bird.

Hard to imagine my father with friends. How likely was it he left behind the snarls of Washington, DC willingly? Or was he someone who liked to grow roses in his greenhouse, or grapes in a vineyard, reclining on a porch in Venezuela or a forgotten part of the world where old hawks fly when the world has done away with them and their service?

What does that tell you, Vitus? came the hot whisper of the Id.

Blackmailed? I wondered. Coerced? I rolled my living tongue in my mouth. In the past, my principal worry would have been the integrity of my teeth, popping out of my jawline like cooked kernels of popcorn. Now they stayed there, fixed as stars.

A car horn brought me back to reality. If I was to be of any use, I would have to learn how to filter out this endless parade of sights and scents vying for my attention.

The garage door lurched open, the motor whirring. The Ford Thunderbird rested there where it had been returned to the house during my stay at prison. The garage door squealed to a stop, followed by the steady beat of wheels and a figure, emerging from the gap.

Geoff Lafferty.

Four feet, five inches. The spokes of his ancient wheelchair high-shine steel. The barrel of his rifle in one hand and his other on the wheel. Bare feet in the stirrups. I stood in my own driveway with my old friend and summed up every hollow excuse to explain myself. Lafferty pointed his rifle up and away from us and said:

"Look what the cat dragged in."

★

"You tell him everything?" I asked Lionel, hooking a thumb in Lafferty's direction.

Inside the confines of the house, the rifle stowed away in the garage, Lafferty sighed and leaned back in his wheelchair with his hands laced over the back of his neck.

From the kitchen table where we gathered, I wanted to be able to appreciate my return home and celebrate it. After all, six months jammed in tight with a hacker's farts and a legion of confused potheads put away on possession and the obligatory crew of mafia and gangster types did not a tropical vacation make. Leaving prison to return here gave me the impression I'd stumbled into a different room and, disoriented, it would take time before I realized I could eat when I felt hungry, sleep when I felt tired, or opt for an all-nighter, open the door, and take in the air when I pleased without it all occurring on someone else's timetable, without McSneer looking over my shoulder. Instead of thugs and prison guards, their faces swapped out with those of Lionel, Elvedina, and Lafferty's.

Geoff Lafferty of the provincial Pleasant Hills Police Department had once been a go-getter, aiming for detective in a town without need of a detective. After years of hard work, unable to climb higher up the rungs of a smothering, tribalistic police department for whom advancing young officers was anathema, Lafferty fell into trouble. Fate threw a kidney stone at him. To allay the pain, his doctor gave him a muscle relaxant. This suited Lafferty just fine. Heavy drugs suited Lafferty better than fine. He took more and more. He manufactured aches and pains and, when he ran out of good will with his doctor, he ferreted out new supply lines to feed his burgeoning addiction. It wasn't that Lafferty was a bad guy. It happens to people all the time. Between the inanity of ordinary life and the interminable waiting for something different to happen, killing time in a small town any way you can becomes the only way to survive it.

Lafferty nearly didn't.

He fell asleep behind the wheel of his cruiser in an ill-fated turn through an intersection. Twisted metal and blown-out headlights. The engine block sitting in his lap with his spine twisted into an emoticon.

He doesn't sit in a cruiser anymore. He sits in a wheelchair. His spinal injury is inoperable, but had an interesting side effect—it broke him of addiction by no longer being able to provide those pleasurable effects of his drug of choice. In one fell swoop, he lost his ability to walk and shook the monkey from his back.

We knew each other in high school. Ran in the same crowds before life took us in different directions and he went to Police Academy and I went to boot camp. We didn't talk deep, but shared the odd drink or two in a lousy dive bar on the county line. Kept our talk light and not about the things haunting us. That's what made our friendship special, by virtue of not being friendly at all.

The police department installed him in the evidence room, where he stowed away bizarre items caught in the scope of burglaries, murders, rapes, and other crimes, many decades old. Mattresses to yield blood for DNA testing, a shoebox filled with human bones of unidentified people, a cast-iron skillet a wife used to kill her husband. Think kindergarten show-and-tell on a grand scale. His evidence room served as the town's dirty closet and charged him with the task of inventorying every skeleton.

He'd known something was wrong with me in my zombie years. Knew my family was in deep with a thousand dirty secrets. Knew I lived in the shadow of the military and knew I had more than a run-of-the mill medical problem I took pills for. He assigned me customers to keep me afloat and feed my investigation business over the years.

But for all that, I kept my one friend at arm's length because to know the truth, for him to know I was more dead than alive was more than I could tolerate. In the midst of that much suffering, I didn't invite others in. Better to deal with it alone than drag them down into the mud.

Now I had to stare him in the face and wonder if he recognized me. Saw the real Vitus through the brand new skin. I had to deal with him in a whole new way and I didn't like it, didn't like the sense of shame bolting up through my blood and turning my face brick red. All my dirty secrets spilled at last. Ashamed to wonder what items the police gave him. Had he looked down in the evidence bag, at the trigger where my finger rested that fateful day, on the gun I fired?

"You know, I had this inclination that we were friends for a hot minute, and then, I get this call from some snot-nosed kid. This kid—this kid whose father I've known since junior high, whose family I've known forever—calls to tell me he'll explain later, but Vitus needs his help. And could I look after his uncle's house while he's in stir on murder one? Next thing I know, I've got spooks crawling all over my ass and this old guy with his lady friend shows up at my evidence room, and I come to realize, hey, maybe we're not friends at all."

I cleared my throat and looked at my shoes. The floor was clean. I tried to imagine him going through each room in his wheelchair, throwing out my trash with Elvedina behind him and maybe Lionel drinking tea at the counter, poring over documents. All of them, cleaning up my messes, the personal ones and the physical ones.

"You never asked."

Lafferty burst out laughing. "You know who else has heard that one before? My wife. Soon to be my fucking ex-wife, because Selina packed her shit and left me. Ten years of helping me around the house was one thing, but having black helicopters use my house as a landing pad while Uncle Sam and his minions explain to me that my good buddy has stolen the body of his nephew—"

"It was given," I gritted through my teeth.

"—yeah, like I 'give' taxes every year, too, I'm sure. Either way, you owe me big for the shit I've been pulling for you. If it wasn't for Lionel here, I'd be in deep with the PD. They'd wanna know why a charged criminal is calling me to be his best man. But they blew down like straw men the second Lionel waved his magic government wand."

Lionel's hands trembled over the kitchen table as he opened up a file and waited for us to have our argument and be done with it. Elvedina still had yet to move an inch. She was a human sun dial with the shadows growing long at her feet.

"You were always a bastard. Snippy and snarky. It was okay. That's just what we did, but when you dropped off the radar and then I find out well, shit, you aren't even really *you* anymore."

Lafferty leaned forward to look at me in the light. A lifetime ago, I took every light bulb out of the house so I could wallow in the darkness where no one could see just how deep my rot went; now I squirmed beneath his scrutiny and longed for the darkness once more.

"I know it's you. It just ain't your face. Ain't your body. The closest thing you got that's recognizable is your fuckin' eyes, which is really saying something since they weren't much more than marbles eaten through with battery acid, but the hate, the spite? Yeah, that's the same."

"Pack it in, Lafferty. You don't have to stay here. Thanks for watching the house and don't let the door hit you on the ass on the way out."

"You don't get it, do you?"

"Get what?"

Lafferty pursed his lips and leaned forward with his elbows digging into his dead legs.

"I give a fuck, asshole. That's why I'm not out the door. I get to have some fun through your cloak and dagger friends, here," Lafferty gestured at Lionel and Elvedina, "I still got my gig with the evidence room, and hey, that's nice, but I'd like to think that maybe you were my friend during all those years. Was that real or made up in my head?"

Bitterness upwelled in me. What was this? Shame? Pride? I heard a voice eating into my head space, sloppy bites and then my Id muscled in: *You're getting the full spectrum of emotion, eh? Don't always make you sensitive. Sometimes, it makes you swing in the other direction. He's the only friend you have, but you can't say it.*

"Was it really worth boosting him from prison?" Lafferty asked Lionel. "Not too late to get a refund and bring him back, is it?"

Lionel's trembling hand ticked out time on the table before he opened his mouth.

"You'll have many hours to work out the subtleties of relationships, and indeed, Vitus will need a primer on how to be human. For now, we have serious work to do. This house will be our headquarters, our home base. I will be sorting and collating data and assisting on the information level and channeling to our friends in Washington. You will all form a cohesive unit. Every second we waste in idle talk is a second in which Jamie's secrets threaten discovery or languish to our detriment. Your task, Vitus, is urgent: discover and identify your brother's monsters."

While Elvedina did her best imitation of my own life-sized, personal gargoyle and planted herself beside the table, the others fixed their coffee. I hoisted myself up onto the counter and reached on top of the ledge above the cabinets. Lafferty watched me with one raised eyebrow when I brought down a pack of cigarettes and nothing else. A Glock 19 should have been waiting for me there, but all I found was a clean outline in the dust.

Lafferty looked like he wanted to say something about the smokes. He knew all the ins and outs of addictions both big and small. I could have pulled out a crack pipe and he probably wouldn't have said anything. Lionel was from a different age— the same age my father came from, when they gave you cigarettes for your fifth birthday. And well, Elvedina looked like she ate tobacco when all the hard drugs were used up .

I lit up and tossed the pack on the counter. I wasn't about to rummage for my gun in front of them, but I wondered if Elvedina would leave me for a spare few seconds to give me the chance. My status as a looked-after government pet was implied: they didn't trust me. I poured a coffee and breathed smoke and felt a fraction like my old self, but with better skin and less gangrene.

"You really have to do that here?" Lafferty asked and waved the air in front of his face.

"I got a headache."

"They prescribe cancer sticks for that?"

Lionel pulled a pillbox from his briefcase and then fumbled around inside. Single serving packets of aspirin and then Tylenol spilled out. A bottle of Ben-Gay. A prescription bottle followed suit, fell on its side and rolled for the edge of the table. I snatched it from the air before it hit the floor and glanced down at it in my hand.

Atroxipine.

I froze. Lionel continued to shift through his haphazard papers in search of a medicine that would satisfy me, but I already held it in my hands. Lafferty dug through a drawer for a coffee spoon, turned away. Elvedina's cold scarecrow eyes distracted elsewhere—staring through the window at the dark shape of the turkey vulture outside.

No one would know if I took it.

I teetered on the brink of decision and desire won out.

I stuffed the pill bottle into my pocket.

Lionel snagged a set of naproxen sodiums and tapped them in front of me with triumph. He began to gather all his medicines and I waited for him to ask, wonder where the Atroxipine was. My sweaty fist locked around the plastic. I couldn't let it go. My throat gone dry.

"I keep a few painkillers on me, for emergencies. This should set you right."

I rolled the naproxen pills into my one hand and sat down while Lafferty wheeled over to the kitchen counter and brought the coffee pot over to the table with a set of cups. Lionel's silver-headed cane leaned against the table and Elvedina had her back to the sink and her arms crossed. The vulture made faces at her through the window. In another world, I had thought my house would be populated by a family. Kids growing up while I grew old. What I had done to deserve this motley crew of fuck-ups eluded me. But with the bottle of my old medication in my pocket, I'd become invincible.

"All right," I clapped my hands, "what do you have, and what the fuck do you want me to do?"

Lionel cleared his throat. "I was going to outline the terms of our arrangement—"

"Fuck it," I said. "Skip the legalese and get on with it. What's the fucking job?"

I got up to lean over the sink and thumb off the cap of Atroxipine. I dropped the generic headache pills where they swirled down the drain, artfully doling Atroxipine into my palm instead and secreting the bottle away again. I knocked the pills into my mouth and washed it down with a swallow of scalding coffee. Two seconds elapsed before the aftertaste swelled through my mouth; I knew that taste. I recognized it with a shiver that turned my arms and legs into rubber and tilted my head back into ecstasy.

Atroxipine. Oh, how I missed you.

"The job," Lionel said and reshuffled a set of papers, "is clean up."

And by "clean up," he's not referring to the shit you do before you invite the Queen over for tea.

"For things Jamie left behind?"

"Yes."

"And he didn't write any of this down? Did he write *me* down?"

"You were in the black. You were very deep in the black. Until you killed Jamie, anyone who knew about you on our end had been killed."

I pointed at the stack of papers nesting in Lionel's briefcase. "Are those case files? Jamie's things?"

"We've had our satellite officers putting together rough outlines. It seems we have a number of things on the loose and out of our control."

"Jamie was initiating projects without permission?"

"I can only speak for so many agencies. No one wants to fess up to rubber-stamping his actions."

I thought of my father and said nothing.

I held up a hand with the burning cigarette in it. Hard to get used to the idea of those fingers being mine. Scars missing from the knuckles, from the fights and knives of my youth. I whistled through a haze of smoke. Being able to taste tobacco again was both delightful and disgusting, and I loved every minute of it.

"Pick the first one off the top," I suggested. "We'll start there, and work our way through, and find our godforsaken monsters."

"Not so easy as all that, sonny," Lionel said, holding up one crooked finger.

"What gives?"

"Is this what passes for the English language these days? What 'gives,' as you so eloquently put it, is a long list of monsters awaits us. We can't simply take them all on at once. This will be done one at a time. We need you to help identify the subject, find the subject, interview them, and at long last, apprehend them."

"How am I supposed to apprehend people who don't even exist?"

"You turn them over to the tender embrace of your dear Uncle Sam, boy. We have the experience, and we have the tools to take care of these unfortunates. Of course, that might be in direct proportion to the damage they've done or the trouble they've gotten themselves into in the course of Jamie's experiments."

"So, one at a time it is, then. Who's our first boogeyman on the Monster Department's most-wanted list?"

The sun set beyond the vulture, who sunned himself with languid black eyes. I moved out the papers from the uppermost file, set them on the table, and passed them one by one—to Geoff, to the space where Elvedina stared, to Lionel, and myself.

I held up a picture to learn the name of my newest job in the fading light.

"Pleased to meet you, Blake Highsmith."

★

You wanna believe that all of life's events come in a series of Cliff's Notes and sound bytes and two-second tag lines, but in real life, complexity is the order of the day. Investigators and police detectives work within a system that's rigid and adversarial. The answers aren't real; they're merely bureaucratic. You hope the perpetrator you arrest is the guy who did the crime, but even if he isn't, he's going to prison. Culpability, not required.

It's not the fault of the men in blue that this happens; that the wrong people find themselves between a set of prison bars or the overworked and underpaid officer doesn't notice the second set of suspicious footsteps leading to the dead body he'll write off as death by misadventure. Before you catch a criminal, the crime must be recognized—it's a thin line between what you perceive and what you don't. This is the dirty underbelly of detection and law enforcement. Just like any complex industry, mistakes happen.

Paperwork filed wrong so John Doe goes to prison instead of John Quincy. The rape kit dropped on the ground or never processed so the perpetrator goes free. The crowded evidence room where files are misplaced and good evidence is thrown out to make room for new cases.

We live in a machine. The only requisite for living in it is to feed anyone who gets in the way into the cogs.

We misfits around a kitchen table, passing flimsy evidence of a secret project that may or may not exist, must now read between the lines. Nothing is linear. It's all scrambled. The puzzles shaken up and mixed together with pieces missing, and now Lionel is asking me to bring together the whole picture.

We pass the pieces back and forth and we do it in silence. Around the table, Lionel and Lafferty come up with lousy ideas to fit their prejudices and biases and filter it through the answers that comfort them the most. I tried to see it with new eyes. As if for the first time. I tried to think without thinking at all and let the picture emerge. I wanted to let Mr. Blake Highsmith tell me what he did, not through his words, but through his evidence.

And bit by bit, the picture coalesced, the narrative formed.

When the documents had finished being passed around and my cigarette burnt down to the pit, the filter smoldering, I plucked it out of my lips and flipped it into my coffee cup with a sizzle. A scrim of ash floated in the brown. Atroxipine buzzed through my veins with a delicious hyper speed that rendered the world into a funhouse carnival ride, faces distorted into carnival masks.

That's a new sensation, I thought.

"You ready for this?"

They were ready.

"I got no fucking idea."

Sighs and groans formed a carousel around the table and after that, we called it a night.

My guests found their places in different corners of the house. Lionel had installed himself in a musty guest bedroom across the hall. Water sang through the pipes as someone ran a shower, Lafferty's chair squealed as he cussed and chivvied it through a close turn, and then I heard the sound of the pull-out couch opening up where Lafferty would count sheep for the remainder of the night. All the noise subsided and faded into the deepening night—except Elvedina's footsteps as she moved through the house with no destination and no seeming end. I counted the times she passed by my door and watched her shadow come and go. She made me uneasy, thinking of what her purpose might be and why she was with us.

My old mattress had seen better days, but the second my spine met the springs, it roused the memory of the narrow prison bunk with Lincoln above me recalling when he used to hack into city grid systems and change the traffic light patterns so he could drive to the local game store without stopping at a red light. After six months, my sleep pattern had started to normalize and now I had to force both mind and body to relearn everything, to remind myself there was no one knocking a baton against the bars or hundreds of snores stitching the air around me. My mattress was so soft, my body refused to recognize it. Sleep would not come without a fight.

Beep beep.

I startled out of my daze. I jerked open the end table drawer and unearthed the source of the noise—my old digital watch. Another second more and I rattled out the prescription bottle

I'd stolen from Lionel. A nice layer of pills at the bottom, sitting in a film of dust. I sat up in bed and disabled the watch alarm, but found internal alarms are harder to get at. I salivated in anticipation of my next dose of Atroxipine, wonder-drug and zombie panacea that once kept my mind limber and stopped me from subsiding into the numb hunger-rage so characteristic of the pre-deceased.

I set the orange pill bottle on the end table. A special space within me opened in the absence of addiction. My private romance with a drug was gone, and there was nothing to replace it with, save an endless stream of cigarettes planting slivers of cancer in my lungs as the seconds passed.

I didn't need it anymore. But having taken it, I appreciated the new perspective. My ordinary swirl of thoughts became fluid. Logical. Inspired and without restraint. All the world and its smallest details highlighted and calling out for my attention. The pain of years past pushed into the background.

Blades of smoke disappeared into the air vent in the ceiling. I tried to imagine what my brother got up to while the government was looking the other way. I could build endless conspiracies on his bones, but did they really matter? What mattered was what the bastard brother of mine left behind—and what he left behind was a man named Blake Highsmith.

Blake Highsmith's file was a patchwork of random statistics. A photo of a smiling business executive. Quiet youth and untroubled childhood with a speed bump of divorce. A latch-key kid. Cliché of disaffected middle-class youth. A million middle-class kids populate the country, becoming alienated adults just like him. Obedient mama's boy did good and rose up through corporate ranks to be a stellar earner for the corporate titans. Shot up the ladder from intern to sales and then to the advertising department.

I imagined Lionel already knew what I was thinking: Blake Highsmith found success working for the same pharmaceutical company that supplied me with Atroxipine: Sisemen Pharma, Inc.

Coincidences have a way of backfiring on you, like a squib load caught in the barrel of a gun. Fools have been known to look inside and get themselves shot in the face. Would I come away with my head blown off when I looked down the barrel for the bullet stuck inside?

Blake Highsmith wasn't a zombie, just a successful man. Freshly divorced, he had then married a beautiful wife who looked prepped for service as a soccer mom—glossy brunette hair and sensible clothing from a conservative catalog. PhD in chemistry. Darling Polly Moore, turned Polly Highsmith.

I shuffled their pictures in my mind. Through the veil of smoke, the sound of Elvedina's footsteps, relentless as hoof beats, an eerie headless horseman riding up and down my haunted hall.

Blake and Polly Highsmith's marriage was a happy one until the police showed up at their door and took Blake away. They didn't drag him out and cuff him like they did me, but then, Highsmith didn't have a gun in his hand at the time. The police department charged him with murder in the first degree, three counts.

While Blake Highsmith settled down into an approaching middle age with his trophy wife, his biggest hobby had been targeting unsuspecting people and killing them. Five people dead of cardiac arrest. They charged him for the three they could prove he'd interacted with the night before their deaths and dropped the other two. The department hadn't been able to come up with a murder weapon, but they had circumstantial evidence and mounting pressure to convict. The flimsiest prosecution in the history of prosecutions, but then, this was the dirty machinery of law.

Someone had to be thrown to the machine, and Highsmith was the sacrifice. If he happened to be guilty, that was just a perk. His wife at home, crying in their empty bed and grieving their long-lost life. My job was not to figure out whether Highsmith was guilty, or to care if he was. My job was to figure out if Jamie had been the one pulling his puppet strings, and then cut them off, one by one.

I fell asleep to the thin comfort of Elvedina's boot steps, thinking of Blake Highsmith. It saved me from thinking of Niko, of Jamie's wife. It was too painful to be left alone inside myself; I realized this whole "living" arrangement would be much harder than I thought.

For lo, the consequence of being human is the birth of conscience.

★

I dreamed I was in Lafferty's wheelchair.

Undead again, surrounded by the claustrophobic walls of my bedroom. The ceaseless beating of my heart, stopped, returning to me the lonesome silence I had not known I missed. Parts of me gone to decay. The smell of me, a rank carrion. The house silent and the door canted open to let the darkness seep into every corner.

When I tried to rise I could not; gravity pinned my every joint to Lafferty's wheelchair while Lafferty slept on. I cried out. Wrenched back and forth so the chair wobbled and still, I could not free myself.

The chair changed. The arms lengthened, forming bony fingers at the end curling over my own, legs transforming from the slats of wood until it was not a chair at all, but Elvedina. Her arms cold as metal, her hands unfurling to lock my arms, my legs paralyzed and crucified on her ruthless and unforgiving body. My mouth evaporated concrete dust, licking the inside of my cheeks for a taste of Atroxipine. Just one dose. A single pill would have me walking again.

In the background, silhouettes. My father, in his black suit. Highsmith, made real from all those pictures I had pored over, his figure bent over and crying softly to himself, with his head down and his hands cuffed with a yellow ziptie.

"Help me, Vitus," he whispered. "Don't you owe me as much?"

I writhed to be free of Elvedina, of her barbed-wire arms. A third figure leaned into the light with his lambent yellow eyes and a neon name tag: INSPECTOR, ECHO. His shadow overwhelmed Highsmith, and Echo reached down to stroke Blake's head. The gesture was meant to be paternalistic, but as he ruffled Highsmith's hair, his forefinger grew in length, extending knuckle after knuckle, sinking into Highsmith's ear until Highsmith's cries became breathy screams. Blood flowed like a tap of maple syrup.

Elvedina turned my head away with a pair of pincer hands. Her mouth was made of knives. She brought me close to kiss me on the forehead, and then to my mouth. Her lips drew blood and I tasted motor oil where her tongue should be. I screamed, and all the spectators laughed and clapped while Lafferty, light years away on the couch, and Lionel locked away in the guest bedroom, slept on.

★

I faded out of blackness as easily as I gave myself to it; but the sense of dreams having elapsed without my comprehension hounded me into my waking hours. As I cracked my eyelids open, Elvedina's rigid figure haunted the threshold of my door.

"Don't you sleep?" I asked.

Her head turned in an angle, as though she could have kept turning it until she wore her skull backwards, looking over her shoulder at me from the corner of one slitted eye. But she dismissed me and faced the hallway once more.

A disorienting attempt to recollect my whereabouts passed—to understand I was no longer in the prison world of snoring, sweaty, rough-edged men. What occupies many a heterosexual man with no hope of conjugal visits is all the women he'll consume when he gets outside. I'd spent hours replaying Niko's body on the kitchen counter, trying to remember how this new body worked. How to lift a hand or make a fist. My arms being a different length than they should be and my new height provided a dizziness that I could only let wash over me, helplessly, until it passed. Sometimes I reached for an object and overshot the mark, clumsily breaking the desired target.

I ran a hand across my chest, feeling skin to skin, hand beneath my shirt—this was not my chest. Not my rib cage. Not my heart—as though by touching it, I could make it real. Even food didn't taste the same—not that prison food was anything worth tasting.

Spent all that time fantasizing about a woman out of my reach, and here I was, waking up to one.

I groaned and rolled with the intention of artfully setting my feet down on the floor. The schism between the body I remembered having and the body I actually owned split wide and I missed, falling to the floor with my breath knocked out of my chest and my spine rattling up to my teeth. I flailed and clutched at the bedspread. When I looked up, Elvedina blocked the light, her head silhouetting a corona of light that transfixed me, mesmerized by her alien presence.

I struggled to rise and missed the mattress for support. My arms and hands and fingers were all in the wrong places and then her hand was before me, fingers splayed.

I hesitated and took it; she lifted me up to my feet. A wave of unreality, of occupying two bodies at once, passed. The bitch made my skin crawl, but I did not let go and neither did she.

We were close as lovers, but sexual tension flatlined. Her nose, inches from mine. Her breath didn't stir the air. Her pupils illimitable and black. I stood there without moving, waiting to see when she would reach the point of maximum awkwardness and walk away, but she did not.

"Are you okay?" I asked.

Was she touched in the head? I'd seen shell-shock like this before, the endless stare and the empty expression, wondered what she'd seen in Sarajevo, if it had been anything like what I had seen—

She said nothing and yanked a drawer out of the dresser and onto the bed. She fished out a shirt and returned to me, smothering and claustrophobic, and shoved it into my chest. I got the distinct impression that if I did not dress, she would do it for me.

"No sleeping on your watch, is that it, Nurse Ratched?"

Immovable, expressionless.

"Think you could give me a few, y'know?"

She did not know.

Again, I suffered the surreal alienation of stripping in front of another woman, and this time I couldn't even say it was because we were in prison—but then again, maybe it was. They held me under lock and key here like any inmate. I pulled off the old shirt from last time and balled it up in my hands, peeled off the shorts, and looked down at myself.

Everything rearranged and different. I'd already had a sexual test run with Niko, but that had been the heat of the moment, unruly and wild sex. Later came the forlorn examinations in the prison cell, staring at everything, the curve of my arms into my shoulder, touching my neck, trying to figure out what Amos had been doing with this body before I intersected it. Scars I would never understand or know the story behind. Like the nick on the side of his ribs, or the strawberry on his hip, a port wine stain on his left shoulder blade. These small things, like coming home to your house with the furniture moved an inch counterclockwise. Nights, I languished on my bunk, touching myself endlessly like I could find the zipper and leave the skin. Running my hands up and down, up and down, and keeping the bubbling frustration of *this is not me, this is not me* underneath where it belonged. Bottling up my helplessness. Relearning how to be me. In time, I imagined the leanness that characterized Amos in life would soon leach away into my trademark rawness hedged by unhealthy habits, too much drinking and smoking, forgotten meals instead of exercise.

I appreciated Amos's Marty Stu, stripper body, but I missed everything that had made it mine. Even below the waist, things were the same. I'd tried jerking off in the prison twice and gave up. Everything felt wrong, nothing in sync, chasing the dragon of pleasure to experience it disintegrate inexplicably, increasing my frustration with no vent to direct it to. A malaise dogged this body, and Elvedina's presence highlighted its weirdness.

I dressed in the quiet. Let myself be naked and raw in front of her and watched her eyes, her face, to meet mine, to react, to express anything at all. She did not see me; studied the light coming through the window until I was done and I felt secretly ashamed of myself, of being not me, of wearing this stolen skin.

Would it ever get better?

I sat heavily on the end of the bed, mattress springs squealing. Elvedina leaned over to push a piece of paper in my hands. I took it from her, staring at the name on the top.

Blake Highsmith's prison record.

I read the name of the prison.

"Well fuck me," I whispered.

★

Blake Highsmith.

He sat down across from me at the terminus of a long steel table from an old interrogation room. A steel chain rattled between his wrists as he sat up straight. If I didn't know better, I'd think this a board meeting and Highsmith the ruling CEO whose off-hand gesture could cut a thousand jobs in an eye blink or order me to fetch him a coffee while he read quarterly financial reports. He moved and walked as though he wore a tie and three piece suit and not the tight, ill–fitting, and often unwashed prison orange.

I'd been sitting in this same spot last week.

He said nothing. I slumped in the chair and folded my hands on the table. Outside the building, Elvedina paced the parking lot. She hadn't followed, and her response had been the usual icy silence.

"You're not a police officer," Blake Highsmith said.

"You're right. I'm not," I said. "I'm what you'd call the clean-up crew. A janitorial service for fuck-ups like you."

Blake Highsmith blinked but his mask held firmly in place. A chin custom-made for superheroes, cleft included, free with every order. Squared face and hair modeled after a Ken doll's. Plasticine and sophisticated. Hannibal Lecter on his day off. It took no great stretch of imagination to think of him poisoning his victims over a cup of tea and quoting obscure classics while listening to Schubert. Or whatever hyper-intelligent serial killers are supposed to spend their time doing.

"I don't leave a mess when I kill."

"You're right, you don't, and that's my problem."

I pulled out the file and pushed it across to him. He looked down at it once, unsure if he should touch an object stained by my peasant taint. His chains rattled as he flipped the first few pages of clipped articles and papers. Fast and intelligent. His blue eyes, positively dreamy. He would have looked great on the cover of *Time* magazine.

"One of the victims' families hire you to question me?"

"I'm an independent contractor. Just trying to figure out what species of monster you are."

He reached the end of the contents, closed it, and pushed the file back to the center of the table. I rose to take it and slide it back to me, but Highsmith held the file down. The wrist chains held taut, winking dull light as I met his persistent gaze.

His mask slipped. Another, different man peered out.

"You Jamie's boy?" he whispered.

Highsmith's eyes flicked to the camera in the corner without moving his head an inch and returned to me in one smooth, undercover motion.

In the deep recesses of memory, I remembered when being this close to a guy's face made me salivate and think about what he'd taste like when I ate him. I grinned.

"Sometimes. Other times, I go by a different name."

"Vitus."

"Where did you hear that?"

"Your brother told me. You have me to thank for your recovery."

The Highsmith I'd traded whispers with two seconds before vanished.

He was acting. Acting for the cameras. Reading off an invisible script. Our pow-wow never happened. We were in the black, now; spilling government secrets had consequences and I had to play the script for the surveillance cameras—but who was writing the lines? My brother, from beyond the grave?

I returned to my walk-on role as indignant interrogator.

"And what is it that you do, exactly?" I tapped the folder as though to bring to life the five victims he'd authored. "Poison? It must be poison, right?"

"No poison," Highsmith said calmly. "All this is on the record. You could very easily ascertain it from my court transcripts."

"I want to hear you tell it."

"I had some obstacles. I eliminated them."

"Oh, come on now; it required a little more effort than that. Why don't you give me the whole shebang? Aren't you itchin' to tell the story? Gimme the *Playboy* interview version?"

He sighed like the ennui of this existence was too much to bear and his schedule was filled. "Nothing to tell. Case is closed, you're the only smartass digging around for gory details. Is that your deal? Torture porn? Get off on this kind of thing?"

"Thought it was the other way around."

"I killed them. Satisfied?"

"Just like that? They spill a latte on your prospectus? Piss on your lawn?"

I goaded him, hoping he might reveal something more that Jamie had buried, but Highsmith's face shut down. The ease of his deception unnerved me. Had my brother employed a psychopath in secret?

He worked with you, *didn't he?*

He shrugged. "They were mean-spirited and useless people who were in my way. Life was more efficient without them."

I opened the folder and held up a picture of one of his mean-spirited and useless people. A smiling man at a bar with several friends. They were all holding drinks with umbrellas in them up to the camera with their faces flushed and ruddy. A New Year's Eve party.

"Jeremy Dietrich. He was mean-spirited and useless, eh? A twenty-eight-year-old business lawyer? What did he do, exactly?"

"I didn't like him."

"You kill everyone you don't like?"

"Like you never told anyone to fuck off and die when you get cut off in traffic."

"Difference being I don't get out of my car and kill them."

"You didn't know Jeremy. I met him through common circles. We'd have conventions and business meetings and he'd show up at the same set of bars and that's how we got to know each other. We'd talk business. But he was a bore. Sexually promiscuous. Made a pass at my wife once. He knew she was married, but still, he persisted. Some people just don't appreciate that what they have can be taken away."

"So you took his life away?"

"But you knew the answer to that. Why are you wasting my time?"

"How'd you do it? If it wasn't poison?"

Highsmith rubbed his hands together through the rattle of his chain and leaned forward. His eyes burned hotter at their centers as they met mine.

"I made their hearts stop."

"Yeah, we got that. It's how you did it that's troubling us."

"I already told them, but no one wanted me to talk about it. My lawyer pressed to get me examined, the usual insanity defense stuff. But I'm not insane. I know exactly what I did. Just because the fools around me don't want to believe it doesn't make it less true."

"What did you tell them? You didn't stab your victims. You didn't shoot them. You didn't poison them. Nobody can prove that you killed them at all. You trying to tell me you killed them with mind bullets?"

The last was meant to be a joke, but when Highsmith didn't laugh or crack a smile, it hung in the air with gathering intensity.

I put the photo down. Faces and identities of his other victims crowded in as I absorbed this in the passing seconds. "Let me get this straight. You believe you killed these people from afar? Like some kinda weird sci-fi bullshit—"

"No bullshit," Highsmith cut in. "I stop your heart, and they find your body miles away from me, stone dead."

Time stopped in the interrogation room. My brain turbo-charged as I quantified this new information. Questions rammed together like rounds in a magazine.

"Okay," I said, "I'll bite. If you can kill just by thinking about it, what's stopping you now, eh, Slick?"

His face, serene, moved not an inch.

"Who said I ever stopped?"

Then, he began to laugh.

★

Elvedina and I stared out through the windshield at the parking lot.

Highsmith's chuckling guffaw followed me like a perfume, haunted the car. The manila folder balanced in my lap beneath the steering wheel. Pages stuck out haphazardly. Five victims. My mind expanded to consider how many went unreported or undiscovered. Each victim had gone to sleep and never made it to morning. Geographically scattered, one in another state. All had the ill fortune to meet Blake Highsmith and offend him in an off-hand or trivial way. Highsmith, with his superhero cleft chin, yukking it up over their dead bodies. A charmer, a go-getter, an all around nice guy, except when he stopped hearts with mind bullets and cured zombies of their pre-deceased condition.

If he was to be believed.

"How did he do it?" I whispered.

Elvedina didn't answer.

I popped the cigarette lighter into the slot and waited for it to warm up. Elvedina stared at the hot blacktop. I offered her a cigarette. She didn't take it. I tucked it into her front pocket. Her gaze followed me with dispassionate aloofness while I set fire to my own, considering if it were possible that I might be driving this car and keel over dead just because Highsmith didn't like me.

"Hocus pocus, Elvedina. That's all it is. A mind trick."

Highsmith could say anything he wanted from the inside of a prison cell, but it was all flotsam and jetsam, a tirade of verbal garbage with nothing to back it up. Magical thinking designed to strike fear into the hearts of others. An elaborate con.

"If he's the real deal, then there will be others. I could just call Lafferty, right? Get his connections at the police department rolling. Get Lionel to run a database check. But, my dear Elvedina, how do you search for something when you don't know what it is you're searching for?"

Nothing.

"So, what would it take to get you to utter a sound, eh?"

I snapped my fingers beside her ear. Not a move or blink. Not a single reflex. I studied her, searched for signs of life. It wasn't as though I hadn't encountered an undercover zombie before, and I wanted to know for myself. I leaned in and sniffed her. For my efforts, I received a nose full of sweat and laundry detergent, but no telltale odor of rot or decay that would have sent my limbic mind into fight or flight.

Yet, she didn't move or stir. She had cold and waxen skin, and she smelled like burnt rubber. On impulse, I leaned in and kissed her on the cheek, pulled away and blew a puff of smoke in her face.

She plucked the cigarette out of my fingers, twisted the butt around, and mashed it into my shirt. The ember burned through the fabric and nailed a ring of fire into the unscarred flesh beneath. I howled and cursed, smacked it away until it fell like a depth charge into my crotch, requiring new, desperate maneuvers to scoop the spark out of my seat and send it sailing out the window so I could extinguish the threads of tobacco smoldering on my burning chest.

Sizzling fabric and the scent of scorched chest hair lingered in the car's stultifying atmosphere. I turned and met Elvedina eye to eye, gunfighters in a spaghetti Western. A bead of sweat scurried out of her hair and down her temple. Jamie's skeleton key dangled inches from the burn beneath my shirt.

The welt from the lit cigarette throbbed and pouted.

I should really stop smoking.

★

Pleasant Hills Funeral Home.

I recognized Niko's shadow as she came around the entrance, through the funnel of back-lit florescence. I trembled inside my new skin, trembled at the sight of her, with the memory of her. Both of us in my kitchen between presses of hot flesh. Her black hair framed her square face. Formaldehyde followed her, sending aromas running away with every draft. It squeezed a sigh from me. My goddess, Niko.

She didn't stop when she saw me, but blood rushed up into her face with an upsurge of passion. She hated me. She loved me.

Her hand flung out and raked across my cheek in a resounding *slap*. I turned my burning face aside to spit blood. One tooth rattled in the socket. Sensation equal parts delicious and agonizing. It hadn't been that long ago when feelings like this were muted and dim, phoned in from another planet. Now, all of it rendered hyper-real and supercharged. Blood rushed south to places it shouldn't. The cigarette burn above my nipple throbbed like a second heart.

"I guess 'I'm sorry' doesn't count for much at this stage."

"You're right," she said, clipped. "It doesn't."

Silence robbed time from us that should have been ours. Elvedina disappeared, became a background fixture, the visible world narrowing before Niko's arctic eyes. Mountain snow embedded in her veins. When she yelled at me again, would her breath come out in frost?

"I meant to call you," I began.

"Why are you really here?"

"I have my reasons. But you came before them all."

She made a derisive noise and looked away.

"I saw Jamie," she said.

I took a cue from Elvedina and decided silence was the better part of valor.

"You're a part of this bigger, more sinister thing. To you, it's just a job. Where I come from, community matters. When I saw Jamie laid out, that was the moment it came home for me. It was fun to pretend, to play the game with you. I always did like your type, but you know what? Girls grow up. And your type sucks."

Being a zombie used to be a less complicated task when talking to her. No pump up in pulse rate, no racing of the blood. No difficult shove-down inside of fulminating passion. All of them, new contraindications I would have to learn to navigate.

"Business, then. I'm looking into a killer."

"I'm looking at one now."

There was more warmth in Elvedina's eyes. I bowed my head and accepted my new outcast status. On the inside, I was knocking over shelves and breaking chairs. I couldn't conceal a tremble in my hand as I spread out the manila folder on a gurney, turning over a clipping for her perusal.

"See this? This guy is a convicted murderer. We don't know how he's doing it. Supposedly, he stops their hearts. But no poison shows up on the tox screen. Have you seen any corpses come through here that might fit the bill?"

She flicked the clipping away and smoothed over a picture. Anna Maison. Jeremy Dietrich. Kylie Stefano. All of them, individuals frozen in time before a camera lens, and the rest of them, gone to dust.

"Heart disease is a big killer, Vitus."

"Can you go back through the funeral director's records and find the names?"

She blew out a breath and nodded. I gathered the papers and stuffed them back into the envelope and closed it.

"I got pulled into this government mess because of you. And up until I heard your case was a wash, I didn't know if I'd be up on conspiracy for murder. Thanks for handcuffing me under a kitchen sink so you could kill your brother."

"I didn't really think it through at the time."

"That's kind of the problem with you, Vitus. You don't think through much of anything. You don't seem to think about anyone but yourself. But I guess it works both ways, because now that you're not dead, I just don't find you that interesting anymore."

I'll admit that during most of my young life, up until my shotgun wedding, I didn't have a chance to "play the field" or sow my wild oats. I guess I'm a massive failure of masculine virility for not having at least several venereal diseases by the time I was in my twenties, but once I turned zombie, dating was relegated to graveyards and well, you grow up with impressions of what sex and love should be, and you discover everything you're taught is bullshit.

Then you meet a nice girl. Try to treat her right. Turns out, you're not her type because you don't have a pulse and a heartbeat. I'd hoped for those to be at least minimum requirements. These were standards I could finally meet!

Now that I had them, it was exactly what she didn't want.

But hadn't I known all along what Niko wanted? She cultivated a taste for the fringe, the strange, the unusual, the morbid. Overnight, everything she found attractive about me had been stripped away. But I hadn't heard her protesting when she let me take her on the kitchen counter before my arrest.

"You're too pretty," she sighed, her eyes flicking up and down my jacket. "You were something else in the days you had scars."

The ghost of anger jittered up my spine. A cold slink of irreparable loss.

"Well, I guess we're over then?"

"You might want to find a new funeral home to skulk around in, Vitus."

"Last time I remember us, it was like you were fixing to move on in."

"I'm not going to be a replacement wife. You already killed your last one."

Oh, now that was a brand new pain, opening my vistas for what pain could be with no pleasure in it. I wanted to disappear into the background, like Elvedina, but there wasn't a single stitch of darkness I could hide within. All I could see were white lights and white tile.

A black belt cinched her bombshell waist into a tight hourglass. She came forward with her tapping heels and grabbed hold of the jacket flap to yank me down so I had no choice but to be face to face. An experience both demeaning and arousing.

She kissed me. Dove in face first. Fast on the heels of bitter rejection, I stared resolutely forward, fixating on the carpeting, the white-washed walls, to find Elvedina at last. Elvedina's stare, drilling through the mentholated air like galvanized nails, Niko's break-up kiss, fathoms away from my thoughts.

"Got what you came for?" I croaked. I tasted lipstick on my tongue.

"I like to break up with people in person. You could learn something from it, Vitus. It's called accountability."

She turned with a flick of her wrist and dismissed me in a royal gesture. I thought of Orpheus. There is a price for looking back.

A cold wind filled her empty space, left me and Elvedina desolate, alone.

"Nothing to say about that, Elvedina?"

Elvedina continued to stare and did not look away. Her hair, the unremarkable brown of a compost heap. Eyes like concrete and just as bland gray. Prison stones.

"I hate you," I whispered.

In the end, I hated myself more.

PART 2

SIDE EFFECTS

lvedina rolled the Crown Vic in the direction of the house.
I read through Niko's intake files. A series of names and
ages. Potential victims. Between the margins, Niko had
written notes on their occupations, what they'd been wearing.
No autopsies. Their heart attacks had been deemed a cut-and-
dried tragedy of biology. One was in his forties, four were in their
late thirties, and one was in her late twenties. Seemed young to
be buying a ticket to the dirt farm on the basis of a heart attack,
and Niko had written beside the youngest "in good shape, looks
healthy, why didn't they autopsy?" Indeed, why didn't they?

I folded the papers and stuffed them into the glove box while
Elvedina pulled up the drive and parked the car with the nose of
the Crown Vic brushing the garage door.

The gloomy ranch seemed replete with sighs, mourning the zombie
resident that used to live here. Surrounded with signs of the living—
Lafferty's unmade pull-out mattress while he worked the evidence
room, the closed laptop where Lionel made his communications to
Washington, Elvedina stalking through like an angry mountain cat,
ranging a peculiar scent—I reminded myself that the ghosts of my
past no longer mattered. The house kept a surreal silence.

Through the interior, to my room. This house had gone
through as many transformations as I had: clutter and discarded
clothes. A thin veil of dust coated every surface. Crumpled letters,
dropped change. The pages of a newspaper I'd never thrown out.
Sheets in a ball at the foot of the bed.

Beside the lamp on the end table, a square of plastic: a cell
phone.

Two minutes of fiddling with the device and I decided I hated
it. A marvelous invention that equated to walking with ten
thousand Roman circuses packed into your hand. Lionel had
taken the time to program phone numbers into it.

While I thumbed through my poverty of acquaintances, I
hesitated, and then punched in the numbers to my brother's cell
phone. Ringing commenced—an ocean roar in my ear.

The line picked up.

I hit END and dropped it onto the end table where the screen
winked into darkness, taking Jamie's name with it.

This was hardly the life I hoped to come back to. I'd received
a new body, been sprung from prison, and I'd had yet to have a
beer or cut loose, but the truth was, that was the type of thing
old me would have done. I wasn't that guy. I'd been pummeled
through the garbage disposal of life and resurrected on the
other side. Trivial pursuits were gonna be a hard sell from here
on out.

How had Blake Highsmith killed them? How?

The door stood open, my prison status affirmed through
Elvedina's constant vigil. Moonlight poured in and washed her in
silver while I spied on her between half-lidded eyes. She did not
move and I fell asleep, stuffing all the things I hated about myself
inside where I couldn't get to them, where no one could get to
them.

I'd forgotten sleep deprivation and exhaustion, forgotten
layers of unconsciousness and slumber. I couldn't remember the
last time I'd turned on the television to lose myself in a black-
and-white patchwork dream.

In my hellion youth, I tasted every fever dream a troubled soul
can own: long-lost fear dreams. Being late for school. Lost in a

building with too many rooms. Teeth falling out. Naked before an auditorium.

This dream resembled none of them.

I dreamed of myself in my own house again. My decay lay heavy in the bottom atmosphere of the room, turning the air fetid, restored to a zombie; I moved my fingers and the flesh split, peeled back like old paint gone brittle on ancient fencing, revealing bones for fingertips. One dream reversed all my medical progress. To my horror, I was not alarmed; on the contrary, I was at home in my rot, comfortable as a dead thing with no feelings and no viable heart.

My Id sighed with pleasure: *This living shit is for the birds. Come back to this. To what we once were. What a glorious monster we made!*

While my dream-self rose from the bed, Elvedina's omnipresent figure vanished from sight. The window yawned open in her place. Curtains trailed fingers over the floor. The screen was knocked out, hanging askew in the frame.

Elvedina?

Listen, a voice answered.

In the dark corner of the room, a shimmering figure resolved and stood at the edge of the moonlight. Polished shoe tips glittered in darkness. The fuzzy fade of his face hovered above the stark white of a shirt collar, the tie cutting blackness like a noose around his neck so his head floated without hinge as though disembodied. *You don't hear her footsteps anymore, do you?*

Footsteps?

All was silent.

Wake up, Vitus, the man said from the deep corner. *I would keep track of that one, if I were you. But it's nice to meet you, after all this time.*

Who are you?

His teeth glistened in the half light.

I'm an Inspector, and that's all you need to know. Wake up, Vitus.

I can't. It's just a dream, anyway.

Some dreams are more real than others. Wake up!

The man darted forward. I crawled backward, caught in the tangled sheets, rising up like tentacles to keep me ensnared. The mattress shuddered as he landed and brought the darkness with him. His hand snaked and grew, knuckling out of his sleeve to push his pinprick finger into my chest. I cried out. He found the hot button mouth of the cigarette burn. A pair of jaundiced eyes burned yellow, his lips forming a rictus, like someone yanked a fish hook in the side of his mouth. He pushed into the burn with his needle finger until pain jittered through me like an arrow.

I shocked upright, straight out of bed—

And woke up into a midnight world. The real world. Gasping and slicked with sweat. Grabbing at my chest to throw my pursuer to the ground. I came away with my hands empty. The decay of my zombie past obliterated as I returned to my racing heart. Adrenaline became ashes in my mouth. I feared his touch would penetrate my soggy and rotten skin. But awake I was, back in Amos's body and with all his borrowed vitality. Cells alive and my cohesion intense and frictive. Not dead. I couldn't tell if I was relieved or disappointed.

Beside me, the ancient alarm clock beat out time. Electric blue letters: 2:42 a.m. My cigarette burn throbbed above my nipple. The window stood open as it had in my dream, the curtains blowing out, but when I blinked, I discovered it had been closed all along. I rubbed my eyes, seeing double images, like photographic exposures blurry and blown out.

Outside in the driveway, a car motor coughed into life.

★

I dropped out of bed. Pain star-bursted through my senses with brand new sensitivity. I couldn't treat my body like butcher's meat anymore. I rolled with gravity and snagged my boots by the door, running, running, down the hall and sliding over wood flooring to the front door. Headlights flashed through the main picture window.

Lafferty jerked upright from the pull-out couch with a garbled shout: *What the hell!* I didn't answer. I gave up on the boots, dropping them at the threshold as I banged out of the front door, sailed down the steps. Sock-clad feet flapping against every painful stone in the driveway as I made out the car there, one amorphous shadow in the dark. My mind forgot which body I inhabited and I twisted my ankle with a yelp, making a clumsy turn to regain my balance, balance that belonged to someone else. Would I ever get used to it, to this body not mine? Double beams of light blinded me, illuminated the closed door of the garage before it. The car reversed, revealing the shape of the Ford Crown Victoria.

I lurched over the hood and slammed my fists on the engine for traction. Pistons rumbled up beneath my hands, radiating heat.

The driver hit the brakes.

I rolled off the engine, moving with the car's momentum. Through the glass, an inscrutable face. Elvedina's heartless smear of lip. Her bared and feral teeth, her black, black eyes.

She reversed the car down the incline of the drive. Lafferty yelled from inside the ranch. I lunged out of the path of the vehicle and back in the direction of the garage. I slapped my hands across the siding until I found the cold brass door knob, wrenched it and pushed inward.

In the cool dark of the concrete flooring and old paint fumes, my Ford Thunderbird rested there. I counted seconds as I slid in, her engine warming up as Elvedina made an inelegant and clumsy K-turn in the street beyond, as though cars were an old muscle she hadn't used in an age.

Fuck it, I thought, and hit the gas.

I converted the garage into my own personal drive-thru. The door collapsed and the Thunderbird tipped up and over the wreckage, its fender crunched obligingly. Sparks scraped along the oil pan to chase the whirling headlights pacing out the street beyond. Hot and burning rubber layered the air as I jerked the wheel out onto the main road. Sweat drenched my spine. My bare foot on the gas pedal, my hand trembling on the wheel.

You'd like to think that tailing someone in a car is easy work. Film has retarded our understanding of invisibility. I hung back. When she turned a corner, I sped up to wheel into the street and prayed I'd be able to find her at the end of it.

Several intersections led us into a ritzy upscale neighborhood that began to look familiar. Newly built McMansions lined the street with landscaping sponsored by the nearest home improvement big box store. Flags hung in the darkness beside smiling and waving gnomes. Postcard perfect houses for postcard perfect lives.

She turned down into the gated community: Ruby's Retreat.

My grip tightened on the wheel. Jamie had lived here before I killed him.

I watched her car pull through the gated entrance. After a minute of tapping my fingers on the wheel and watching her headlights make their way behind the white fenced-in gate, I edged forward, trying out lies inside my mouth.

An underpaid Rent-A-Cop in uncomfortable security gear leaned out the window to get a better look at me.

"Oh! Amos!"

I smiled and waved.

"I, uh, see you've been released. That's good. You were always such a good kid, you know I didn't believe it when they told me . . . "

Rent-A-Cop pushed a button and the bar rolled up. I nodded thanks with relief, pushing my bare foot against the pedal and the car into Elvedina's back draft. By the time I turned down that familiar road, I already knew her destination:

Elvedina's car sat in Jamie's driveway.

I idled from the street.

Figures moved back and forth past the windows like shadow puppets. Between the gap in the curtains, Megan held out a glass to Elvedina. From here it could have been apple juice or whiskey. Elvedina took it but did not drink. And unbelievably, she was speaking. A hot sting of resentment and jealousy sank in—she spoke to *her*, but not to me? I rolled down the window as though I could pick up the sound through the glass over the distance.

Crickets outsang her. I leaned with my hand resting on the side of the car door and my head out the window, my other hand on the wheel. A film of sweat formed beneath my fingers.

I would never characterize my brother as a loving man, though he pretended at warmth. Played off the extrovert. Went golfing with buddies, displayed a useful wit to dazzle high-society friends where needed, but it was Megan who went home with him, Megan who stayed with him, Megan who saw the deep and dark underbelly of her husband while she raised the son she loved. She loved her husband, even when he was cruel, but she adored and worshiped her son. Her dear Amos.

I wore her son's skin, now. Owned his body. My hands tightened on the wheel even though the car was off and the engine silent. I'd known Megan since the beginning of their relationship and did my best to be kind at every reunion. Helped her out of a jam in Atlantic City once when she didn't want Jamie to know she had a gambling problem. Now, watching her through the curtains brought to life the immensity of what Jamie had done to all of us, the consequences of Amos's sacrifice. Had Megan known? Been complicit? Blessed her son in his journey? I couldn't imagine it, but I didn't know. And not knowing, I suffered in silence.

Her son was gone, her husband was gone. The totality of my final crime hit me and I retreated, leaning back into the darkness to stare at the road. I'd taken something from her I could never return. I hadn't stopped and thought about how it would affect her, change her, and turn her world upside down— that she might never recover from this loss.

And Elvedina stood in her living room where I should have stood, begging her forgiveness.

The McMansion sported a lavish picture window in imitation of Atomic era houses. It lent the effect of a movie screen framing two pivotal characters, allowing me to view them in detail even from the distance the modest front lawn and street provided. Megan moved her hands as she spoke. Tears scaled down her cheeks and smeared her mascara. Her lower lip trembled and her curls shivered and shook with her unnameable grief. Dead-eyed

Elvedina looked as sympathetic as the guy who breaks legs for the mob. She reached around her chest to a space beneath her armpit. Elvedina's fingers sank into shadow along her ribs, the place a person might stow a firearm for safekeeping, and my legs lost feeling, paralyzed on the floor of the car. I sat up straight, my hand on the door handle. If Elvedina had come to kill Megan, it was not within my power to outrun a bullet to save her.

Instead, Elvedina brought an envelope out of her pocket.

I breathed out a long, whistling sigh of relief and collapsed back on the seat. She set the envelope on the counter. Beside the envelope, a red folder marked a square in the polished oak of the table. Elvedina switched the envelope for the red folder, slipped it into her interior jacket, smoothing the front down over her breasts to her belly in a gesture like a mountain cat, oblivious to her own lethal intensity and made more frightening by its lack of sexuality. Elvedina snatched up her whiskey glass and downed the contents in one swallow. She didn't even put the glass all the way down when she turned, set her palms at both sides of Megan's face, and then kissed her on the forehead.

Megan sobbed harder.

The farewell over, Elvedina stepped away toward the door.

I needed to get a move on. Any second she'd be out the door and would find me in the street gutter, slapping mosquitoes away from my gaping mouth.

I could just drive away into the night, blazing taillights down the forlorn streets until I was a set of fuzzy glowing red eyes in the distance. But who was I fooling with the world's shittiest attempt to shadow another person? Did I really think she hadn't heard the car crash out onto the street, hadn't seen me weaving after her down the roads? I could stay here and get it over with, confront her and demand to know what kind of business she had with my brother's wife. She could investigate me all she wanted, but leave my family out of it.

I kicked open the door and slammed it shut, leaned against it to wait for her.

Elvedina stepped into the circle of a lamplight, illuminated in neon before blending into darkness. Her eyes met mine. She cocked her head, lips parted, and destroyed a patch of zinnias beneath her heel, staining the concrete with their petals until she came to a stop before me.

"What are you doing here?" I asked.

She opened up her jacket and pulled out the red folder, shoving it against my chest. I reached for it, our fingers brushing. Her flesh was greasy to the touch. I itched to get away from her, sliding farther down the car from her path with the red folder in hand, papers shifting as I tried to keep them in my grasp. When I looked up, her car door slammed closed, ensconced in tinted glass.

I held the folder up in the feeble light. Stamped across the front, CONFIDENTIAL, and a name typed on the tab: VALENS, LIONEL.

I hitched a breath. This was Jamie's file. From his office. Through the curtains, Megan's figure wafted back and forth like a haunt through a sepulcher. Finding answers was as easy as ascending the steps to her door and daring to knock.

And what would I tell her? Me, the killer of her husband. Me, the wearer of her son's skin?

Nothing. Absolutely nothing.

I climbed into the car and hit the gas, gliding down the street. Street lamps cut orange circles over my face as though I were floating underwater in a subterranean ocean. My breath quickening, burning. I wanted to plug my mouth with a cigarette, but left wanting, I swallowed the vast and empty night instead.

★

In the dark and amid the cricket song, I took the steps up the porch. I shoved the red envelope beneath my shirt, between the uncomfortable rub of my waistband and against my spine. My jeans didn't fit me right with this body and I missed my unhealthy, unmuscular body. Someone attempted to reconstruct the broken garage with a creative mish-mash of plywood and duct tape. I passed the sleeping figure of the vulture who did not stir either feather or wing. The steady, faithful presence of the ugly bird comforted me as I jangled out a house key and opened the door.

Two steps into the darkness and the lamp flicked on.

Geoff Lafferty sat in his wheelchair—holes in the chest of his yellowed shirt, hand on his chair wheels, and sweat glistening on his forehead, ready to hoist himself from the chair onto the pull-out bed.

I wanted to offer help in a piss-poor gesture of rebuilding the friendship I'd destroyed. Geoff had been living with his disability a long time; he also knew the ins and outs of addiction, a pain we shared but did not speak of. His wheelchair, however, was another matter.

He put his hands on the armrests and locked his elbows, raising himself out of the seat. Straining muscles bore testament to long hours teaching himself how to do this hard work and to do it alone. While I had learned how to deal with my own wasting ailment of Virus X and my new zombie status, he had not wanted my help even then. Visits to his hospital bedside with my hat pulled low over my face had been among the first unsupervised visits that Jamie had allowed me when they finally had a fix on my dosage, on keeping the beast at bay. I had sat chewing my medication and waiting for Lafferty to wake up and discover he no longer had feeling in his legs. His wife, Selina, had her face in her hands in the hallway, saying she didn't know how to tell him, over and over. And she didn't have to; I did it for her. In those suspended hours of pain and interminable waiting, there'd never been time to tell him what really happened to me, and I wasn't there for sympathy. When he woke up, we cracked jokes and kept our tragedies dialed low.

Those hospital days were far behind us.

"You gonna stare all night or sit a spell?" Lafferty asked.

He'd tumbled himself onto the pull-out and patted the mattress with mocking wink. "Come on over and braid my hair while you spill your woes. I ain't going back to sleep anytime soon."

I sank into the mattress. Lafferty produced a bottle of whiskey from beneath and twirled off the cap. We traded the bottle in the silence.

"You get free refills of this at the gas station?" I asked.

"Tastes like shit, right?"

"Sorry about the garage."

"Your government spook is paying me three times what I make at the station for doing monkey work. Nothing to be sorry about. Keep destroying things. I fuckin' love it. Place will be rubble by the time it's all said and done."

"Sorry about Selina."

"*Sorry* never was a word Selina liked, and I guess she heard it from me too many times. Don't go picking up my bad habits."

"Not gonna divorce me, are you?"

"No, actually, I'm moving in. Need a roommate?"

I choked on my drink and managed to spray us both in a varnish of whiskey.

"Oh, you are gross dead or alive, for the love of Christ," he muttered as he palmed a fine misting of liquor from his eyes. I finished a long incendiary swallow.

"Maybe I just need a good friend," I said.

Lafferty took the bottle from me. Cold wind lanced up from the door, cracked open. The night was cool and kept me awake through my exhaustion. Every muscle ached and stretched on a rack of pain; and while it was pain, it was also pleasure. To be dead for so long, agony transforms into ecstasy. I thought about Niko. The slap, her stinging fingers on my skin. I tried to find the words to frame what I had witnessed moments before. There were none.

"You're a bastard," Lafferty began. "You gonna still go on being a bastard?"

"I don't know. I'm not a zombie anymore. And it's taking me awhile for my body to catch up with my brain."

"Do me a favor, while you're psychoanalyzing yourself and all that boring shit?"

"What?"

"Just, don't get in so deep that you lose sight of what's around you. Keep your eye on Elvedina."

"Oh?" I raised an eyebrow. Thready moonlight painted the walls through the blinds.

"I hear the old man talking on the phone sometimes," Lafferty said. His voice sank below the hum of the refrigerator. I leaned close to listen. "She's not with him, if you know what I mean. Like, not part of his command. She's a free agent."

"What, like a soldier of fortune? And you're worried about that?"

"You lose your logic muscle? You stop taking the zombie pills and get your refill of stupid? She's a fuckin' cleaner if ever there was one. Button man—woman, whatever. Doesn't talk. Doesn't want to know your name. You look me in the eye and tell me it's not possible she's here to kill you, or even me, just for being here. Maybe even the old man, too."

The whiskey cap fell to the floor and rolled away from my fingers and beneath the hungry shadow of a chair. My pupils contracted in the dark. The pucker of fear moved through the center of me as my bowels coiled tight into a seething snake. Lafferty's eyes glowed as fierce lodestones. For this man, undone by his broken spine years ago, optimism wasn't a part of his vocabulary. He spent his life looking for the darkness in the sun's rays, hunting out the seam of unreality behind everyone's mask.

Me, I was buoyed by the false sense of optimism that being in a new body bought me when I should've been looking at the world with Lafferty's keen eye. I thought of the red folder digging into my back.

I had thought Elvedina a babysitter, an inconvenient gargoyle to hound me and keep me in line, but her real purpose stayed secreted inside the black depths of her sunless and granite eyes, her slashed mouth, her unbearable and pitiless silence. Everything about her, a blank and mercenary tool to do someone else's bidding.

To kill—and not ask questions.

To kill me, after I had given them all they needed to know about Jamie's work.

I'm proud of you, son.

A fetid whisper drifted in from my unconscious Id: *The old gray fox, eh?*

I snatched the bottle from Lafferty. Elvedina's headlights broke over the rise of the driveway and through the hedges so it cast scratching fingers over the wall before extinguishing.

"Don't let on," Lafferty whispered in my ear.

He took the bottle from my numb fingers. A car door slammed through the cricket song. Tree frogs cried, peeping wails through the pine barrens. Her footsteps pistoned, machine-like, over concrete, crushing the grass beneath her tread to appear as a shadow at the door. Monolithic. A sphinx made human. Her eyes possessed the vitality of a car's dashboard gauge: chrome circles of black. She occupied the porch beside the bleak figure of the vulture on the rail and did not move.

In the silence of the slumbering house, a ringing phone sounded, the tinny old style telephone rending the air. All of us at distant points snapped to the center, where the ringing bleated, invisible.

"Well, answer it," Lafferty suggested.

I didn't realize I still had a telephone. I hopped a chair, overturned a table, and at last fished it out from under the pull-out mattress while Lafferty watched, enduring my clumsy efforts. I took up the receiver and answered.

"Hello?"

"Is this Mr. Valens?"

I whirled with the handset dangling from one finger, the receiver crushed between my chin and shoulder, and stared down the hallway. Lionel must be sleeping in the guest bedroom and the hallway remained empty, all the doors closed.

"This is Lionel Valens," I said.

Lafferty lifted one eyebrow and I put a finger at my lips, leaning down to hold the phone out. He inched toward the offered receiver and listened beside me as I crouched.

"Yeah, well, I wanted to let you know that there was a fight today while the inmates were getting their meals. A prisoner doing time for grand theft auto, name is Gunther, got into some kind of altercation with Highsmith. There was an assault, looks like Gunther was sent to solitary."

"I'm sorry. This concerns me how?"

"You paid me money to know, buddy, but that's not the juicy part. The fight was around five or so. Gunther was trapped in solitary about five hours until now, and he ain't trapped no more. Found his body in the cell. We think he hanged himself, but everything's being processed now. You want more info, price goes up, got it?"

"Yeah, thanks for your help, and don't call again."

Click. The connection cut and I set down the phone on the base and put it back on the floor.

"What's that supposed to mean?" Lafferty asked.

"I don't know," but all the same, I didn't like it. I would have to tell Lionel in the morning, despite the deception. Paying prison guards to get information is small stuff, but it put me at ease about Lionel's presence, as though he was on the level, actively helping, not conducting anything untoward behind my back I would come to regret later. In the morning then, I promised myself, I would fill him in.

I stumbled to bed in a drunken haze. Lafferty hid the bottle back under the couch. I hit the mattress with my shoes still on my feet, dangling in thin air. I twisted to sprawl on my back, staring at the ceiling, counting her footsteps out to the entrance of my door and then back again. They receded down the hall. I reached into my pocket and brought out my pills.

I held the prescription bottle up into the light. Pills caught in the orange cylinder like fireflies.

It was different, when you were a zombie, my Id pointed out. *Didn't matter about the side effects. So what if it ruined your kidneys, pitted holes in your stomach lining, or increased your chances of cancer? But you ain't a zombie no more, Vitus.*

I spun off the cap and jammed a dose down my throat. A hammer blow to my mouth. I dropped the bottle and it rolled into darkness.

On a night like this, I would have driven past the funeral home. Would have watched Niko, hidden among the cemetery stones, playing the radio to an audience of corpses. She could have been my new addiction, but I'd used her up, ran down the supply. All I had left was this bottle to soothe the withdrawal.

I contorted, bed springs squealing beneath me, and brought forth the red folder. Papers spilled out across the sheets. I held the first sheet to my nose in the dim light, working out word by painful word through my drug-addled brain. Atroxipine heated the bottom layer of my stomach with steady pulses, feeding me as I read. Jamie's handwriting decorated the margins, shorthand codes he utilized when he worked out puzzles in his mind.

The handwriting the dead leave behind is irrevocable—it subsists like a spell, waiting to take effect long after they're passed. From end to end, the pages packed with old-style type—the kind pressed into the tooth of the page from old typewriters. Sheets of flimsy onion skin, yellowed at the edges. The date at the top read AUGUST, 1958. Above the heading: PFC, VALENS, LIONEL—TRANSCRIPT.

I read and my brain snapped and crackled, Atroxipine raising up a euphoria amid the quickening, a thousand cups of coffee and a heroin shot rolled into one.

The sheaf of papers formed an old report, purloined from Jamie's locked filing cabinet, if I had to guess. What other secrets were buried in that house that might leak out if someone put the thumbscrews to Megan? I pushed the thought aside to examine the contents.

A simple report, a transcript of an interrogation—deposition? The origins unclear, as though someone preferred not to reveal to what purpose the information had been recorded, and then disappeared into my brother's possession. It stood to reason this had been my father's, passed down from father to son.

Naturally, I'd never been the recipient of my father's trust, nor his hidden reports.

Typed, Spartan questions, supplied with long-winded answers from Lionel Valens. A mission in North Korea gone awry. It started off in the same monotone filling a thousand and one encyclopedias, the naming of trivial tasks and listing of various goals, missions, contingencies. Typical protocols to be followed, in what order.

Then, things queered and a weirdness began and ended with the one person most capable of fucking up any mission: my father, the wily gray fox, Todd Adamson.

I bared my teeth to think on him—our endless fights, his condescension as he asked me to explain myself, account for my savagery, my coarseness. Why could I not do what was best for the family, why could I not respect him?

Because you're a snake with a human face, I had told him and received a ringing slap across the cheek for my troubles. A glitter in his eyes, a breathlessness as he shook his hand in the air to free it of my stain, the sharp ring turned out, my face bleeding.

He'd been an old man at my birth. Yet, in this report, he would have been closer to my age. In my mind's eye, I melted away his wizened old man's mask. Smoothed the wrinkles, the way my mother had laid out a pie crust when it broke, rubbing the dough back together, brand new.

Thinking about family and home made the cocktail of whiskey and Atroxipine heave deep in my stomach. The ceiling revolved above me. I shut my eyes, holding my father's face there, firm, like an ancient god. Saturn, with his mouth forming a sickle.

Younger, younger.

Clean shaven and in an army uniform, jouncing along unknown roads in the back of an all-terrain army vehicle in olive drab. Another man beside him. I grasped after the figment of imagined memory, building it from scratch out of Lionel's face, moving him backward as I had my father until he, too, became a slight youth in my mind's eye, his whole life ahead of him.

I tried to taste the heat of the wind curling up thick from the Sea of Japan. Recalled maps from my military years. Almost heard the sound of Lionel narrating to a disembodied presence in the room; a bright light occulted by an interrogator; the hot, sticky sweat of soldiers and tobacco from someone's cigarette. Lionel, a young and shivering soldier, pressing out the words between puffs of smoke.

The transcript text went missing where the action intensified. Redacted with a black marker—all my attempts to bend the page in the light revealed nothing. I managed to extract enough to know Lionel and my father left the relative safety of their banal intelligence gathering from their office desks and went joyriding with necessary fieldwork being the pretense. They played hookey and got caught. Someone from the North Korean side, an agent named Jin. The black marker turned more blocks of text into massive squares of black. Midnight swallowed up the paper and my father's secrets with it.

But imagination could suffice. The empty space made rich with unspoken affairs, clandestine or perhaps considered too improper to put into writing. Had my father been affiliated with the enemy in some other fashion? I wondered if it were scandalous. My father's amoral bent bore allegiance to no one. Perhaps the answer was more mundane—Jin and my father could have been lovers. Not the first nor the last time his dick had gotten him into trouble. I wished I could say my father was the product of a repressed generation that could not fully appreciate all forms of love, but the reality gave no respect to the lofty ideal of love itself—my father was an omnivore. He did not love people. He loved himself. And if he could get what he wanted with sex, he wouldn't think twice. No doubt he left a legion of broken hearts behind in his wake on either side of the gender divide.

Elvedina's footsteps echoed back and forth across my door. I peered over the top edge of the paper to catch her face before looking away. Why give this to me? To let me know where Lionel's loyalties resided?

I closed my eyes, pressed the paper to my forehead.

I reached the end and let the final page float down to the floor. I dropped the others over the mattress until I was papered in Lionel's old transcript, floating on a high that made me not give a single care for anything around me, for the dirty socks I still wore or my rank-smelling shirt. I curled on the bed and pictured the transcript text floating before my eyes, laid out across the paper-white ceiling like a flat screen, waiting for oblivion to arrive, waiting for the dreams on the inside of me to come roiling up out of my own leviathan.

I woke up, and when I woke up, I knew I was not awake.

Lucid dreaming. In a distant point in the universe, I was sleeping in my humble ranch surrounded by my father's once right-hand man, my good friend, and my terrifying automaton of a babysitter.

I woke up lying on a field of green and fragrant grass with a cerulean sky above.

I've been waiting.

The field extended into vast open spaces in all directions with the faint smudge of buildings in the distance to the left of me and an ocean to the right. Forests of unknown plants, and just beside me, the figure of a man in a dark suit encased in a living shadow. Surrounded by a corona of darkness consuming the sunlight around him. A black hole threatened to open up beneath his feet. He stared out at the vista with his arms crossed, tapping one shoe, impatient.

I don't have all day.

"You're him. You're the Inspector."

He put a finger to his lips and turned to me in a snarl.

Others are listening, fool! Silence. I have better things to do than make small talk with a whelp such as yourself!

He leaned down, grabbed my shirt by the collar. I dangled in thin space before he deposited me on my feet. The shadow passed over me, nipped at my neck where his fingers had gripped me, became spears of ice.

Come now. It's happening.

"What? What's happening?" I asked, but he did not answer. He turned his back to me and paced forward, bringing the shadow engulfing him like coils of unending smoke. I ran to keep up. He glided, an arc of blackness at his feet, his shoes never touching the ground and speeding up, even as I ran faster.

He went down a dirt path between arching trees. His back rigid, arrow-straight and discordant with the stride of a normal man. I closed the distance, taking a bend in the road, when the sound of a sputtering engine broke the silence. I stopped and faded into the shoulder of the road, out from the tunnel of trees. A shape moved through the dappled light, bursting out to the other side where the Inspector and I stood.

You see those men in the car?

"Yes."

An all-terrain 1950s army Jeep jounced over the imitation road. This model had the top taken off so it looked like an opened tackle box, square and compartmentalized, the windows discarded so the passengers rode exposed to the elements. A trio of men rode in the car, one in the front behind the wheel. I saw the Asian. His hair dark, his skin tanned by long hours out in the sun. He took the corner with his face grim, wearing the North Korean uniform. The two young men in the back, equally grim. Their eyes passed over us.

"They can't see us, can they?"

No. You're the one here to see. Now keep quiet and truly look.

The two men in the back wore Russian uniforms. Their light-colored eyes, their hair—maybe it was the cowboy in their tilted shoulders that gave it away. American. American posing as Russian.

Everything locked into place:

"That's my father."

The Inspector offered nothing. Distant trees rustled, complemented the sound of the army vehicle, the lilt of foreign languages. My father, one arm slung across the back of the seat and surveying the countryside like a lord, with Lionel beside him.

Jin, his face turned to the sun beneath the shadow of his military cap, pressed the pedal so the Jeep gave a burst of speed before he stomped on the brakes, carving deep brown swaths of earth into the land where they stopped.

I abandoned the Inspector, running to draw closer to the Jeep. I heard yelling. My father, sulking beside Lionel with his teeth gritted, whispering into Lionel's ear, I mapped the movement of his lips to read the words: *Just give it a minute, we'll get out of this,* and then the Jeep's engine stopped. Lionel and Todd, small and fragile in their flak jackets, unarmed.

"Go ahead," Jin said. Jin pulled the brake to seat the car in place and stood up on the seat with his back to the idling engine and the wheel, turning with my father's .22 in his hand. Jin spoke perfect English in an Oxford accent. He spoke better than my father. "Get out and take it off."

Jin made them undress. They trundled out of the vehicle to stand at the side of the road. The process rendered awkward, stilted as men are when forced to abandoned their armor. How young, how unthreatening this young version of my father was, as he stripped down to his underwear, with Lionel beside him doing the same. Unarmed along an unfamiliar road. Jin tossed them two Korean uniforms from his superior position at the helm of the car, and they began the tedious process of getting dressed into ill-fitting clothing. This was the man I had feared for all my life? Cowered before, forced on my knees before, broken and killed before? Disgusted, I watched Todd's impassive expression. But for that, I never would have realized this man was my father. Even with our features so well-matched.

Jin climbed into the front seat proper, facing the road ahead with my father and his friend to the side. I discerned the nature of his intentions. In all likelihood, Lionel and Todd's own men would mistake them for enemy soldiers and cut them to pieces with friendly fire. They wouldn't realize their error until they got close enough, and even then, may never realize their error.

My father opened his mouth and a tirade issued forth. Sharp, commanding barks and this, this I recognized anywhere, in any language—my father was cursing his head off. He was cursing at Jin. In Korean.

My father hurled insults with his mouth twisted on one side like he always did when he was in the heat of it. Obscenities Lionel failed to include in the secret report. I tried to retrieve the transcript from memory but what I witnessed was part of no report. This—all this—had been redacted. The Inspector brought me here for the live performance.

Todd knew Jin—knew what things to say, and about whom he should say it, to get Jin to wheel his vehicle back around. The same way he always knew what to say, to anyone, to hit their soft spots and get them to go from zero to sixty in no time. I'd played this game with my old man before. I knew how good he was at it.

Jin turned away from my father, but his ears flamed red. He revved the engine and then hit the gas. Tires spun in Korean mud, trails of earth, Jin's mouth a flat line. I tried to imagine my father's enemy, a man I could empathize with for our mutual hatred of Todd, the wily gray fox, who in this time was not so gray, but still wily. Jin with his mouth pressed together so thin and small his lips disappeared from the map of his face.

Jin yanked the wheel and the Jeep cut a doughnut until it faced back at my father. Todd perfected the art of venom. My old man with his hands on his hips and facing down a Korean soldier who wrestled the humming engine of the all-terrain beneath his hips, waiting to drive it right over my father's face.

The grenade, though? the Inspector said with a sigh. *I don't think Todd expected that.*

"Grenade?" I asked. "What grenade?"

Jin hauled himself up to stand on the front seat, reached down to his well-armored vest and ammunition belts, took an object off his flak jacket, pulled the pin, and threw it.

Handheld one second and airborne the next, sailing through the brilliant blue sky and past the foliage, the diesel fume of the running vehicle bringing tears to their eyes as Todd tracked it against the sun.

Jin had thrown it at Lionel.

I admired Jin. He estimated my father's character and decided the best jab at Todd he could make was going after his friend. I held my breath, forgot Lionel lived, unable to understand how time would coalesce to the present, when—

Todd reached out a hand and caught it.

The grenade made contact in the soft meat of his palm. He thrust forward with a gasp, launching into a sprint. By my birth, all his youth and athleticism would be gone, save the burning vitality in his eyes. Here in the bendable past, my father was a different animal. He pounded up the road with the live grenade, arms and legs pumping.

Jin stood poised at the helm of his stolen vehicle like a captain who only begins to realize his ship is sinking. Five seconds stood between my father and explosion. Five seconds until detonation; my father making those five seconds count, eating the meters fast.

Jin startled, scrambling to return to the driver's seat.

Todd launched onto the front of the jeep. A howling commenced, the marriage of sounds betwixt desperate men—

Jin's howl, Todd's snarl, the guttering engine as Jin tried to reach the gas and use momentum to tumble my father off the vehicle. Too late. Todd hurdled the engine like a Goliath with one distance-eating stride, grabbed Jin by the scruff of his collar, and sent him reeling back.

Jin shrieked. Todd laid out the agent on the back seat and snatched a pin out of one of Jin's vest grenades. My father didn't hesitate, though for one second, I thought it wouldn't fit. That maybe the hole for the pin wouldn't be the same size and shape. I wondered if Todd could feel through his fingers, down deep through cast iron, the grenade expand a fraction of an inch before he shoved the pin back into the hole and it held true.

Leaving the one on Jin's vest ticking, surrounded by yet more grenades and munitions, to cook its way to detonation.

Todd hopped off the back of the truck with Jin's pin in his hand.

Behind him, the horizon exploded.

✹

I woke up with a monster in my face.

I grasped reflexively for the weapon that was no longer at my bedside. The creature flew up into the air, morning light filtering through the windows: the vulture squawked and flapped his massive wings with gusts of wind, sending black feathers into the air as he perched on the back of an old chair. He settled into place with his beak open, his tongue darting like a viper's, agitated and annoyed. If I'd had my gun, I would have shot him and been able to stuff my pillows.

I sat up against the headboard. The adrenaline made my mouth bitter, my breath rancid. The bird must have crawled in during the early morning hours, which meant Elvedina still haunted the porch with the door open. I imagined her with dew clinging to her iron figure, her eyes like marbles. I reached for the pack of cigarettes and then put them down. Debated quitting again. This wasn't like being dead when smoking didn't matter; shit mattered now in ways they hadn't before. The pill bottle from last night had rolled against the wall.

The vulture sunned himself lazily.

"Couldn't bring me coffee or anything useful like that, eh?"

The cell phone beside the bed vibrated, lighting up like a strobe. My brain couldn't catch up to my eyes. Time to be a functioning member of the twenty-first century, I decided, and lifted it into the air to punch the unlock button and cease its irritating chatter.

The vulture took flight. One second I held the cell phone in my sleep-numb fingers and in the next, it was gone—the vulture winging through the room and into the hall with the cell phone still ringing and blinking in the cage of his talons. Wing beats buffeted me. I held onto emptiness like a man trying to hail a cab while the vulture busily tapped it with his beak on the floor until the screen cracked and the ringing stopped. Plastic bits flew.

I nearly fell out of bed in a half-hearted attempt to stop the avian theft. The world turned hostile. The horizon, suddenly optional. I was sick and nauseated, like when Jamie and me used to raid our father's liquor cabinet. My brain slammed against my skull in one endless ricochet.

"You look quite under the weather."

I pirouetted to face the voice and discovered Lionel beyond the threshold in the hall, the fringes of his hair ruffled and uncombed, staring at me over the rim of his glasses, reflecting light within light. Pinning down his gaze became difficult, sickened me with speed. Was this Atroxipine withdrawal? His left hand trembled while he balanced a pen and a book in the other, each line in his face like the scar on the surface of a deeply rutted mountain.

"Had a shitty night's sleep."

"Come now, boy, I was just about to chase some coffee. I dare say, I know you're an adult, but you look something like a lost child."

Lionel crooked one paper-dry claw over my bare arm. Tensile strength flowed through him, as though the old man were made of rebar underneath his wrinkled skin and his flagging heart. He used me in place of his cane, and together we tottered down the long hall. The vulture squawked after me.

"Who is that?" Lionel asked, tremulous.

"Oh, uh, Fluffy."

"I didn't know you had a cat."

"I didn't, either. Let me get you a chair."

The vulture followed us down the hall and took flight to make a home of my shoulder. Each time I shoved him away, he refused to leave, persistent, annoying, and morbid. I let him, unwilling to interrupt the conversation to school the recalcitrant bird, and most of all, because I felt sorry for him. Unwanted, unloved, ugly. He reminded me of myself, of all those years undead, and I didn't have the heart to shove him out into the wilderness. Normal people had dogs and cats. But I could no longer make claim to their charmed ranks. Yet, wasn't I fit for a companion? Did I not deserve company to allay my dark hours? And if this scavenger of the dead chose me, who was I to refuse him?

I pulled a chair out for Lionel. He sank into it and slid his paper and book onto the table. I threw the coffee pot in the sink to fill it. A rumpled coverlet and the unmade sofa bed gave mute testament to Lafferty's midnight drunk and his warning: *She's a fuckin' cleaner if ever there as one.*

The night seemed a decade long in retrospect. How many dreams did I have between here and there? They numbered in the thousands I thought, pouring coffee grinds into the basket. I remembered Elvedina's kiss to Megan—that inscrutable woman suddenly so intimate with my brother's wife—and Lafferty's face, earnest and worried. *You look me in the eye and tell me it's not possible she's here to kill you, or even me, just for being here. Maybe even the old man, too.*

I set the coffee and sat down across from Lionel. From where I took my seat, Elvedina's starved shadow stretched taut like a wire across the floor from the porch. I kept her in my sight line, and halting, told Lionel about the prison guard who called last night, relating the strange incident of Gunther, the prisoner who assaulted Highsmith over dinner, who killed himself later that same night in solitary.

"Omens and portents," Lionel muttered, drumming his fingers on the table in deep thought. "This does not bode well. Coincidences are never good."

"You thinking that Highsmith put him down?"

"I think it's a reasonable suspicion, but through a locked room?"

"Could have bribed a guard . . . You did."

"Hmmm, yes. Maybe. We'll have to look into it later when the facts are in and accounted for. If it wasn't a bribe—if it wasn't a guard aiding him—"

The unfinished thought took sinister form. What, exactly? What was Highsmith up to? How many suspicious deaths were occurring at the prison with every second we failed to prove Highsmith's culpability and allowed him free reign to do as he pleased, kill as he pleased?

What of us? Which of us would be next in line if we vexed him?

I left it, but in the same way a splinter itches beneath the skin, knowing it would return with a welter of pus and poison besides.

"So, you knew my father."

"Oh yes," Lionel nodded. "We met each other a long time ago. We were young, it was the forties and we lost touch for a bit. Ran into each again over in Korea, later, Vietnam. We built our careers together, you might say. We had an overlap in political and military applications."

"I can't imagine my father young."

I did not speak of the dream. I failed to mention the classified report. I hadn't known my father to be friends with anybody. There were merely people he used, and people he kept close, and all the rest he kept as enemies. Now, I had a chance to get closer to Lionel, to get under his skin and see what mettle he was made of. Yet, in the diffuse light of the morning and the locusts warming up outside, the smell of coffee drifting in, I realized there was nothing to discover. Oh sure, the old man had stories to share by the dozen, no doubt.

But the evil spy with the hidden agenda I'd been looking to uncover wasn't here. In front of me was a tired old man who was little more than a glorified warden. I'd thought he'd been up to no good, but what, exactly? Was I about to uncover his secret conspiracy to use the extra flyer miles on his AARP card or get his senior discount at the local diner?

This was a man at the end of his life. Look, how he trembled. His glassy eyes hidden behind the thick lenses. What could he see, if anything? I'd been able to turn the clock back on my own biology, but nothing would stop his relentless spin of entropy. One day, I would be in Lionel's place—an old spook at the end of his life, wanting to get back down south to Columbia, to Guam, to forget about The World and the arthritis biting into my joints.

There was no conspiracy here.

The woman outside was a different story.

I became aware of Lionel, aware of his fragility and what an easy target it made him for any would-be assassin. My sense of protectiveness came to the fore, shifting this confidante of my father into a different role. His failing sight, his trembling grip— could any of it measure to Elvedina's steely composure, her well-muscled strength?

"Oh yes, he was something else, your father. Everyone knew it. He had quite a following of hangers-on. He had charisma, a deft politician, was your father. I know it's hard to picture, seeing as how your mother married him so much younger. You were born, what—when he was forty? I wouldn't expect you to know of him, the way he used to be. He's much more serious now, but back then, ah, your father was very energetic. Would get up to all kinds of pranks. I understand you and he are not on the best of terms."

"He burned bridges. Exiled my mother."

Lionel inclined his head. The morning sun made his wrinkles seem as mighty river paths in a folded map. Monkish. He drew his chair closer to me so our elbows brushed. I froze, thinking he would take my hand in grandfatherly fashion, and then he relented at the last and was still.

"I will not lie to you, Vitus," he said. "In my past, I did terrible things. I've seen things, all the things old men don't talk about. And some of us, we grow more distant and hard with every passing year. Men like your father. Some of us—men like me—sometimes, standing witness to all that terror and heartbreak, it does something else to you. Makes you realize there's nothing to be gained from all that pain. The pain opens you up on the inside, instead of closing you off. It's what makes it hard for me, to see how much pain your father has inflicted on you, and know there's nothing I can do to repair it. And indeed, I do not think you would want that from me, and I do not think there is anything that can be done for it."

He reached into his suit pocket then, withdrew a ball in his hand, and set it down on the kitchen table with a *tap!* And I saw it was not a ball at all.

It was a World War II–style grenade. A ring of yellow around the top gave it a high explosive wartime designation. A fragmentation grenade like this had not been in production since the 1970s. My breath and heart stopped in tandem. The pin and the ring gleamed like razor wire in the light. It was older than I was.

It was the grenade from my dream.

"Bet there's a story there," I croaked, coughing to make my voice work right again, choking out my surprise.

"You know your father and I conducted special intelligence projects during Korea and Vietnam, didn't you? You father must have told you about that."

"No. He never talked about work much. You saw more of him than I did."

"Well, that was how I ended up with this beauty," Lionel said and tapped the grenade. I nearly choked again, wondering if the thing were still safe to handle after all those years. In theory, it should be, but munitions have a way of betraying you as they get older.

"What kind of work was it you and Todd did?"

"Most of what we did was observation. Todd was restless. Didn't like being put behind a desk. He'd invent reasons to go out and explore the countryside. I told him, what are we supposed to do if we get caught?"

"With my father? Pray."

Lionel ignored the deadpan. "Oh, nothing so dire. He just laughed and gave me a passport. Your father was very good that way. It was a Russian passport—during the day, I pretended to be Pyotr Ivanovich."

I remembered the dream, the Russian uniforms young Todd and young Lionel wore as they sat together in the car.

"At night, when we found ourselves too far out and getting lost on unpaved roads, I unfolded the passport. Do you know, it was stained with old blood on the edge, just a sliver of rust. I wondered what had happened to Pyotr Ivanovich. It occurred to me much later that Todd had been what happened to Pyotr Ivanovich. He had a way of making things happen, turning miseries and tragedies to his advantage. Only later, when I had the time, when things were calm and he was far away, did I deduce how these things came to pass. In some ways, I am frightened of him."

"Then there's hope yet."

"I don't blame you for your antagonism toward you father. But I would never dare tell him. At the core of him, he was a deeply lonely man. That happens when your greatest talent in life is running headfirst into the maw of danger. The people you love tend to disappear off the edge of a cliff. And more often than not, it's your fault. I sometimes wonder if he loved me as a friend if only because I survived longer than all of them. And am surviving still. Though what dubious accomplishment that may be, you may debate."

I made a mental note to treat Lafferty better than my father had treated Lionel.

"During one of those projects—one of the unofficial ones in which Todd could not seem to sit still behind a desk for more than ten minutes at a time without bemoaning the torture of paperwork—we decided to chase down a figure who kept reappearing in our transmissions. We drove out and took on our Russian identities and Todd delighted in the roleplay. I noticed the small efforts he made, taking on the appearance of Pyotr Ivanovich's comrade, Vlad Nicholavich. Combing his hair a certain way, smoking cigarettes with his opposite hand, as though he were becoming and assuming totally the personality of this made-up identity. And later, as with Pyotr Ivanovich, I realized it likely Vlad was no imaginary figure, but a soldier lost from his Soviet Empire, rotting in a ditch beside Pyotr Ivanovich in Korea. Todd was becoming Vlad and, even at night, when he arose, he kept the pretense, speaking Russian, affecting a heavy accent. I would have told him to stop but we were stopped by guards a time or two. His flawless performance allowed us to slip through the cracks. Chameleon like. Reptilian.

"I don't even think the man we were tracking down mattered in the scheme of things. Todd liked to take on challenges merely to do them, to engage in high-risk activities for the satisfaction it brought him to beat the odds. We found a lady of the evening. He went to bed with her while I waited and disapproved. She led us to a middle man, and that man led us to an agent who had regular contact with Kim il-Sung. We were going off the map on this one. Todd said he wanted to talk to him, probe him discreetly, and I believed it. He had a natural, seductive charm. A rendezvous point was agreed to, and this man was going to meet us under the impression we were passing him sensitive information from the American side.

"Close enough. Though it is one thing to say it—another to experience the horror of realizing the house of cards is made of stones and about to topple over you. And we did not quite appreciate the trap. I think the principal problem lay with our target agent—he was a man very like Todd.

"Jin, his name was, though if that were his first or last, I cannot quite wrestle it from memory. In the end, your father planted the seeds of his own undoing. Jin and Todd had met before. So his Russian sham fell apart when they were close enough to stare each other in the face. Naturally, that did not go well. We scrambled and retreated. Jin could have satisfied himself with shooting us as we ran, but instead, he stripped us of our passports. We would not survive ten minutes without our cover, unless we wanted to lie low as fugitives in North Korea indefinitely."

"And then . . ." I pantomimed pulling a pin with my teeth, throwing an imaginary grenade.

Lionel nodded.

"Sometimes, I don't think that day really happened. I wouldn't be sitting here, if not for your father."

And that's how he bought you, I thought, but did not say. *That's how he owns you. How he commands your loyalty.*

Lionel took the grenade back in his trembling hands and pushed it back into his pocket where it disappeared with a slight bulge. Easy enough to overlook, when he walked with a distracting silver-headed cane to obscure the unusual cargo at his side.

"Once upon a time, your father cared about people. He'd do the impossible to save the lives of the people he cared about. And that's why I carry the grenade with me. So I never forget that day, and how he saved my life."

"It's what he does to people he doesn't care about that worries me, Lionel."

"I won't pretend that he's a good man. But he's been a good man to me. And you should think about times you don't know about, that he might have been a good father to you, and you never know it."

The coffee machine breathed a hiss of steam and I retrieved two clean cups from the drain board, snatched a bottle of generic pills for the headache, and counted out two. They buzzed the ancient memory of Atroxipine. Like cigarettes, I felt the seismic pull of that old addiction, the pills in the back of my jagged throat, blazing a pathway down into my bowels. I thought of Todd, of Lionel, of Jin. I thought that if Elvedina had planted the red folder in the hopes of shoving a wedge between me and Lionel—in a desperate attempt to prove that Lionel was untrustworthy, that he had been keeping secrets from me—well, it failed miserably. Clearly, I held his confidence. He'd handed me all the redacted information, and who knows, perhaps that dream had been nothing more than my subconscious, stitching together a reasonable turn of events from the available information.

Elvedina, I thought, *you'll have to try harder than that.*

I palmed a dose out of my pocket and shoved two Atroxipine into my mouth, guilty and savage. Taste buds opened up to receive it, salivary glands working overtime. I poured coffee for

Lionel as though everything were natural. At all costs, I decided, he could not know about my burgeoning addiction.

"Yeah, well, I'm sure he was a lot more fun back in the day."

That's right, my Id whispered, *just like nothing happened, eh?*

"He must have passed something on to you. It's in your blood, this work. You're a quick study. I imagine you'll make quick work of Highsmith."

I said nothing. I drank the coffee black.

"You don't know yet, do you, how he's killing them?"

I didn't know how to tell him that if Highsmith was to be believed, the man himself was the murder weapon and I was looking for mind bullets.

"Be careful, Vitus," Lionel said. "You father would never forgive me if anything happened to you. One small detail could unravel the entire thing."

I hid behind the coffee and kept my eye on Elvedina through the curtain. Again, I thought of her secret kiss with Megan. I wondered if the same hands that held her face were hands that pulled triggers and assassinated with cold ease. What had Megan seen, in all her time with Jamie? What battle stories did she have to tell? A silent witness to his crimes?

I jerked upright. Coffee sloshed over my chin and down my shirt with the coordination worthy of my old zombie skill set. I wiped burning coffee off my face. Everything was on fire, and behind my eyes, my brain generating smoke.

The wife, of course. *The wife.*

Highsmith's wife.

★

Polly Highsmith.

When you think "serial killer," you conjure a series of composite images manufactured by Hollywood. An intelligence tempered with animal ruthlessness and cultivated as roses with thorns twice as sharp. Killing machines become breathtaking and beautiful in their violence, like gladiators of old, their circuses become private arenas. Even the violence takes on sexual undertones, as though killing someone is tantamount to sexual conquest. The line blurs and you're not sure anymore if being the focus of a serial killer's wrath is to be flattered and desired, or feared and terrified.

Glamour shots on the cover of a magazine of the serial killer's face, isolated and lonely. You forget that most of the real ones, not the Hollywood-crafted villains, have wives. They have parents. They have siblings. They have children. Swallowed up by the shadow of their husband's infamy, the wives of serial killers occupy the background as victims by proxy. How could they have known, seen the path of destruction unfolding before them?

This, in turn, led me down into memories of my own, my long lost wife and child. They never had a choice in what the fates decided for us. I signed up for the military experiment my brother helmed, the infusion of Virus X, the experiment that turned me from human to monster when it should have made me a better, more able soldier and cemented my rise through the ranks. My family hadn't signed on for madness and mayhem, just as Polly had never conceded to a life such as this. Like my wife and son, Polly was forced to stand witness to the casualties of her husband's choices. Unlike my wife and son, she lived still.

I had no preconception of who Polly Highsmith would be. Would she be the female version of Blake Highsmith? Part of me expected the door to open and that I'd be confronted with a gorgeous widowmaker, desperate to wrap me in her silk and suck me dry. Ruthless and cold, maybe even colder than Elvedina.

But Polly Highsmith was small. So diminished, she seemed to shrink beneath my gaze as the door opened. From the corner of my eye, even Elvedina looked flummoxed as she stared straight ahead into empty space before realizing our host was two feet shorter. I anticipated well-appointed high-end clothing to suit the part of the wife of a powerful man, and what I got was Wal-Mart sweatpants and a scrubbed-raw face with mouse-brown hair pulled back into a ponytail.

"Who are you?" she asked.

Who was I, indeed? I stumbled and nearly said *Vitus*, but that wouldn't do anymore, would it? In private, I could be known for who I really was, but if I so much as applied for a library card or social security, I wasn't Vitus anymore, was I? Vitus was lost, buried deep in the body of my nephew.

"My name is Amos Adamson," I said and gestured to Elvedina, "this is my assistant. I'm a private investigator, and ma'am, I know—"

But Polly Highsmith was already retreating into the interior with her faded mouth peeling down into a scowl. I talked faster into the disappearing gap of the door.

"—I know this is difficult but I have reason to believe your husband is innocent and we're just trying to ascertain how to help you both."

The door slammed shut in my face then bounced back open. Polly's eyes glittered, but her mouth was still grim-set, adding twenty years to her age. Her petite frame buried in the layers of dingy-colored sweatpants and a shirt that looked like it worked overtime as a table cloth.

She invited me in. The rest of the palatial house was sterile and cold: vaulted ceilings and massive entry foyers so the wind revolved in an endless polar vortex. Marble countertops stolen from *Scarface*'s movie set. Wall-to-wall Berber carpeting a celestial white, spun out of cotton candy. Elvedina followed me in and we were led to a room with a coffee table and a gas fireplace with fake logs resting in the center, a world where everything is reduced to cartoon status. Even fire, fabricated.

"Nice home," I said. It wasn't. It felt like a science lab.

"I'm trying to keep everything maintained for when Blake comes back."

She set out several glasses and turned away to unearth a liquor bottle from the cabinet.

Comes back? I mouthed. Didn't she know her husband had been sentenced for life?

Elvedina arched one eyebrow and said nothing.

Polly returned. We sat like children in a church pew on our best behavior. In the next second, clinking glasses and the slosh of liquor. She did not meet our eyes. Everything about her shuffled through each moment in a half-daze. Medicated, I concluded.

Had I been like this in those months after I had become a zombie? Tethered in a straightjacket and mewling like an incomprehensible beast? And afterward, when I discovered what my wife had become, the horror and the outrage had been far too large to absorb.

"They asked me everything already."

She sat on the couch across from us. Her hands fidgeting in her lap. One knuckle over the other, wringing them. She turned her wedding band 'round and 'round.

"I don't think they asked you the right questions."

"You said your name was Adamson?"

"Yes. That's right."

"As in, Jamie Adamson?"

A power surge worked up my spine and lit up my brain. The connection between Atroxipine and Highsmith. There are times working cases when nothing fits or makes sense or amounts to anything. Chasing shadows to no avail. Other times, the synchronicity comes on hot and thick as syrup, and I licked my lips with anticipation.

"I'm his son," I said. "He's been recently deceased."

"I saw the obituary. Naturally, I imagine they weren't about to publicize his death in great detail. The government knows how to shelter their own."

"They want me to take a closer look at his projects. And I know, Mrs. Highsmith, that he often conducted business with your husband."

"I really can't talk about it," she said.

Oh, but she could. I looked over at the blank television screen and noted the picture of her husband, his arm flung back along the couch while she rested her head on his shoulder. I reclined, letting my body stretch and become expansive in imitation of the missing husband. Giving her a gentle psychological comfort, to ease her into familiarity with me that I had not earned.

A ticking clock. The fridge hum filled the emptiness with a depressing soundtrack of desolation. All of us ensconced in silence like a tomb until every word echoed back to us with ten-fold sound.

"I don't want to reopen old wounds. I know you met my father. He spoke well of you and Blake. You can be safe in the knowledge that, as Jamie's son, whatever secrecy he held with you and your husband, I am bound to as well. No court can steal it away, you know. If he ever put you under such a restriction."

Some people are taciturn; others wait to be unlocked with the right combination of looks and words, gestures and touches. The road to Polly's heart required me to play a compassionate husband to replace the one she lost—and it wasn't hard to do, to fill that ache if only for a fraction of a second. But unlike Polly, I could lie to myself only so much. When the time came, all my gestures of compassion were nothing but weaponry to get what I really wanted from her.

I sat forward to put my hand on hers. I steadied her fingers with a touch and she stared at the bottom of her glass and did not move. Her lower lip trembled.

"You build a life together," she whispered. "People get married for love all the time, but I wasn't like that. I think that's naive. I wanted more. I wanted a foundation. Blake understood that. We wanted to have our careers but go on to bigger things. We wanted to be a force. Husband and wife. We wanted to be a business. We wanted to change the world together. Do you know what it's like, Mr. Adamson, to build a foundation for the future, and watch it be dismantled right in front of your eyes? One strip at a time?"

"I think I do," I said.

She put the glass down. I followed her as she poured herself another glass and I masked my surprise. The glass went straight to her lips with a hefty swallow.

"Everyone asked. They said I had to have known. Had to have been involved. How could I suffer evil in my own home and never know it wore the face of my husband? And it's just not that simple. And I couldn't make it simple enough for them to understand."

I squeezed her hand and took both of them in my own over the coffee table. The grasp didn't last long. If I was hoping to gain a foothold into her private thoughts, this would not be it. Instead, she topped off her glass. Again. Liquor, apparently, was the path to this woman's confidence.

Elvedina leaned back and watched us in her typical silence.

"You don't have to make it simple, Polly," I assured her, watching her drink down her third glass. "Give it to me complicated. I'll put it together. That's what I do."

"He changed, after he got his promotion. He was gone all the time. Do you know that? Hour upon hour. Night after night. I used to think it was an affair. Some other woman. I kept sniffing his collar for a mistress's perfume and looking for lipstick stains and there was nothing. I followed him, too."

She laughed, and the laughter came out thin. Her voice wavered, her words slurring at the edges.

"He was always at work. In some ways, that was worse. Another woman, I would have understood. But he didn't have another woman. He really loved me, and only me. But then there was his work, his career. And I could suffer that. I could sacrifice our time to that because I was banking on a future. A future that never arrived."

"Do you think he killed those people?"

She looked away. She closed her eyes and seconds dragged out upon seconds. Her head tilted downward, her chin flirting with her collar until she came awake, suddenly, her eyes widening to keep herself aware.

"I don't know. The law says he did. They destroyed us, in that court. We laughed it off at first, because it was just so silly. I mean, who gets taken to court with such little evidence? Our lawyer promised us the case would be dismissed before we even got that far."

"But you did go to court."

"Rumor is one of the victims had a relative working out of the county prosecution. They wouldn't let up. Kept pushing and pushing. So even though there was barely a case against my husband, they pushed it through. You know how it is in New Jersey."

I nodded. It's who you know that makes and unmakes laws in this state. That answered one thing, at least.

"We didn't take it seriously. I know now, we should have. But because we didn't, we didn't get our defense down. We had people left and right assuring us it would never come to pass because it was ridiculous and then . . . right before my eyes, the world turned upside down overnight. One day, the sky is blue. The next, I can't be certain of what color it is anymore. And I lost him. Just like that."

"Did he ever give you any reason to believe he'd killed anyone?"

"He wasn't always nice. I mean, to most people. He was nice to me. He never said a mean thing to me in my life. Never raised a hand to me. Reporters were all over me trying to get me to admit to some kind of transgression in our home life. Like he would come back from killing people and take it out on me. There wasn't anything like that. He ran his mouth sometimes. He was under tremendous pressure at work, constantly under deadlines. There were people in life he had to please, who expected results. If he failed to deliver, there was a lot at stake. He could lose everything. Naturally he'd say incredibly stupid things, like, 'I wish Dietrich was dead, I could kill him.' All bluff, like no one ever says that kind of thing when they're angry, and then forgets about it later?"

"I spoke to your husband," I said. "He says he killed Dietrich."

Polly put her head in her hands and stayed there for long minutes. The clock ticked and ticked.

"Doesn't he care? Doesn't he love me at all?"

She scrubbed and raked at her face with her hands. Her wedding ring was a cool, pale gold disc. She leaned against the couch with a sigh, closing her eyes.

I waited to see if she would speak again.

"Polly?" I said.

Elvedina sat where she was without commentary, oblivious to us both. I ignored her in turn, leaning forward to tap Polly on the knee. Polly's leg moved with the force of my tap, but she did not stir. In between the ambient sounds of the ticking clock and the refrigerator hum, she let out a whistle through her lips, sucked in breath. Her eyes searched from beneath the lids. Polly had nodded off.

I informed Elvedina. She stared at the sleeping woman as though she had never seen such a thing before.

I stood and took quick inventory of my surroundings. I shook off the taste of the whiskey and inhaled all the scents of this empty home. Mentally, I mapped out a rough draft of its layout. I looked up the stairs and saw doors ajar. Up there would be a master bedroom where Blake Highsmith slept beside his wife. I gauged the value of the second floor against the eroding seconds. Polly could wake up at any time. I turned away from the stairs and, instead, chose the long hall that arrowed away from the heart of the house and into spaces unknown.

I passed a bathroom, shelves affixed to the wall like slashes, adorned with vases and fake flowers. In another time, this must have been an attractive place, a place one wanted to come home to. Now the silence and the emptiness clamored with despair, gave voice to a throbbing sorrow.

I forged on. I opened a closed door and saw it led to a basement. Several steps down the narrow wooden stairs, a concrete floor loomed up and I made out the shapes of a washer and dryer, an old industrial sink. Empty and unwelcoming. I left it, closing the door behind me.

At the same time, the door seemed to slam shut an instant too soon, nearly catching my finger. Subsidence, I consoled myself, but the sense of the house willing to shut me out, conspiring with some ancient damage, persisted. Some places take on the stain of past crimes, but I'm not one to bother with ghosts and such nonsense.

And yet, my collar formed a tight noose around my neck and I reached up, loosening it. I wanted to get out of here—this place where the doors shut in on you too quickly and the lady of the house drinks herself into oblivion and her husband thinks he kills people with mind bullets.

I found a guest bedroom, a storage closet, and then faced the last door tacked onto the end of the hallway, like an afterthought. I stepped up to the brass knob and twisted, throwing it open.

Cool air flowed over me, chilly at the bottom against the concrete slab. Darkness pervaded beyond my gaze, and I could not penetrate, but I knew the atmosphere of a room like this. An attached garage.

I couldn't see into the room, but a burning in my nostrils, the smell of spilled gasoline and paint fumes—and more than that. The stitch of goosebumps up my arm filled me with anticipation.

No murders occurred in this house; all the victims died in their own residences or hospitals. All the same, I intuited latent malice within the molecules of the disturbed air, confirming for me what I already knew: something had transpired here. The room, heavy and overfilled with presence as I reached around the jamb to flick the lightswitch.

The light switched on—and then blew out, extinguishing into darkness.

In the brief illumination, I had expected to see a car. An expensive model would have suited the likes of Highsmith. I pictured a Nissan Z, or a Mercedes, BMW. Empty concrete greeted me, stained and with tread marks from cars past, and then the darkness cut off my sight and left me blind.

I fumbled for my car keys and found the key chain flash light, lifting it to shed a cone of light on the floor. I thought of horror movies past and waited for the light to flicker, burn out and die, signaling my fate. Perhaps I'd be chopped into little bits by an ax murderer. I'd scream good enough to be one of the B-Movie queens, and Lionel and Lafferty would shake their heads in disappointment that I was had so easily. Elvedina, well, she'd say nothing.

None of those things happened. Instead, I brought light to the square of concrete before me and I drew the light forward, over marks and ridges. A dark pattern etched in the stone.

I frowned.

Squares. Big squares, in a line, formed against the wall and kept going beyond where my little light could reach. A shape darted along the wall, and I snared it in a circle of light. It reared up on hind legs, a white rat, nose twitching to regard me with beady eyes, and then dismissed me to scamper into the corner.

I flicked off the light. The square marks embedded in the concrete stayed with me. I conjured mental images, fitting objects into the shape. One after the other, a time clock ticking in the back of my head. When would Polly awake?

"Cages," I said. "Kennel cages."

And since when were houses infested with white rats?

★

Elvedina and I packed into the Ford Crown Vic. We sat in the car together; I felt uneasy and sick.

A rational person might wonder why I'm sitting shotgun with a woman who may or may not kill people for fun and profit. Real life is not so simple. Since Lionel established her purpose as my shadow and prison warden, weaseling out of her care was going to take more political finesse than I had the power to wield. Like a kid hiding beneath the covers, the only certain death is letting the monster know you're on to him. Or in this case, her.

She'd kill me after this was solved. It wasn't personal; she wouldn't waste her time with her hands. I bet she'd put a bullet through me while I slept and leave my remains for the vulture. Fluffy would tear me to shreds and think of all the good times we had together. A New Jersey bastard getting a sky burial without the fanfare.

I reached into my pocket, tripped a finger over smooth plastic, and then brought out the pill bottle. Elvedina started the car and the engine sputtered; the radio buzzed a tune into stale air. Her eyes were lost and burnt out asteroids hurtling through space. I should not be doing this—I told myself this refrain every time. And like every time, I opened the cap.

I tipped the bottle to my mouth, tumbled three pills onto my tongue, and snapped the bottle shut with my eyes closed, listening to the engine underneath the radio noise as Elvedina backed out of the driveway. Drugs did funny things in my blood stream, sent every synapse in my brain running on rocket fuel.

As we drove, Polly Highsmith's house became small in a landscape of abandoned homes waiting to be filled with families that would never arrive, awaiting a return of stock investments and market prices.

Familiar landmarks of the place I spent most of my life: old restaurants, shopping malls. House after house, boarded up and foreclosed. All of New Jersey collapsing in on itself as though the state had become a black hole. Every now and then, a lone person walking along the shoulder flashed by, and homeless faces in abandoned homes peered out from broken windows.

Then, as though someone had simply hit the RESET button, the gated community rose up from the detritus, whitewashed and pearlescent in the coastal sun; houses rising from sugar sand like ancient citadels overseeing the flotsam and jetsam. Box stores and shopping centers.

She took us back through suburban sprawl, lurching to a stop in front of Pleasant Hills Pharmacy. She killed the engine. Up close, scar tissue webbed between her fingers, burn marks when she pulled out the car keys.

I wondered what—who—had given her those.

"What the fuck are we doing here," I hissed. This was the same pharmacy where I used to pick up my refills.

You know, my Id pointed out with acid, *she is a woman, she probably has needs.*

Oh, I realized. Had I been so detached from female company so long that I forgot about the mundane realities that came with?

Or, you're just an asshole.

Or, maybe I can just take another pill.

I fiddled with the bottle. Less in it than before. What would I do when I ran out?

The car door slammed. Elvedina's figure receded as she went up the steps and disappeared from view. This is what dogs must feel like when their owners leave them in the car on a hot day, tongue lolling and sweating in the sun. There was a time when each and every pore stitched in my skin didn't breathe or sweat. Was a time when I could almost hear and feel the bacteria eating at me and advancing the decay of my body. Now everything was thrown into reverse and I rippled with renewed cell growth. The thrum of my blood and the stretch of my ligaments.

Fluid drumming up through my spinal cord in an unreal flux. The assumption of my living body had taken place nearly simultaneously with killing my brother, inextricably linking the two events within my mind and leaving me with scant time to appreciate the changes as they rained down upon me. Roughly six months later, now that I was out of prison and free, was not enough time; and I was coming to realize that a thousand years may not be enough time either.

I closed my eyes and forced a thousand and one raucous sensations to dim, to return me to my quiet, undead life from before. Listening to street traffic, kids laughing in the cul-de-sac. In between the pleasant heat and the sweat trickling down from the inside of my elbows, I drifted into a place that wasn't quite sleep, but not wakefulness, either.

I went on like this, half-sleeping in the car with the scent of the leather interior in my nostrils. I came to by degrees—up and up through the waves and to the surface. Woke to a sound beneath my seat without sense of how much time had passed.

I opened my eyes. The sky was saturated into a blinding blue. The sound again, louder. A scratching beneath the seat, down deep beneath the metal of the car. Was there a cat underneath the chassis? *Scritch scritch.* The scratching again. Daylight blinded me, and I twisted in place. It moved beneath me, dear god, what was it? It pushed up the seat. A long and strangled groan I mistook for my own vibrated up through the metal in an inhuman growl. I jerked upright, fighting to unlock the seat belt. The metal squealed, the car rocked on all four tires with a force pushing up from under to get at me with tooth and claw. The seat churned. A ghostly form ripping through the fabric from within.

The seat belt jammed, my fingers slipping against the lock. The seat leather split beneath me and broke apart into a pair of lips, revealing a hand through foam stuffing, fingertips white with ragged flesh and bone. The grave odor of week-old pus in a hospital, a dead hand. I recognized the wedding ring on the left.

Jamie. Jamie was coming for me.

He grabbed my thigh, fingertips punctured straight into the meat. Next would be his face, pushing up through the seat as though being birthed through the car itself. I scrabbled over the dashboard, blistered in the sun, and yanked open the glove box. Papers flew. The face of the brother I murdered, rising through the leather like a drowning man with his lips pulled back over his teeth.

I blinked. My brother's face shifted into Blake Highsmith's, laughing, laughing, laughing as he reached up and looped the seat belt around my neck and began to strangle me.

★

I woke up screaming. In my thrashing, I must have kicked open the car door and slumped, half-in, half-out. Ass to the pavement. The seat belt snarled around my throat so I dangled out of the passenger seat with my upper half caught in the vehicle, drawing in struggling breaths through the thick, syrupy heat. Jamie was gone, but my vision reported burnt out silhouettes of his grisly form when I closed my eyes, like staring at the sun too long. Footsteps penetrated through the rushing blood thumping in my ears.

Elvedina's boots filled my vision in front of me, her snapping arms and her grim face with the cut-throat grimace. She'd come to gut me and truss me while Jamie and Blake Highsmith looked on and laughed. Bleed me out and mount my head on the wall. Kill me right here in broad daylight and let my father know it had been a job well done. He'd celebrate with a glass of whiskey with chilled stones and do the kinda shit elite scumbags like him do when they're not running a hegemony.

Elvedina's figure blotted out the sun. I flailed for a weapon. Fingernails eroded against the concrete and came away empty. She leaned down. *Get away from me!* I wheezed, but all that came out was a strangled whistle. With one efficient motion, she unlooped the seat belt from my neck. My skin burned. I fell over, kicking, with my spine against the roadside and the hot surface broiling my new skin. I crowed breath in and out in throat-singeing scrapes. She bent over me and dragged me up, her fists in my shirt.

I collapsed into her long enough for me to feel the press of her against me, and the sensation of her sent every hair needling on end. With anyone else, I would have been asking for her number and her astrological signs, but touching Elvedina was like being skin-to-skin with a reptile. Cold skin. Hard and rubber, a waxy grease membrane between my fingers where I'd touched her. She piled me into the passenger seat.

She looked up and down the street, back at the line of corporate box stores, scanning the horizon. Then she returned to me.

"Fuck you, you're probably just going to kill me anyway," I wheezed.

She closed the door on me, leaving me with two seconds to jerk my hand out of the gap before they were jelly.

★

If I thought I felt sick after I woke up this morning, it was nothing compared to now. My bleached face in the sideview mirror while I hung onto the door of the car without strength, strapped in without motivation. My spineless head rolling from shoulder to shoulder as Elvedina veered down the street and back to the house.

She slapped me. I hissed and threw up my hands and came fully awake. Her knuckles pressed white against the steering wheel, her face in profile as it cut through sunlight. I felt as though I should know her—the cast of her features, the suggestion of her Balkan background, summoned all the ferocious memories of Sarajevo, but I was not ready for Sarajevo and never would be, so I buried it.

Elvedina dragged me out. I listed and slid, collapsing out of the car. My neck burned with the memory of the seat belt. Every spoken word came attached with a fish hook. Up close, I could smell her. Gun oil and lead off a firing range. I wanted to vomit all over her shirt in a desperate bid to express my disgust and fear of her. Or was I thinking of Jessica, my long lost wife? My head swam and my eyes rolled to look at her, and still, it was only Elvedina. She hoisted me up by my shirt so I hung in the air like a marionette and then herded me into the house. Fever broiled in my mouth. Sweat rolled off my skin. My head on a balloon string far above the earth.

We burst through the door and I found the couch. Voices. Lionel's query, a trembling question. The sound of Lafferty's wheels *rap-rap-rapping* over the floorboards as he rolled to me. Someone pressed a cloth to my forehead. Elvedina, her hand on my head, her lips colorless and her eyes like surgical lasers.

"Get away from me," I croaked. "Get her away from me."

Lionel cut through the fray and his voice gave me focus. His face loomed above me and Elevedina subsided into the background.

"What happened?" Lionel asked.

I opened my mouth to tell him and instead the world came rushing out of my throat and spilling all over the floor.

★

After my embarrassing vomiting episode, Lionel scrubbed his shoes free of backsplash at the table where we all sat, while I sipped a glass of water and recovered.

Elvedina paced back and forth outside on the porch. My hands were clammy, my forehead cold and waxen where I pressed the glass to it to cool the fever inside. The vulture migrated out of my bedroom and invited himself to the countertop, flapping his wings and beating the air to get closer to the table. He settled beside the trash can to preen his feathers and peck at leftover Chinese takeout. Lafferty stared at it with one eyebrow raised. Lionel was absorbed in maintaining his shoes with his trembling hands. I could see the bulge in his pocket where his ancient grenade resided.

"Highsmith did this?" Lafferty said.

"It was just a dream," I said and set the glass down. With a slip of my eyelids, I could drift off into sleep. My catnap in the car had counted for nothing. "A really vivid dream."

Lionel nodded while he buffed one shoe and finally the old
man set it down and stepped into it, pulling up his pant leg to set
the heel.

"There was another casualty at the prison again, Vitus," Lionel
said.

"Another prisoner? Someone crossed him?"

"Not quite," and Lionel's pronunciation came out slow,
labored as though he did not like to think on the news he intended
to deliver. "No, I'm afraid the prison guard I bribed to report
to me is dead. He apparently passed out from unknown causes,
which this alone would not have proved fatal. He happened to be
taking a bath, however, when he went under."

"He drowned?"

"They'll be doing an autopsy," Lionel said.

"His heart. They're gonna cut him open and, if they're smart,
they won't stop at his lungs. They'll see his heart stopped."

"You know, Vitus," Lionel began, "you seemed quite sick when
you awoke this morning. What did you dream of last night?"

I waved a hand in the air to indicate vagueness. "Nothing,
really."

"Or nothing you'd like to share," Lafferty pointed out. He
gave me just what I needed—a helping of acid with the main
course.

"They were strange. Disjointed. My father. Highsmith. Some
other guy I dreamt of once before. Just meaningless psychobabble
from the brain."

"Highsmith again?" Lafferty said, but not at me. He spoke
over my head to Lionel as though I were a child and they were
my parents discussing sex. "I don't believe in coincidences."

"I'm right here," I said.

"Vitus," Lionel began slowly, his voice reminding me of the
smell of old libraries and the sound of paper in a world before
phones and cell phones and neon distractions. "Did you ever
consider that Highsmith is killing people through dreams?"

"That's your theory? That's the best you got?" I stared,
incredulous.

The vulture squawked and leapt into the air to land on the counter.

Talons tapped over the surface and he ambled over to drink out of the sink. His head like raw hamburger with a beak pressed in and his black eyes, staring at me. I would have to feed him if he was going to stay, but I couldn't concentrate on the damn bird and untangle the newest knot of bullshit presented to me at the same time.

"Look, I know how it sounds—" Lafferty began.

"No, I don't think you do," I snapped. "Mind bullets and bad dreams? Where are you getting this crap?"

"Highsmith said he'd killed with the power of his mind, didn't he? And we got nothing else for a weapon. No poison, nothing on toxicology."

"Don't feed me shit and say you baked brownies, Geoff," I said. "You know they don't test for everything."

"There is quite a lot of literature on incubi and their ill effects," Lionel added, leaning forward across the table to stare at me like those people who casually talk about sex demons between sports stats and weather reports. He reached out and set the back of his hand against my forehead. The touch of his hand, cool. He then leaned back and away. I didn't even let my father touch me. "Your fever is down," Lionel said, wiping his hand off with a napkin.

"Incubi? Oh good. We can read exorcisms next. You do know it's the twenty-first century, right? That we left the Dark Ages behind five hundred years ago?"

"Have we?" Lionel said, mild. "With modern-day crusades in the Middle East alive and well?"

"Look, I'm pretty sure I didn't have weird kinky sex dreams with Highsmith, so consider your bullshit theory debunked. My father was the one who used to argue politics, but I don't have to put up with it now."

"Not so fast," Lionel said. "It doesn't have to be sex that does you in. There are things undiscovered yet that could just drain you of your vitality. It doesn't have to be an incubus, but the idea is similar, is it not? To feed off you, as a parasite."

"Well it looks like you got the whole thing solved and you don't need me anymore."

"It doesn't take a doctor to see that you're sickening."

Lionel lifted a trembling hand. He looked feeble at the table but the small shift in motion commanded our attention and rendered us silent. He tapped his forehead, wrinkled like the pages of a book when you hold it on one side—etched horizontal lines, timeless wisdom sandwiched between.

"What I am about to tell you, you never heard me tell you," Lionel whispered. "What I am about to say has never existed."

The vulture squawked and lifted into the air, landing clumsily on the back of my chair and beating his wings against my head. I cursed and pushed at him for space and he ignored me, brushing his talons over my shoulder and standing close to me so his feathers rested against one ear where he sat, contented. He smelled like yesterday's garbage, but I'd spent years saturated in my own decay so I suffered it, riveted to Lionel. Lafferty and I understood without speaking that what he would say next was classified information. What happens in Vegas—or in government operations—stays there.

"We ran programs involving out-of-body experiences," Lionel said gently.

And this, my friends, is how your tax dollars get spent, so people can pretend they're ghosts and call it a full-time job.

The Dark Ages, indeed.

★

Out-of-Body Experience—or OBE, as it's commonly known—belongs in the world of government conspiracy theorists who like their paranoia thick and their tinfoil hats thicker. Fringe groups intersecting between hackers, hippies, and goths. Neo-witches playing around with colored bits of paper for love spells and lighting candles on the full moon, hoping maybe Stacy in Biology 101 will let him get to second base.

When Lionel spoke the words *out-of-body experiences*, I tumbled back in memory to find myself beside Jamie once more.

Our years reduced to fractions and divided up into moments, all the way back to childhood. Our mother, winding the phone cord around one arm and talking in earnest whispers over the wires. Our father, away politicking in Washington. We were Roman Centurions. We were native braves, outwitting Custer. We were plotting elaborate fantasies and schemes to free the dinosaurs trapped in the center of the earth.

We hadn't quite reached that inimitable place when you discover desire, frustration, sex. People tell themselves they stop daydreaming once they hit puberty, but that's not true. We go right on daydreaming into adulthood—it just complicates things when they hoist you up by your puppy scruff and throw you out into a world filled with guns and knives, and worse yet, people wearing three-piece suits more dangerous than any street thug. Women whose lipstick is just a smattering of war paint. Broken hearts, broken promises, and the lies we tell ourselves. Welcome to adulthood, kid. You can dream, but it's the cost that breaks you.

Before we hit those dubious rites of passage, our favorite pastime was breaking into our old man's library because it was there, and we could. Because it smelled and felt like a place we shouldn't be. Because we were forbidden and it was rich with the promise of opportunities, of ghosts that needed banishing and secrets in need of liberation.

Our father kept books and papers everywhere. The room had an exoskeleton of leather-bound volumes, tomes nicked straight from the library of Alexandria before it burned. Foreign language dictionaries open on the desk. A gun sitting on the ink blotter as though that was the instrument our father used to sign papers. Civil War–era colonels' swords, one from each side of the conflict.

Here we discovered moldy chapters on lore long forgotten. We laughed and scoffed and called it crazy. Laughing and scoffing our way into our teenage years and into adulthood, but deep down inside, we struggled not to think deeply about it.

Jamie and I had a long way to go yet from the library room in our father's house to a full-fledged spook curating the very books we spent our childhood mocking. Back then, we used to trade old texts with Victorian illustrations back and forth between us. A man sleeping on a bed and his ghostly double rising up from the mattress while his other self slept on, connected only by a thin thread of consciousness. Detailed instructions on how the subject should recline, how much they should eat the night before (little if anything), their mindset, tricks on how to ease into the state. Charts on chakras and how they opened a seam down the body to allow the other self to eject from the physical shell. Seriously metaphysical shit that made us jumpy. Jamie would stand lookout in the mahogany planked hall while I read a passage out loud to him in a whisper. We laughed and cracked jokes and later on in the night, we stayed awake, wondering if twins of ourselves were escaping our bodies in our dreams and playing pranks on the rest of the world, ghosts connected by a thin silver cord while we slept. Wondering if those dreams of flying were stand-ins for when we ourselves had left our bodies. And we kept on wondering, right up until I started to get into too many knife fights in school and Jamie wanted to excel and be the good son, thumbing his nose at our long lost brotherhood in favor of pushing me out of the imperial nest so he could preen before Father. Such was Jamie.

And now he was gone. I'd pushed him out of the nest for good. We weren't boys anymore. The allure of breaking into the library was not nearly exciting as once we entered the disappointing and cursed land of adulthood and responsibility.

The day before I left to join the military, I visited my father in his office to give him a stiff and formal goodbye, but the old gray fox had slipped away. I never did tell Jamie how I opened up the door into a cold and sterile room. Civil War blades spotted and tarnished with the blood of dead legions. Our father, vanished. Left me standing over his desk filled with papers and stacked books.

I pulled out a photo of a man lying on a bed. Naked. Electrodes pasted down his bird-thin chest. His eyes hollowed and closed into black circles. A scientist with a clipboard in his white lab coat. I need but listen, and I can summon the sound of machinery calculating mathematics and imagine the sound of my father's voice, his steps on the linoleum, commanding, holding papers in his hand and signing away other people's lives. My father. The quintessential desk murderer.

And the smudge of smoke, levitating just above the body of the patient, giving thin suggestion to a set of eyes, a slant of mouth.

A faint silver cord between.

Fast forward to the present: I reflected on the questionable heart attack victims Niko had taken in to her mortuary. Their hearts stopped in their chests. Their eyes open wide and the capillaries burst as though someone had reached in through their throats and squeezed until there was no more blood left to milk. I wondered if when Blake Highsmith fell asleep, he rose from himself like a fading Polaroid photo and walked out of his own cell and down the lonesome halls of the prison and out the front door and into the pale moonlight. Hummed to himself. I imagined a tune to complement his classical tastes, like Beethoven's "Ode To Joy," as he glided with a smile on his face and a vacant expression in his eyes suitable to the kind of psychopath who was absent of feeling and had always been that way. Perhaps Mommy hadn't hugged him enough. Daddy didn't buy him that pop-gun for Christmas. Now his eyes reduced to buttons of glass without feeling, his heart filled with high-test hate simmering through every chamber and waiting for the chance to swallow another life.

My brother's voice from the past: *Beware the echoes and specters!*

If Lionel was right, this is what Highsmith had been doing. Becoming a ghost between his eight-hundred-count cotton sheets. Treating his sleep like a business proposition, the date of my attempted murder another action item in his schedule book. He'd slip down the streets in the high noon heat, find me sleeping like a babe with my head tilted back on the headrest, mouth half open, unaware of the pseudo-ghost hovering near. This is how it played out. This is how the seat belt came loose, unspooling to snarl and brand a burn around my throat while Highsmith violated my dreams to kill me, dead.

I couldn't lay my hands on this knot to unravel it. I couldn't logic it. How do I put an end to something I couldn't see or detect with the naked eye? How did I square this with known reality?

The vulture squawked behind me from a distant galaxy. I reached up behind me to stroke him absently while Lionel and Lafferty argued over out-of-body-experiences and their validity.

Smoke and mirrors, my Id whispered. *You've seen the road this leads down, if you buy into the occult. Remember Jessica? She used belief to control people. Like all clever politicians do. This man-made fantasy leads us down the treacherous path of obscurantism.*

The type of thing my father would have done. Did I dare believe the impossible only to have it used in turn to control me? I was not so confident and self-assured to believe that I too was not used as a pawn. That's how fools are made, by their hubris. Even now, how did I know I was not carefully being placed on the chessboard set by my father's own hand?

Let Todd think that. Just up until the knight stands up and walks right off the board and out of sight.

But had he foreseen even that?

Would I die with Highsmith's hand jammed down my throat, strangling my heart?

The vulture shook me off. Down the line of Lionel and Lafferty, the old man's hands trembling as he continued to argue and tried to articulate that there might be other victims as of yet undiscovered. Across the table and through the door, Elvedina stood in the threshold. Her eyes as bullets, the rims primed and ready to explode.

Who would get to me first? Elvedina, or Highsmith?

★

Lionel outlined his speculation while the vulture abandoned the chair and high-stepped onto my shoulder, kneading me like the world's ugliest cat.

The vulture and I listened, attentive, as Lionel narrated his speculation for us. If the old man was unnerved by my newfound psychopomp, he said nothing of it. Highsmith, Lionel went on, must be a subsidiary of the OBE program—the program we have to pretend doesn't exist and that we can't ever speak of or write down.

I lit a cigarette and wondered how Jamie went about it. Did he create a drug to facilitate the lucid state required for out-of-body experiences? Smoke curled out of my mouth. I considered if I could be as fluid as that smoke, as free and dispersing. Allowed myself to consider the impossible. And the impossible proved seductive. For the hardened cynic, there was nothing more alluring than illusion. Than the thing you *want* to believe. True love, fairy tales, happy endings. Romance is the ultimate weak spot of any hard-nosed pragmatist.

My father counted on it. So close, I could smell him in the room, or maybe that shadowed presence of the lone Inspector, watching us even now. I waved a hand through the smoke and it vanished. The vulture cooed and squawked and shifted on my shoulder.

"I don't believe it, and it's not good enough. We have to go to the source."

"Highsmith?" Lafferty said.

"No, my dead fucking brother of course, Highsmith."

"Elvedina will take you to the prison again. I'll arrange a more private meeting, shall I? I can't have you asking sensitive questions while being surveilled."

I wanted to protest Elvedina's presence, but decided it would seem suspicious. Lionel had made it clear he would not relent in this.

Lionel and Lafferty argued with the contents of Highsmith's folder spread out before them. I got up and sent the vulture reeling to the kitchen counter, his wings raised before he flattened them against his back and closed his eyes with his beak pulsing open, pale pink tongue like a sewing needle. The creature flapped behind me, talons awkward and tearing at my shirt before I steadied him with one hand. He settled on my shoulder as easily as a telephone wire, cooing deep in his throat like a purr.

I slipped down the hall and faded into the familiar darkness of my house. These places I'd once roamed, these places in total midnight black when I'd been undead and haunted, lamenting my long lost human-life and all the things I once had loved, or not loved well enough: my wife, my son. What did I have left to lament, now that humanity was returned to me? To weep over Niko, what we lost or the many ways I'd wronged her? Things that were never meant to be?

From a distance behind, coming for me across the floor, I heard Elvedina's steady and relentless tread.

I turned the corner into my room and the bird moved with me, riding shotgun on my shoulder still and determined to make this his new home. I counted the seconds I had remaining to me. I knew this room of old. After a quick calculation, I knocked over a shelf of books. In the empty space behind the boards where I kept a Glock 19 duct taped, there was nothing. Nothing but the pale and shining threads of ripped tape. I stared at it and reconstructed the intrusion, someone quietly pulling out the books and stripping the gun out. It could have been Lafferty, it could have been Lionel.

Or Elvedina.

Her steps beat out time, closer. I thrust a hand up into the box spring of the mattress. I fumbled for a hidden weapon. Instead, an old Atroxipine bottle spilled out and rolled along the floor. The vulture flew from my shoulder, attacking the bottle until it bounced to the other side of the room.

I had made a mental note to buy the bastard a mouse from the pet store when Elvedina reached the doorway.

I turned and found myself toe to toe with Elvedina. I took in her face from our intimate proximity. Sexless in the dim light. A winding scar rising up out of her shirt collar and twisting its path to the space behind her ear; as though her entire face was a mask that I need only reach around to unclasp and pull away to see the real Elvedina hiding within. Gun oil wafted from her. She packed a weapon where I couldn't see.

"Why not just gun me down now? Instead of feeding me to Highsmith, you could be done with it and back from whatever godforsaken place things like you come from. You could do it now," I suggested. I pitched my voice soft. If one didn't know better, we'd be mistaken for lovers arranging a secret tryst. "You could pull out your weapon and stop my heart. Think of how easy it would be, think of the relief. I've killed. Oh sure, our circumstances are different. But the anxiety is the same. Even a stoic feels it, deep in their cold heart."

The vulture scrabbled at the pill bottle in the corner.

I drew closer, close enough to point my finger and tap her chest once. Her skin, permafrost. "That fear-sweat that creeps out cold over your skin. Your heart picks up extra beats you didn't know you had, just before it evens out and gets real still. You could put an end to all that, right now. And I'd probably fucking deserve it."

An inch of space enough for a snake to crawl through was all that was left between us. Not a molecule stirred between. The slick membrane of the Jersey humidity plastering clothes to flesh and making my every breath sluggish, but of her, nothing. I sensed her attention slipping, a low-level boredom, and I played my last card.

Her chest did not even seem to rise and fall with respiration, no increased heartbeat or breath. Ice cold and steady through and through.

"Maybe you're here for something else, huh?" I leered.

This quickened her; she shoved a hand into her shirt and pulled out the Sig. She planted the gun into my chest and used it to push me back, driving the barrel into the old cigarette burn so I hissed. She swept my legs out so I fell backward onto the bed.

I wish I could say it was foreplay but there was an edge of darkness to her that sent me crawling back. She held up her thumb and forefinger with a bare millimeter between the two, her stare withering me even after she left the room.

The burn still itched and throbbed over my nipple. The door slammed in the wind of her absence, left the vulture and

me behind, rattling the prescription bottle with the damning
reminder of my past.

★

"You look like shit," Lafferty said.

I sat on the edge of Lafferty's pull-out mattress and ran my
hands through my hair. I'd have to get a cut soon. This was
something I'd never had to worry about before. That, and eating.

Lionel's biggest contribution to the case was a conspiracy
theory based on old CIA programs that probably hadn't been
relevant since the Cold War. Lionel made sandwiches in the
kitchen as though he belonged in some faraway cabin, vacationing
with his grand kids and teaching them how to fish.

"I feel like it, too. What a coincidence." The burn marks from
the seatbelt stood out in hyper contrast on my throat. I skated
my fingers over the ring of it. "I never thanked you."

"For what?"

"For taking care of the evidence for me. You didn't have to
do that. You could get in big trouble for hiding something like
that. And they could have sent me away for a long time if they
had found it. Thanks for not spilling it to Lionel and Elvedina,
either."

He laughed, quiet while he looked at the floor between
his useless legs. "They tried. Came with a search warrant and
everything."

Coldness overtook me at the thought. If they had found what
I'd hidden—but that was a road not taken. And it would do me
no good to think on it now. For now, Lafferty held it safe and
secret. When this was all over, I could return to the evidence
room and face all the things I'd left behind.

"Take this," Lafferty said, and he looked away and down the
hall for Elvedina as he pressed something into my palm.

Cold metal burned a line into my hand. I yanked my shirt
up and stuffed it into my belt. The size and shape of a folding
knife.

"Thanks."

"That bitch comes for you, give her hell. I'll be watching. You scream, I come."

"You don't really think Highsmith is leaving his body at night and slapping me around while I sleep, do you?"

He snorted laughter. "If he is, you got a helluva lot more than Elvedina to worry about."

★

The gloaming descended. Night came with slick and humid breath, oven hot winds and the cicadas whining in the trees.

Fluffy found the back of my bed post and dug his talons into the wood so they left flecks of cheap white fiber beneath. I discovered red welts on my shoulder where his talons bit in. Elvedina's heavy tread made every floorboard squeal and rock. The shower ran while I sat cross-legged on the mattress, turning a pack of cigarettes over in my hand and contemplating all the things that make life worth living.

You mean like pain, the death of loved ones, and the people you betrayed? My Id suggested with sarcasm.

My old zombie self had a point and left me ruminating on the bad more than the good. Niko telling me she liked me better when I had scars. I thumbed the hot ring of the cigarette burn Elvedina branded into my chest. Maybe in a year or two, Niko and I could try again. At the rate I was going, I'd have plenty of new scars to make up for the old ones.

I reclined, palming the burn, but there was no comfort in these coiled springs, no good memories between them. The room became a prison cell and my bed a tomb.

"Come on, Highsmith. I'm waiting," I hissed to the ceiling.

Jamie's murder key slid across my collarbone, metal alternating between hot and cold. I reached up and unclasped it, set it down on the end table. One more mystery I couldn't solve.

Sleep did not come. The sunlight faded and brought mosquitoes and tree frogs singing into the heat. The moon, splitting the sky with a muggy corona like a single, bleary eye surveilling us. I tossed and turned on sheets dipped in swamp land, the marsh in my mouth. Elvedina's shadow revolved like a clockface, ticking back and forth until I finally dug out the spare bottle of Laphroaig in the bottom of my sock drawer and jammed it down my mouth in a desperate bid to get it over with. To get to the battle ground.

Alcohol burned a stinging pathway down my throat. The bottle fell from my outstretched hand, rolled under the bed. The vulture, flitting his wings to settle into a better position on the headboard, and focusing one eye on me like a cracked marble floating in viscera.

I wanted the drink to be good enough, good enough to forget the persistent itch of my ravenous hunger, a hunger so reminiscent of my zombie days. And then it came, the rattle of the prescription bottle like music, the twirl of the cap and the bitter pills under my tongue. I increased the dose and took four together, one after the other like mints. How far could I push it? Did I dare? Was it possible to overdose? I was hurtling into a world of unknowns headfirst without a helmet. And I didn't care.

I closed my eyes. The cigarette burn, throbbing until the pulse of Elvedina's footsteps blurred, became one with my heartbeat.

Back and forth. Footstep layered on footstep until the drumming beat lifted me through semiconsciousness. I grew light and insubstantial. The relief of slumber, finally. Let me forget everything and subside into darkness.

Void and blackness. Then something woke me to myself.

I plummeted out of dreamless serenity. Opened my eyes and stared up at the cracks mutilating the ceiling. The moving curtain at the window. I registered a silence that marked Elvedina's absence. Counted my breaths and listened for her. Counted heartbeats. I could not detect her footsteps anywhere throughout the old and settling ranch. Distant snores escaped Lafferty on the pull-out couch.

A shadow occupied the corner of the room.

I sat up in the darkness, confusing reality with shapes that weren't there. I rubbed my eyes and waited for the shadows to move. They did not. The wind and the moonlight shifted, brought with it bare illumination and caught the glitter of peering eyes in the dark.

"Highsmith," I growled.

The shadow morphed and lengthened, delineating a human shape. A swipe of a hand. From thick coils of darkness, it stood— rising and sliding like a box turning inside out. The figure gained cohesion, rested before a band of moonlight so only the curve of his jaw, the jut of his shoulder in a suit, became visible.

"You're not Highsmith."

A grin divided the dark. His teeth were bleached white and concealing endless rows of sharpened canines behind the first.

Highsmith's a naughty one. Talking too much when he should be grateful for what he still has. Namely, his life. Which brings us to you. You've made it quite far, for an upstart.

"Tell me about it, whoever you are."

I don't deal in names.

"What are you then? You're the one they call the Inspector, aren't you?"

The grin stretched wider like an elastic band testing the limits of breaking.

"What do you care if I live or die?"

The same reason some men put money on horses, he answered. *It's how we put irrational and uncontrollable fate in a controlled setting. Our humanity's acknowledgment to free-wheeling fortune, that force we cannot tame with all our science and technology.*

"So you're saying you gamble your money on me living or dying, just to comfort you in the face of an indifferent universe?"

Essentially, peasant.

"Which one was it? Which did you put money on?"

The Inspector leaned forward out of the darkness.

Moonlight tiger-striped his face, pulsing in and out of reality like a strobe giving brief flashes of things carouseling out of my vision—warped skin over bone, flaking flesh in striations that immediately faded and gave way to smooth youthful skin in a whirling dervish of disease and vitality unified. A face in flux and howling.

His knee hit the mattress as he landed. Springs squealed. Every perception intensified, from the crease in his suit pants to the bony wrist curling out from his sleeve. My lips curled up away from my teeth as I scrabbled backward along rough and dirty sheets, away from him, but he advanced, inexorable.

Time reversed upon itself. Imprisoned in dream time speed. The bed no longer a bed, but a conveyor belt forcing me to move closer even as I shrank before the Inspector's pursuit. His mouth flew open, hissing.

This is real, I thought. Jesus Christ, *this is really real.*

The flash and gleam of something in his right hand. He laid the other across my chest to bar me. My limbs stricken, tied down with hundred-pound weights at the wrist. The touch of him featherlight at first and then pressing with the force of megatons. Fingers weighed me down like ancient ritual stones in human sacrifices. For the first time in my life, it occurred to me, with his undulating snaking roll across my body, that I could be raped. A fate I'd ignorantly thought was only reserved for women could also be mine to suffer.

His movement was undeniably sexual, but conquest was not his goal; he instead laid the flat of the knife blade across my belly and held it there. Put his lips directly at my ear and held me taut and listening. I longed to hear Elvedina's footfalls like thunder, to break the spell. Where was the calvary? And the rushing emptiness of realization: there is no calvary. No one is coming to save me.

Vitus, I know it doesn't seem like it, but I'm betting on life.

I laughed through the fear. "I know what people like you do, people like my father."

And what is it we do, exactly?

"You bet on both sides and tell me how you were pulling for me all along."

Surprise. Even a hint of pride, as though he perceived me for who I am, for the very first time.

Very good, Vitus. Very good, indeed.
And then, he sank a knife into my belly.

★

Liquid fire opened up a seam across my abdomen. I followed the line of agony out of the dream and into the screaming dawn burning over the horizon. The folding knife Lafferty gave me hours before clattered out of my midsection and to the floor.

The vulture screamed, his wings unfurled at the window and sunlight slanted through his feathers. My return to the waking world left me alone; abandoned save the vulture, the Inspector evaporated into the shadows. I clutched my belly, holding in the blood with a torment so deep it leached through the soles of my feet and into the ground. Fracked through bone and marrow. My spine rattled against the headboard as I struggled to rise— every instinct pushing me from paralysis to action and failing miserably. Strategies took form and burst apart before I could act on them. Find a phone. Find a person.

But the vulture ate the phone and nothing remained.

The door burst wide. Elvedina filled the threshold, all six-foot Balkan length of her, her eyes, mercury-burst thermometers. She lurched into the room like a loping wolf, snarling, latched a hand around my bare ankle and dragged me bodily to the end of the bed while I writhed and screamed. My voice blew out, extinguished into a pitiful gurgle of desolate noise.

I couldn't fight her and hold my guts in at the same time.

She grabbed at my wrists; I fought with her, stubborn, until she succeeded in tearing them away from my middle. My ripped shirt, the open, oozing wound exposed.

I remembered Niko, when I first came to the funeral home with my jaw bone in hand and hope in my heart, her levelheaded stare when I expected screaming. Niko surprised me with tenderness where I deserved none, kindness when I'd used up all good will.

Elvedina plotted to kill me behind cold assassin's eyes. Calculations stacked up behind her gaze as she scanned the room for useful items, discarded the sheets as too bulky, and instead tore her shirt off over her head, shoved the shirt down into the bleeding center of me, hard, a lit stick of dynamite exploded in my guts. I loosed a new scream of agony. She took the long sleeves of her shirt and wrapped them around my center, binding me fast. I fell back, sweating out my pain and shivering out my agony. Jamie's voice was at my ear as though I stood outside of myself on some distant shore, watching this wash of a boy, flailing and convulsing with pain, my brother narrating for me the extent of my damage with detached, medical interest. Noting the coldness in my fingers, the numbness, the creeping shock. Taking my pulse with scientific detachment.

She slapped me.

The distant fantasy of my brother diagnosing me from afar evaporated. I skyrocketed back to the screaming present. I cursed at her and she slapped me again. Either she was keeping me alive by preventing me from passing out or she moonlighted as a dominatrix and was clocking in extra hours. She could delay the others, delay the help. Let me bleed out while the EMTs were en route. Leave me with my guts tumbling onto the floor like telephone wires. Of course, that didn't seem to jibe with her irritating, albeit charming slaps to the face jolting me from the brink of gray-tinged vision, threatening to consume me and lead me onward to blissful shock-sleep, perhaps never to awaken.

She grabbed my face in her hand and squeezed. Brutal and dirty fingers painted lines of ice into my sweating skin. Her palm bit like the rubber heel of a stilletto shoe.

"You gonna kill me, just you fucking try," I husked.

Doors banged open in the hall. Lafferty's chair rolled over the planks like a freight train racing down the tracks, *thawk thawk thawk thawk*. A rifle shot cracked through the morning bird song. The birds fell silent. The vulture's beak opened and closed beneath rolling eyes as he danced, agitated, from one leg to the other, worrying the bed post, his half furled wings throwing a shadow over me.

Elvedina revolved, catching the door with her fingers and slamming it shut on the racing wheelchair charging down the hall. The door buckled as he rammed it, and his wheels squealed when he bounced backward.

I tried to yell. Each word came with a sucker punch. "The damn bitch has me—"

Elvedina snarled and reached over to pick up the end table. The lamp went crashing to the floor. The lightbulb popped like a firecracker and sprayed glass. My voice lost all strength as she swung the end table by the leg and threw it into the window. More glass shattered, fragmented into the dawn.

Lafferty's voice filled the hall in a relentless echo. "*Get down!*"

A shotgun blast. The bedroom knob blew out. Innards of the lock uncorked across the floor.

Elvedina turned and scooped me up. I seesawed in her grasp. The world revolved in confusing kaleidoscope and confounding fever. Wasn't I supposed to be picking *her* up off the floor? What was next, the godforsaken smelling salts?

If I'd had masculine pride, it must have fallen out of my pocket where Elvedina crushed it beneath her heel as she took me, shivering and dying, directly out the broken window. Lafferty yelled for her to stop or he'd shoot, *by god, he'd chase us in the fuckin' wheelchair if he had to.*

My head tilted back. The rushing sky filled my vision; Elvedina half-naked with her own shirt wrapped around me like a swaddling child. A living sphinx. Every stride of her legs and pump of her heart a bellows. *This is how I'm going to die.* Staring at the sky where the scratching tree limbs cut light into prison bars. The shadow of a vulture, tracking us with his lambent eyes, crying out into the wilderness.

PART 3

DEUS EX MACHINA

O nce upon a time, as all the fairy tales go, I was a zombie. They called my condition *pre-deceased* to describe the state in which I was legally dead but still conscious, as though it made the indignity of my arrested mortality easier to bear—made it easier to ignore the limbs that would become loose in my joints and the teeth that would unceremoniously eject from my jaw, make it easier to suffer the tears that would form in my flesh, like flaking lead paint on a fence post.

Zombie sounded too grindhouse for my brother, so he slapped a title on it, the same way he would a medal of honor on a soldier. Like I should be thankful to experience every trivial ache and monstrous agony of death in slow-mo.

They distilled chemicals from puffer fish. From the spotted mushroom *Amanita Muscaria* and *Atropa Belladonna,* deadly nightshade. A witches' brew they named Atroxipine. They gave me endless refills. With this prescription, I could ape and mime all the rituals and habits of any living human (except for the living part). It gave me a subzero blood flow, but lit up the reactors in my brain like a Christmas tree. Restrained me from sideslipping in that feral state known from every zombie movie.

But the time between one pill and another sustaining my upright animation would stretch thin and perilous. An itch came over me as one dose ended and I readied to take another, timed out to the alarm on my wristwatch. The consequences if I skipped a dose were extreme. I could not decide to discontinue my treatment and bargain with myself for a medication-free life just to come crawling back to the pill bottle once I'd learned my lesson. To forget was to devolve. To forget was to fall through the abyss of my psyche and never find my way back again, and I would be reduced to a jaw-snapping, teeth-clattering hunger that could never be satisfied and never be filled.

I never skipped a dose. Never played with the milligrams just to see what would happen. But as the deadline approached and I waited for my watch's interminable *beep beep* and felt the sheen of moisture in the back of my throat churn in anticipation of a raw meal, I intuited a darkness welling up all around me and contracting my vision to narrow pinpoints. Could sense and taste my backslide into the less than human. Falling through a hole in myself to land in the deepest and darkest ninth circle of Dante's Inferno where I could not remember who I was, how I got there, or anything other than satisfying this endless hunger.

The times I fell through the hole were rare; but they stuck out in memory like old silent films with their washed-out silver celluloid. Broken frames. Herky-jerky sounds. Some frames sped up, others slowed down, and the central narrative lost, so when I finally did recover, I was left to piece together the broken memories. No amount of deduction could reverse engineer my personal tragedies. All that was left behind were useless bits and pieces of an engine that would never run again.

When finally I woke from a nightmare Inspector shoving his knife into my bowels, I thought myself returned to the past, drifting back and forth through my own timeline. A zombie one second, human in another. A ceiling avalanched above me in blinding white. When I turned my head, a row of gurneys stacked in an infinite line, one after the other.

I recognized the interior of Pleasant Hills Funeral Home. Bodies awaiting burial, awaiting the strict attention of my Underworld

Queen, Niko. Had Elvedina brought me here? Questions crowded in and stacked up, one fast upon the other. I stretched back into memory to understand how I had arrived here, who had taken me, and if I were still in danger. My head sluggish as the result of a deep anesthesia, threatening to pull me back into the dark.

A singular memory of Elvedina carrying me, the halls and rooms of the funeral home and Niko's voice, unintelligible—afraid? Terrified?—and then, a mask closed over my mouth, spitting noxious fumes into my lungs. When I turned to face this new assault, I held onto a second of consciousness to stare into Elvedina's heartless and cruel face, her mouth flat as a blade and their seam the sword-gutter through which the blood of enemies is designed to run. A flashing scalpel in one hand, the doctor's mask engulfing her rigid face into a sinister doctor with Niko's tools at her disposal, and Niko, where was Niko?

Not here. I fought to wake. My purpose should be to protect her even if she resented me and resented my protection. What had Elvedina done with her, to her?

But there descended blackness, and no room for Niko in the black.

Voices penetrated into the leviathan through which I'd fallen. The squawking vulture. Images of my brother. Memories of my father. Dreams of Highsmith laughing at me as usual but this time he stopped laughing and begged me to help him until his face distorted into the snout of a pig, snorting. Tears ran down his face and his laugh crossed the boundary into screams.

The dreams ended. Hands pressing on my belly—deep and seismic tremblings through my solar plexus. I vomited into the mask. Someone turned me over and cleaned me up. The long and narrow line of a hand pulled a rug needle away from my stomach.

Stitching me back together.

Don't you know? My Id whispered. *You died. This is where people go when they are dead. To the funeral home. Won't that make you so pleased, to have one last night together with her?*

Every stitch pull was another in a long line of embalming. Fingers too rough to be Niko's. Every time I opened my eyes, I waited to discover myself inside a coffin, to wake up to my own funeral. Soon, the embalming pump would sound and deliver formaldehyde into my veins and preserve my worthless heart.

But every time I opened my eyes, I was still on the table, and still not quite dead enough. Elvedina skirted the edges of my vision with her teeth bared like knives and bent over me. She wore the look of kamikaze determination, turning her blank face into a rictus. Her desperation mesmerized me in its raw ugliness. Each time her fist disappeared into the mound of my ruined guts, warmth spread out until I could only writhe beneath her stare.

Whispers cosseted me. A brisk command: *"More ether, please"* and the steady *blip blip* of my pulse rate tracking on a third-world veterinarian's heart monitor.

Elvedina wavered into view as though I were staring up at her through the bottom of a lake.

She lifted a wand of black iron in her hand; a foot's length of sinister metal radiated heat and turned glowing red. Elvedina grinned. The red glow lit her smile like a jack-o'-lantern's as she laid the end of the burning wand on my belly and I understood, then: she was using a cautery.

I smelled myself burning.

Beware the echoes and specters

I passed out.

★

No matter to me the blood in my mouth or the broken bones. Years without dreaming in my zombie state made me hungry for it now. I closed my eyes, reeling back into darkness and counting sheep with abandon.

Long ago, all I had was the cold comfort of late-night television. Old noirs, black and whites on the silver screen. The dead don't sleep; and now I floated on a wave of syrup in a vast ocean. My only complaint is I can't change the programming, and I have to take the nightmares with the dreams.

Sometimes the nightmares seem so like real life. A shadow of a memory. Of a thing I did that I cannot take back, a decision committed that cannot be unmade. The fates, conspiring against my better self and forcing my hand into murder. My father had a term for this: *iacta alea est*. The die is cast.

When they questioned me at the police station, I said I did not know what I had done. I did not remember killing my brother. I could even believe my own lie to buy me some peace. But here in dreams, I could not relent. The memory, like a freshly printed photo:

I've got a gun in my hand pressed to my brother's chest and his wife yells at us, chucking ugly knickknacks and figurines at us. They shatter on the hardwood flooring until we're covered in ceramic and blood. We're eye to eye. Jamie shaking and spitting blood while I press the tip of the Glock over his heart. He reaches up and I'm ready to do it again, take our sprawling fistfight right over broken glass and drop us straight off a cliff into hell, if there is one.

"Why wait?"

He guides the muzzle into the path of his heart. Presses it there. Jamie doesn't take a swing at me. Doesn't close his eyes. He doesn't look angry or sorry or sad. He looks like a man about to go on his way to the most important board meeting of his career. He reaches up at his neck and grabs at a chain, a necklace glinting with blood and light. He snaps it off into his fist and loops it over the muzzle of my gun.

At the end of it, a black skeleton key sits along the side of the firearm. My key, my murder key.

"Take care of her," Jamie said. "I love you, brother. Beware the echoes and specters. Beware the echoes and specters!"

His voice, climbing in volume, and I killed him. Blood spray coating me through and through and the errant buzzing of the fly in my grip. The fly that wants to eat, infect, and give away this zombie magic to another.

Her? What did he mean, her? Megan? Our mother?

And who were the echoes and specters?

★

Through the never ending blackness, I came back from
eternity.

I woke up on a gurney, alone in the white rooms and halls
of Pleasant Hills Funeral Home. The concrete floors with their
chromium drains like deep-set eyes in the ground filled me with
familiarity, with homecoming. The white sheets and the Tyvek,
fungicide, menthol and ammonia marrying in the air. All of it
filled me with a satisfaction so deep, I held myself still until it
passed from me and I knew it was not a dream.

But Niko had cast me out of her life. Exiled me from the
underworld. And she had every right to. I was not a good man,
and sometimes, this is how the fates draw us. Life destroys us
and makes us into unrecognizable shapes; and we have no other
choice but to continue on as best we can, as neither good nor
bad, but eking out existence in the terrifying in-between.

Niko deserved someone better. Someone not tainted by so
much pain and bad choices.

I grabbed hold of the rail on the gurney. Embalming machines
pumped in tandem. Corpses at the end of the room with their
faces covered by long, white, plasticine sheets. Groggy, my body
moving at triple time with my brain playing catch up.

I tried to hoist myself up and failed. I swallowed back a cry. I
must get used to pain, I thought. Pain is what living is all about.
But I never had to feel pain when I'd been a zombie. I had grown
spoiled—mistaken numbness for strength and courage. I'd never
felt fear because I was already dead, never shed tears because I
lacked the mechanics of crying. But now I felt everything. It
made me wonder if I had been capable of things like compassion
and love before. If maybe I'd been too desensitized to really
know the difference; made psychopathic by the very nature of
my unnatural biology.

They gave me bodily life in an instant, but my soul was taking
longer, coming back by degrees.

What would be the cost when I was human all the way?

I had to get off this gurney.

I tried again and leveraged the gurney rail with trembling fists.
Spiderwebs of agony cascaded through my middle and, when I

sat up, my sweat gone cold with the pain, I groped my abdomen. Feverish and healing. Beneath the fabric of the shirt I wore, someone had stitched out the equator. How long had I been here?

Long enough to endure surgery and recover while the wounds themselves were still knitting together.

Every sound echoed into infinity and bounced back from the dim corners. Swabs and scalpels laid out as though someone had stepped out and would return any moment. Beside me, a push cart with a stainless steel top beside twists of wire and medical tape, a pair of medical scissors, an orange prescription bottle.

Atroxipine.

My breath caught in my throat and I snatched the bottle up in my hand. Pills bounced back and forth in a rattle with satisfying fullness. I held it up and read the label. It was written out for Lionel. The date on the side indicated it was from last year. Lionel was taking Atroxipine?

But Lionel wasn't a zombie. What use would he have for Atroxipine if he wasn't dead?

I turned the label around. SIDE EFFECTS, it read, followed by mouse print detailing a laundry list of the many agonies that will prevail upon you should you dare use this medication without the advice of a medical professional—all the sort of shit you don't worry about when you're dead anyway.

I stuffed it into my pocket. I didn't have time to puzzle over why Lionel was mainlining Atroxipine like a twenty-year-old smoking bath salts. I had more pressing concerns involving my survival. Was Elvedina still here? Did she have Niko? I cursed.

I hauled myself up with every sense and nerve stretched out and open to the world around me. Listening for voices and sounds, confirming distant traffic beyond the mortuary doors. I reached a hand out across a lab table to stand straighter and knocked over a pair of scissors, sheets of paper, the sound like a subatomic explosion in the frozen and silent atmosphere. I stared down at the bleached paper and stepped on it with my naked toe, examining the sloppy scrawl beneath:

Beware the echoes and specters!

I must have been saying it in my sleep. Someone wrote it down, puzzling my brother's last words. I kneeled, taking a pen from the gurney, and uncapped it. I should have been looking for my boots, should have been picking a scalpel as a weapon from among the instruments, but the sight of that final line that I, as yet, could not decipher, held me with more efficiency than any cage.

I wrote the same line beneath the original scrawl in my own hash mark of illegible writing:

Beware the echoes and specters!

I frowned. I scratched out the first word, pared down the line until all that remained was a skeleton of the phrase:

Beware the echoes and specters!

I circled the last three words.

echo and specter

"The Echo Inspector," I whispered.

A wind filled my ears, pummeled me with ocean noise until I dropped the pen and it skittered across tiles and ground, beneath the gurney legs and under the shadows of waiting corpses, until the silence returned once more; left me on the verge of understanding at last what Jamie had been trying so hard to tell me.

"Beware the Echo Inspector. Beware the Echo Inspector!"

In my rage and my anger, I had not truly heard him, misinterpreted the line until it came out sideways and buried what last truth he tried to impart to me, killed him and forgot about it. But I did not forget. I heard it in my head, listened to my ferocious Id mock it, and screamed it even when I was put to sleep.

Lionel, I decided, and Lafferty—they would know what to do about this. It was Lafferty, after all, who knew before I did that Elvedina was not all she appeared. I could count on my friends.

I wheeled a gurney over to the basement window and climbed on top of it. I moved fast and yanked the window open, punching out the cursory screen. I considered my size and took a breath and I knew if I thought about squeezing through the opening, my thin courage would fail me and I wouldn't do it.

I gripped the window frame and pulled myself through with every muscle in my belly rebelling and screaming defiance and testing the limits of its stitches.

I don't know if you've ever truly swallowed a scream. But it tastes a lot like blood.

✳

I went crashing through backyards and past angry barking dogs through chain-link fences. The world took on a funny haze in the hundred-degree heat. Blood began to spot my shirt as my breath hitched in and out. I held the wound together with my palm plastered flat on my bloody belly and took each step with gritted teeth. I heard fluttering wings and the scream of a hawk or raptor and realized it was the scavenger bird that had taken such a liking to me—the turkey vulture, shadowing me in wide and fractal circles from above before he finally descended, digging his insistent talons into the meat of my shoulder. I did not possess the strength or will to shrug him away. *You and me again, my friend?* And he seemed to wrench me back true when I drifted in the wrong direction or sagged and slowed. Every windshield, window, and metal fence linking stabbed spots of blinding light into my eyes before I finally stumbled up my own driveway and burst through the door.

Lionel sat at the table with a cup of tea at one hand. A file spread open when he stood up from the table, shaking with his old man's quiver. Lafferty took a seat beside Lionel at the table, his hair wet, slicked back fresh from a shower, doing his best imitation of a mob boss's hired help. Only his glittering intelligence nestled in his eyes gave Lafferty away because, hell, you have a lot of time to read when you're recovering from a spinal injury and you can't leave a wheelchair. A cigarette dangled from his—no, dear lord and god Christ almighty, it was a vapor cigarette.

This *must* be hell, I thought.

"When did you start smoking?" I asked Lafferty.

"Fuck my habits," he said and jabbed a finger at me. "Where the hell have you been? I've been looking everywhere for you! Wondered what shit from your past finally caught up to you and good riddance," Lafferty sneered. "Tell him all about how we were planning his funeral."

Lionel cleaned his glasses off with the edge of his shirt, as fastidious old men are prone to do, with his fingers beating a devil's tattoo on the air in his state of agitation.

"I'd thought the worst," Lionel said grimly after he perched his glasses on his face. Moisture glimmered there, threatening tears as he turned away, unable to look at me. "I could not stand to think of what I would tell your father."

The vulture at my shoulder squawked once and flapped his wings. No response offered itself at this display of worry and concern. I had forgotten, after so many years of being a lone wolf with nothing but a gun to keep me company, that people fall into the bad habit of caring for you.

"I'm here now," I sputtered and pulled one bloody palm away from my bleeding middle. Drops of blood spattered on the ground between my bare and blistered feet. The vulture screeched.

"Help?"

★

"Elvedina is here to kill me," I snapped.

My shirt sat in a sad puddle of blood where I'd thrown it on the counter. The vulture wrestled with it, darting in to stab it with his beak and then dancing backward with his wings raised, as though he expected it to take on life and fight back.

"My boy," Lionel said, and his voice took on the lilt of a tired but concerned parent, "I thought we agreed Blake Highsmith was the one with diabolical designs upon your well-being."

"Him, too," Lafferty agreed around a mouthful of surgical thread.

I laid on the kitchen table. The ceiling fan spun shadows 'round the room while he mopped up my blood with a coffee filter. We'd run out of paper towels. A pleasant numbness settled around my middle where he'd injected a local analgesic, and even better, the unnamed pill he'd passed me that made my head float around like a cork in the ocean. Because if there was one thing Lafferty knew, it was his drugs.

My Atroxipine bottle rattled like a pocketful of cobras. I dared not part with it.

"And your supposition is that Highsmith wishes to kill you for sport and amusement, and Elvedina wishes to kill you for . . ." Lionel let the thought float on the air, unanswered.

"Because the government has no other use for me," I said.

Lafferty snorted and began his first stitch. "They ain't the only ones."

"Don't you think that motive's a bit thin? After all, why not send me for that task? If that logic holds, surely, someone would have informed me and I'm sure I don't have to tell you, I've been asked to kill for my country a time or two as the occasion calls for it. Do you think they would have hesitated to ask me to get rid of you, instead of sending Elvedina?"

I bit my lip to keep the demarcation between my thoughts and my tongue. I did not want to say that he was too old to be running these dangerous games. I did not want to say that not only did I think him—the old man with tears in his eyes to think me dead—too old, but too weak, too useful as an information collector, to serve as a collector of bones.

"Elvedina came with you. Who is she? This government's got drones and pills, enough weaponry to blow up the world, and no one knows who the fuck she is?"

Lionel sank into the chair beside my head. He picked up a wet rag, and from the corner of my eye, I watched him pat the sweat from my brow before sighing and sitting back in his chair as though all of this pained him so, and most of all, to watch me suffer. The vulture squawked and I heard the tinny rattle of his beak as he missed the bloody shirt and hit the sink. Lafferty bit off the thread with the sharp edge of his teeth and began a new stitch.

"Maybe Highsmith's a part of it. Good Lord, does being living make you obtuse?" Lafferty asked.

"Spell it out for me like I'm stupid," I snapped.

"I regret to tell you, but Elvedina is here to investigate Jamie's death," Lionel said.

"I know that. Wasn't the police report enough?"

"Maybe she ain't here just for you, *prima donna*. Maybe you're not the center of the fucking universe," Lafferty jeered and jabbed the needle into me. With all the drugs pumping through this body, I could not feel it.

"Highsmith?" I asked. "You think she's here for Highsmith?"

"All due respect, Mr. Lionel," Lafferty said as he unspooled more surgical thread and tossed a wad of bloody coffee filters to the floor, "but maybe they didn't tell you about Elvedina. Maybe that's why Vitus's dear old dad sent you. Because he knows what people like Elvedina are sent for, and he wanted an extra pair of his eyes on his dear and sainted son."

The tremor in Lionel's hand seemed then to increase. His eyes lost a fraction of their vibrancy in the face of this new disenchantment.

"To be cut out," Lionel whispered, "just like that. So quickly, our time passes and eclipses, and then, we are discarded."

I sneered. "Some sooner than others."

"Hey," Lafferty said, "she ain't here to kill you, Lionel. But if I were a betting man, I would say she's killing anyone and everyone that was Jamie's brainchild. Government has enough scandals between torture sites and whistle blowers, they don't need more. So she'll kill each one, and then anyone who knows about it. And like the tool you are, you gave the confirmation she needed, and now she's gonna go around and clean the slate in her own good time, and just circle back around to Vitus, like a person does when they're going down a shopping list."

The bottom dropped out from beneath my spine as though there were no table beneath me, and beneath that, no floor, and beneath that, no ground. I could sink and subside into a great yawning emptiness until I came flooding back to myself at the thin edge of Lafferty's stitch, gasping.

"Niko," I husked. "She's got Niko."

★

Ever watch a spiderweb? A fat, juicy wood spider hanging in the center of it like a berry. It's a story as classic as boy-meets-girl. A hapless insect falls across a thread and jiggles the structure. Struggle ensues. It seems like a straightforward operation— get caught in the net, and the spider swiftly smothers you in his version of Saran Wrap to seal in the flavor. Y'know, for that midnight snack.

It's a bit more complicated than that.

If you pay attention, it isn't falling into the web that kills you. It's the struggle. The more you thrash, the more threads you pick up, binding you to your ultimate end. It's not really the spider that does you in—it's you.

Niko fell into the web. A chance misalignment of the stars. She happened to be working the shift at Pleasant Hills Funeral Home when she took in the dubious remains of my wife and son. From there, the first thrashing was Jamie presenting her with a government nondisclosure form forbidding her to discuss me only to discover later, that contract served double duty as a CIA recruitment form.

Taken to the logical conclusion, if Elvedina was here to clean up after Jamie's messes and his loose threads, Niko would be farther down on her shopping list—sandwiched somewhere between myself and Highsmith, after rolls of toilet paper and kitty litter.

★

"Because you've been so good to her up to now, you're gonna wave your hand and make it all better. That's gonna be a challenge with your guts falling out of your stomach."

Lafferty leaned into my face, wheeling his chair to stare at me laid out on the table. He loomed wrong-side up with my head screwed on upside down. White spots in my vision, creating a snow globe. Lafferty had the last remnants of surgical thread between his fingers.

"Picture this." Flecks of blood caught in the hairs of his knuckles. "You show up, and instead of doing her any good and playing Billy Bad-Ass, you get her killed. Isn't that some great relationship?"

"She doesn't want me anymore."

"Like I haven't been singing that song since Selina left. Cry the blues with me, brother. What makes you so sure Elvedina didn't just drop you off at the funeral home and leave? She could be over at the prison, creeping up on Highsmith as we speak. Ever think of that? We got two potential targets spread across town and the last time I checked, there's only one of you."

Lafferty set his roll of medical tape and gauze on my chest. A noise funneled out of me similar to what a sheep makes when it's caught in barbed wire. A spiderweb of agony rippled through my skin, forming tendrils of fire. His wheels rapped against the hardwood as he rolled back my way with a Glock 19 in his lap.

"You'll go to the funeral home?"

"No, I like to spend my spare hours square dancing at the local dive—yes, I'm going! Do I look like your fucking sidekick? I'm gonna save the damsel, who probably doesn't need the help of trifling fools like us, and you go get Highsmith before Elvedina dusts him."

He stuffed the magazine into the gun. I realized it was one of mine that I'd been searching for. Was everybody but me allowed to be armed? Or were they afraid I'd shoot everything I saw in a temper tantrum? He weighed the benefits of my Glock over his battered rifle, and abandoned one in favor of the other, giving the Glock to Lionel and ensuring it would remain out of my reach.

"You can't drive," I pointed out.

"Like hell I can't. You haven't seen my horse."

★

My greatest range of movement was remaining prone on the table while Lafferty wheeled his way to the door, shrugging off Lionel's hand with anger.

"I can do it myself, watch the fuck-up on the table, why don't you."

He knocked open the door with the snout of the rifle and rolled himself out onto my porch. His wheels racketed down the steps like a sack of bones gone a'clatter. I tracked him through the kitchen window, his shape receding as he tucked the rifle beneath the seat of his chair and out of sight.

"He can't go down the main drag in a wheelchair," I protested.

Thunder rumbled. A roar engulfed the house and shuddered the window panes. Lafferty's empty wheelchair was turned on its side on the pavement, one wheel spinning and sending rainbows of light off the spokes. The roar continued on, and I heard a healthy yell of exalted triumph when the sound multiplied and followed a streak of black and red past the kitchen window—a modified motorcycle painted in flames with Lafferty riding solo and his useless legs strapped to the side. His hands rotated the grip. He shot forward with a grin. He and the machine united, as he leaned into the speed. I stared, mouth open, tracking his motion from window to window until there were no more windows as Lafferty broke the speed limit and whizzed out of view.

"Maybe if I'm nice he'll let me ride on the bitch seat," I groaned.

The vulture squawked in response and flew over to the table, stalking around the profusion of medical supplies, dropped medical tape, and coffee cups, and swayed over me, alert. I wondered if he would try to take a swipe at me, but he stared at Lionel with livid and atavistic eyes as though the old man would suit his appetite just fine.

The last of the lidocaine ebbed through my blood. I rolled to my side. Deep prickles inside my skin and stabbing fathoms beneath. Tears issued from the corner of my eyes as I set two feet on solid ground and lurched to a standing position. I longed for the fatty padding of a hard-won beer belly.

Lionel watched me, his eyes ringed in dark circles, magnified by his glasses.

"Have you dreamt of Highsmith?"

"Not this again," I sighed and rubbed my eyes, clasping both my hands over my face as though I could corral the darkness and hold it. Never come out from under it.

I opened the dish cabinet over the kitchen counter to the indignant squawking of the vulture. The bird sought to find a comfortable position at my shoulder and I let him. I reached up and searched the inside of the cabinet.

"We stripped the house, Vitus," Lionel said. He kept his voice amiable as I cursed and smashed my fist on the counter. Plates stacked on one side clattered.

"This is my house," I snapped. "I need a weapon. Going with nothing and running into Elvedina on the way, how should I defend myself? With hopes and dreams? Government forms?"

"The decision has been made," Lionel said. "It just means you should stay here. You'll be safer. We don't need your muscle, Vitus. We need your brain."

"Zombies need brains," I muttered.

I thrust a hand into my pocket. The familiar rattle of the prescription bottle stabilized me with its siren song. The bird nuzzled against my head as though it could give comfort through feather and skin.

"No one seems interested in my opinion. No one wants to hear that out-of-body experiences are fairy tales, and as menacing as Highsmith may be, there has to be a better explanation."

Lionel spread his hands. His fingertips vibrating as though on strings.

"And that would be?"

"Someone else."

"And yet, it is true we ran such OBE programs."

"That proves nothing."

"Stay," Lionel said and approached me with his arms out. "You need sleep. You need to recover. Don't take on Highsmith or Elvedina without taking your badly needed rest. The man I retrieved from prison is not the same man before me now. You look like you're ready for the vultures."

"No," I said. My skin felt hot and taut against my skull, taking up all this unneeded space between me and the rest of the world. "No!" Again, louder. Frantic. "Where's my gun? Why have you taken my weapons? Are you afraid I'll hurt you? That my judgment's been compromised?"

I made a tight fist around the bottle. My throat burned for a taste.

"You're a part of it," I whispered.

"Vitus," Lionel said, his voice pitched soft and his gaze struggling to hold my stare. "Be reasonable; you're too sleep deprived to take this on. Can't you see I'm trying to be sensible, to take care of you—"

"No, no, no! You want me to go to sleep! Go to sleep and then it'll be Highsmith, no, not Highsmith, that thing, that . . . Inspector," I hissed.

"Vitus, what are you talking about? What's wrong? We can solve this together, but you need to stay here and recover—"

"You need me to go to sleep and die," I hissed again, but the hiss became a long moan. Fire buried in my bowels, every breath a stabbing pain. A nest of pit vipers lazing in my belly and rattling their tails. "Sleep and die!" I yelled.

The entire world took on a frenzied quality. The same delirious haze I'd experienced earlier as I stumbled home. I no longer knew if Lionel was a friend or enemy, with his bulging grenade in one pocket and his helpless, fragile hands opening to take mine.

"You said yourself that you don't believe in out-of-body experiences, there's nothing to fear—"

All my thoughts jumbled together and disintegrated. Nothing made sense. Only when Lionel touched his gentle hand to my shoulder did I explode. The vulture squawked and muttered. I stumbled away from Lionel with my hands out and my teeth bared, brandishing a coffee spoon.

"Stay away from me."

I dropped the spoon and sped through the kitchen, tripping over a chair and kicking it away. I moved to the door, through the bleached hot square of blinding light, and outside into the unforgiving sun. I reached into my pocket for my car keys, blood in my mouth. When I opened my hand, the bottle of pills sat there instead.

Exhausted. Groggy with lidocaine and the ether they pumped into me at the funeral home. I could barely stand on my feet and Lionel was right—I needed to stay and recover. Everything in my guts and my senses pointed me in the other direction. I could trust no one in my vulnerable state, and the space of my dreams was forbidden to me—it was the single place I was most in danger. Highsmith or no, OBE or no, someone stuck a knife into my guts. Dream killers did not exist, but the wound in my middle was real, the only concrete fact I had.

Elvedina. She had been there that night and every night. She had access and opportunity while I explored nightmares with a made-up villain. She had stabbed me, conveniently spinning my fantasy and reality in contrary directions, until I could no longer tell which was which. How could I fight if I could barely stand?

I popped the top off the bottle. A satisfying rattle sent my salivary glands singing and filling my mouth with wet. Like a drunk breathing in the spirits. Beloved poison. I closed my eyes and tipped the bottle back, pills pinballing a path of fire down my throat. I swallowed as though at the brink of some holy transubstantiation.

✦

Events then and the events now swapped places like spokes on a spinning wheel. I'd been in Kosovo, Yugoslavia, served in those broken lands. Nights in a foreign country where I stood watch for hours upon hours with no sleep, consulting with Jamie with no understanding that very soon I would not be alive, but not all the way dead, either. That Jamie would press a needle into my arm delivering Virus X and all the consequences to me.

Present-day Jersey was no Balkan country, but my car looked like it'd been through war. Dented, the fender hanging on like a crooked thumbnail. I pressed my foot to the gas and lurched through the streets, my focus broken and distracted between the mundane details of operating heavy machinery, the hot blazing sun, and the struggle to keep straight in my mind my mission, my goal.

Highsmith, I reminded myself. *Elvedina's going to kill Highsmith.*

In my old zombie days, I could have made an argument to let Elvedina take her pound of flesh and leave it be. She'd eliminate Highsmith without qualms or quibbles, hit the street again, and go on to her next bucket-list item. This idea was not without an element of attractiveness—didn't it take care of all my sticky problems?

Except, I wasn't a zombie anymore, being a death machine was no longer my primary business, and now that I was human, all my problems were sticky. Everything was sticky. Everything came with morals and ethics and complicated questions of law and justice. Highsmith had been tried for murder—he was serving out justice as the law dictated, by judges expected to do good by the public. If I let Elvedina stomp into the prison with all her Frankenstein charm, *knowingly* let her kill Highsmith— this would be a corruption. My job was thug work: apprehend the real killer and turn them over to Lionel. And odds were good the killer was Highsmith.

What happened to him after that could be Lionel's burden, I decided. Until then, I had a responsibility to make sure Highsmith was alive for it.

Above me, the vulture tracked a black shadow back and forth over the car. His scavenger presence comforted me. Who could hate the lowly bottom feeder of all the birds? This animal who takes from the dead when no others will? Who is to say his occupation is less noble than any raptor or bird of prey? He became a pinpoint of midnight to lead me on, to keep me steady and my direction true. Slowly, my thoughts and wrecked cognition straightened out.

It's the pills, my Id breathed as the car rocked to a stop at a red light. I grabbed the bottle on the seat beside me and held it up to the light above the steering wheel.

SIDE EFFECTS: MAY CAUSE SLEEPLESSNESS, IRRITABILITY, HIGH BLOOD PRESSURE, HEART PALPITATIONS, RACING THOUGHTS, PARANOIA, DEPRESSION, ANXIETY, NERVOUSNESS, VERTIGO. SHOULD ANY OF THESE SYMPTOMS BECOME A PROBLEM, CONTACT YOUR PHYSICIAN OR GENERAL PRACTITIONER.

I dropped the bottle down to the floor where it rolled back and forth with each turn of the car. My drunken weaving steadied, I gripped the wheel with renewed intensity. The world around me stood out in hyper contrast and high definition, so it seemed I could penetrate the pore of every leaf hanging from the trees, differentiate every blade of grass from their fellows. I casually committed to memory the license plates of cars I passed, reeling off their makes and models for my own amusement: Chrysler, Volkswagen, Ford, another Ford, Chevy Silverado, and on and on I went.

Giddy and euphoric.

I looked down at the bottle.

If Atroxipine had kept me functioning when I was a zombie, what the hell was this shit doing to me now that I was alive?

I grinned and pushed the car faster down the asphalt.

I passed through the gate of the county prison. Employees smoked by the entrance doors with their identification tags dangling around their necks, vehicles parked in orderly fashion and none of them the Ford Crown Victoria Elvedina might be in possession of. A knot formed in my chest, beating like rapid-fire gun shots. *Oh, that's just my heart*, I remembered, and it picked up speed as the medication gripped me in full swing, turning my life into a hyper-speed carnival ride.

I nodded to the employees in the front and entered the cinderblock building. I logged in, signed my name on the form, and extracted my keys. Spilled loose change into a dish. They yanked me through the detector and slapped a visitor's pass on my chest, sending me to the next room. I'd wait there until they fetched Highsmith from his hamster wheel and then we'd both meet with a pane of glass between us, a telephone line.

"*You.*"

I turned around as the door snicked shut behind me, closing out the hustle and bustle of the prison administration.

McSneer.

He overfilled his uniform and had the vague pastiness of mild ill-health—staring down the road of heart disease. A few too many beers at the bar? Or maybe a coke habit to get him through the interminable hours until he could escape his soul-crushing job of herding two-legged rats all day? It made for an unpleasant, hot-tempered individual. A square of a bandage in the spot where Elvedina had broken his nose gave me a thrill of satisfaction. In his eyes, I discerned every green shade of envy. I had gotten free of this place. Why hadn't he?

"How's it hanging?"

I even managed to sound jovial. I wondered what Atroxipine would be like if I tapped a vein? How much faster if I eliminated the time-release pill coating and went straight to the brain?

"Maybe you. Maybe you'll be hanging soon."

Well, that's more sinister than I'm used to.

"Can hardly wait. Lead on."

McSneer beckoned me. I'd been through this routine before, though usually from the opposite angle. This would be the room where I would normally be strip-searched if the visit was more personal, but now it would serve as a waiting room.

Except, that's not quite what happened.

He held open the door to wave me through with a weary gesture. The room awaiting me plunged into ominous, teneberous dark. A footstep in, and McSneer pushed me from behind. I stumbled into the cold concrete holding cell. I spun with my hands out. The door slammed shut and McSneer flicked on the overhead light.

In the corner of the room, Elvedina sat in a chair. But I wouldn't call *sitting* what she was doing. Not when your feet are duct taped to the chair legs and your wrists are cuffed behind you, your mouth gagged into a terminal smile. Sweat plastered her forehead and her eyes glittered like a resentful snake's.

McSneer hit me from behind. I sank to my knees. Reality wobbled along with the horizon. Seconds of time went missing in the darkness but those fractional seconds cost me my freedom as I came to, my skull a cracked egg shell rolling on my popsicle stick spine. Fire stapled through my belly where the stitches tested the limits of stretching flesh. Fresh flowers of blood dotted my shirt once more.

Knuckles pounded into my face, mashing my features into new areas. I spat blood onto the concrete, turning red to black, the floor so cold my blood danced like water on a griddle. My wrists were jammed together and bound, forcing my joints to snap and strain.

McSneer cut a silhouette above me, backlit by the bulb. He slapped a square of duct tape over my mouth. I tasted plastic and glue. Elvedina listed into view, collapsed in her seat and her eyes half-lidded. But she did not look defeated, though her cheek sported a split purple knot, her swollen eye becoming a persimmon. Her wound amplified her into sinister dimensions. Though her hands were cuffed behind the chair, she was moving them in circles as though she believed she could work free of the high-tensile steel with will alone.

I returned my gaze to McSneer.

"Two for the price of one. This bitch here, would you believe it—came in here packing. And we know she came with you. Was here when that old man sprung you out. And now both of you are here together."

I didn't even bother to speak with my lips sealed together with the tape.

"Ain't found where she's hiding her piece yet, though. That's troubling us quite a bit. She comes here, goes through the detector, and rings for metal. She gives us keys. Goes through the hoop a second time, rings for metal again. Turns out, she rings every fuckin' time. So we get her in here where we can make a proper examination."

McSneer's lips oozed into a greasy smile. The stitches in my belly turned cold. I imagined, with delicious clarity, what it would be like to break every bone in his body. I'd start with his nose, since Elvedina had done such a good job there first.

"And then *you* show up. So now you can watch me, eh?"

McSneer leaned down and put his hands on my knees. Hot lightning bolts poured into my bones from his palms. His fingers gripped with alarming possession. This was the prelude to some greater indignity. It wasn't as if there were any secret about the rumors and lawsuits that surrounded the county prison.

Allegations of withheld medical treatments, run-of-the-mill rape.

This didn't feel run-of-the-mill to me.

I blinked to force McSneer's face into focus. When I had him firmly dead center, I jerked my entire body. The chair rocked forth and sent scissors of pain through every wound. I pounded my head into his nose.

McSneer screamed. I laughed in muffled *hyuk hyuks* behind my duct tape. Though I couldn't tell from the way her lips were twisted out of shape by the gag, I'd like to think Elvedina was grinning.

McSneer cupped his broken nose and swiped a handful of blood off his face so it spattered to the floor. I could cross that off my bucket list.

"If you wonder why later on," McSneer said, toneless and dead, "it's just because I can."

McSneer pushed aside the pin of his belt and whipped it from his pants with a slap, letting it fall to the concrete like a limp snake. I smelled old sweat, mingled aromas of day old food and blood, his overwhelmingly bad breath.

He turned his back on me, toward Elvedina.

I stopped laughing.

From where he'd trussed me in the chair like Elvedina's forlorn shadow, I could see the line of his back blocking my view of her. He pulled up his shirt so it ballooned around him while he unbuttoned his pants. Rustling cloth. He kneeled to the concrete to huddle between her legs. I contorted as though by magic, some *deus ex machina* might descend from the heavens and set us free. Our eyes met above McSneer. It was Elvedina who stabbed me in the middle of the night, Elvedina who'd probably been gunning for me on the basis of some executive order but all lost urgency. Her attempts to kill me seemed not to matter now. Afterward, we could go back to killing each other.

I rocked the chair in protest. I called him dirty names reduced to garbled muffles from behind the duct tape. Drops of blood formed on the floor and I tracked them back to Elvedina, back to her black and illimitable eyes and her busted lip and split cheek.

One of her heels smeared in blood, tracking ghostly footprints around the room where he'd beaten the blood from her.

She did not look away. McSneer tugged her pants, reaching out to unbutton them, moving the zipper down. Pulling at the fabric to free her hips with a grunt. The clothing came loose as though what he did was of no more consequence than shucking an ear of corn. I looked away.

As he bent over, stared down at what he must have considered to be his prize—his right to take, his right to control—he rocked backward.

"What the fuck."

The atmosphere in the room shifted, humming electric. I leaned in my chair but saw nothing beyond the shadow of McSneer's bowed head. I heard the syncopated creaking of Elvedina shifting her weight, saw her arch her back and curve her spine at an angle that stretched the limits of the human body. Her trapped fingers strained and waved in the air like jellyfish tendrils.

Bones in her hand broke and gave way. Her elbow jerked as she freed one hand and then the other and gripped McSneer around the face to bring him forward so she could stare him in the eyes. He didn't move—pinioned and paralyzed by fear and awe.

I did not see so much as hear the sound of her pressing her thumbs into his eyes. Heard him suck in a breath and heard the rattle in his throat as she continued to push and push until his eyes popped. Her thumbs found his gray matter and she lobotomized him with surgical precision.

The scene elapsed as though from the far end of a telescope. Everything a film reel, a movie in which I was an audience member, unable to move from my seat. McSneer sank to the floor to his knees, then collapsed farther still. He twitched on the concrete, his hands curled and his spine hooked and his mouth open. Small moans escaped his twisted lips.

I forgot Elvedina, forgot about the case, forgot about Niko and Lafferty and Lionel. All of reality reduced to this room with this prone and ruined body and the shadow rising from the chair before me. Goliath-sized. Immense.

Elvedina stepped over McSneer and into my vision. I started at
her shoes, tracking up the stained folds of her black jeans to her
knees to her thighs and then to the wide open V of her pants. She
hadn't bothered to zip up. I could not look away. Her presence
commanded my audience and held me under a ferocious spell.

From that open flap of fabric where human flesh should be, a
nest of wires stood revealed. Input and output jacks. A rat-king
of electronic trappings that made what should have been tender
female sex no more than the back of a television set.

She leaned down to rip the duct tape off my face. It stung like
I'd tongue-kissed a hornets nest but I said nothing, staring at her
while she stared at me until I believed I could see my face in the
reflection of her eyes, diminished and small and going on forever
in that smallness. Like convex television screens instead of eyes.

"*What* are you?" I whispered.

She let the flap of tape fall to the concrete and left me there.

★

All the world around me revolved as though the room itself spun
on the head of a pin. Corners swapping with corners. The gray
concrete blocks fading into their fellows as though this were not
a prison but a maze that went on into infinity.

And here I was, at the center of it.

A uniformed officer cuffed me with the new and improved
version of handcuffs—yellow zip ties. Lionel could pull his
government favors to expunge my record all he wanted, but there
were no magic tricks to fool the prison guards into forgetting my
face. My status as an ex-con, coupled with my poor interactions
with McSneer during my stay there, lead them to restrain me until
they could figure out my level of involvement in the homicide
and finish questioning the staff and thereupon either arrest or let
me go. They left me in the chair where I'd watched Elvedina blind
and damage McSneer, whom they picked up and loaded onto a
gurney and wheeled away, his pained mewling diminishing and
then disappearing from my sight. I floated on the outer edges

of my Atroxipine high and clung to the last vestiges of euphoria against the final image of Elvedina blinding McSneer.

Blood stains on the floor formed curlicues and semicolons. An officer reported into his mic every small detail in a buzzing drone. A janitor appeared, moving a mop and bucket across the floor, pushing around dirty water and looking at me, from time to time, with weary eyes.

It gave me all the time in the world to think of how miserably I'd failed so many people and hurt them with no thought to their future or even mine. The manner in which I left Niko, and in the state I left her, when the right conduct had been obvious—I should have stayed in the circle of her arms. Surrendered my newfound life to love and happiness. Instead, I turned away from Niko to pursue vengeance in the blind killing of my own brother. In this way, I'd likewise given no thought to his wife. All these women, littered in my wake, as though their lives were spent engaging in damage control for every dumb-fuck decision I made. Had Highsmith even considered Polly's heart, her feelings, when he decided to kill Dietrich?

Had I considered anyone's when I cut Jamie down?

A set of brown trousers appeared before me. An old and trembling hand leaned down to take my wrists up by the yellow zip tie. In his other, a pair of scissors. It should have frightened me—should have worried me that such an old and frail gentleman be sent into the maw of dirty secrets—but Lionel paused with the jaws of the scissors balanced over my wrist. Great will gathered within him, amassing force until his trembling leveled out and became steady. His breathing changed, every breath like a slow-turning clockwork. He cut, and the yellow zip tie fell to my feet in a curl of ribbon.

I stared at the blood spots on the belly of my shirt. Pain roiled all through me like bursting bubbles of champagne and I could not bring myself to look up. I kept rerunning Elvedina through my head with obsessive compulsion—watching the unfolded flap of her jeans, the seductive fold of human skin, opening up into . . . wires. Loops and snarls of unknowable circuitry.

A robot.

Lionel leaned his cane against my chair. The janitor left with a nod, shuffling down the hall with his bucket. We were alone with the four institutional walls.

"What happened here, Vitus?"

"Did you know?" I asked thickly. "Did you know what she was?"

The old man frowned, stooped over to put a hand on my arm. It beat out a metronome tremor against my skin. Owlish eyes. With a beard, he might have been an ancient Merlin figure, stuffed full of secrets and wisdom in his hideous polyester suit.

"Vitus," Lionel said, "I am not your father. I am merely an old soldier, boy. They send me out with company and tell me not to ask questions. Now tell me everything that happened. Tell me what you discovered. And let's see if we can't untangle this monstrosity on our own, eh?"

Deep within me nestled and birthed the fear that all of this was by someone's design. If not my father, then Lionel, or even Lafferty. Everyone in my sphere became a suspect, but that logic too would only destroy any chance I had of survival.

"I'm tired of being the one always putting up the collateral in every relationship," I snapped. "You want me to trust you, you have to earn it, old man."

Lionel nodded as though this did not surprise him. He collected himself and spoke with resignation.

"Elvedina intercepted me in DC, where I confirmed her assignment. I was told her function was to investigate Jamie's death and your involvement in it, as an overseer, an objective observer. Do I seem a fool to you, Vitus? Do you think I believe every lie I am told? I was told she was to be a part of my contingent and I was not to question her presence among us. It makes it hard, you understand, for me to figure out what I can and cannot trust her with. But these were not decisions I had control of."

"My father," I whispered.

Lionel gave affirmation, his head glowing white like a halo. The overhanging bulb, creaking as it swung, lit each hair in filaments of fire.

"Do not read too much conspiracy into it, lest you be swallowed whole by it," Lionel said. "If your father had not sent me and Elvedina to investigate your brother's projects, it would have been someone else making the order. The machine is bigger than all of us."

"Crimes," I said.

"What?"

"Not projects. What my brother conducted were not projects. They were *crimes*. And so what if I believe you? You haven't told me anything I couldn't have surmised on my own."

"Let us leave off your troubling legal judgments. After your murder, *your* credibility is lacking, Vitus. But for this one thing," he said, and held up one finger, trembling with each beat of his old and weary and stubborn heart. "There was another part of this mission. I am to observe you, Vitus. Did you not think there would be grave consequences to your newfound humanity? You may not know it, Vitus, but your case is being studied in the halls of power where only the few are allowed to walk. And there is more than one file on you. The file of the man you were when you went into the service, when you were not much more than a young and brash boy playing soldier. A file of you when you became a zombie, and now—"

"A file for now," I finished for him and looked up, gripping the arms of the chair with my hands in fists. The lines where the zip tie held me burned red in the light. "And what have you decided about me now?"

"Before, you were a psychopath. Despicable, heartless, a ruthless shadow of a human being. And this was not your fault. This was the side effect of your disintegrating brain. How were you to know? All Atroxipine could do was restore a mere shadow of the boy you were— and really, the boy you were was not much better. You may not know this, Vitus—but the human mammal does not come with a manual on kindness and compassion. It's a thing that must be taught."

"A philosopher, how nice," I said.

"I won't lie, Vitus. They want you put down if you cannot be brought back from the brink."

Shocked. I reeled and felt as though the floor itself buckled until the room became straight again.

I wanted another dose. To taste the Atroxipine melting under my tongue. Wanted to know what it would be like to cook it inside the silver lining of a spoon and tap the fount of my vein.

"Who was going to pull the trigger? It was Elvedina, wasn't it?"

"What do you think, Vitus?"

"Elvedina's the red button. But you're here to reform me."

Lionel nodded with long suffering eyes, the flaps of his eyelids like the weather-worn saddles of old western cowboys. Forgotten Americana.

"I have been your kind and caring ghost these days. I think your father thought an old man might be the order of the day, to bring you from the brink. You're not a soldier anymore. You can retire, you know. The government will pay it. You won't be rich, but there's a place, down in Venezuela, where I live. The Margarita Islands. The sun is forever, there by the equator. You can have a life where no one knows who you are. You're just another drunk *gringo*, lazing in the sun. You can forget your father, for though he is my friend, I can't say he has always made me proud."

"He cheated on my mother," I said suddenly.

Lionel's eyebrows lifted.

I looked away. "My mother ran abroad. It was the thing that broke us all apart. It took us all the way to Sarajevo."

"I saw the file," he said.

"It's incomplete."

"Your name wasn't in it."

"I was too young," I said, my throat gone dry. "I was sixteen, and Jamie and I got caught in Sarajevo."

"The siege?" I could see Lionel doing the calculation of years in his head and his mouth pulled back into a half circle, a cup of pain. "The siege, boy? They brought you to the siege?"

Lionel could not summon the words to describe his horror. But I had been there. I had been there for the Siege of Sarajevo, where the army surrounded the city and the people inside were dying from mortar blasts and sniper shots while Jamie and I hunted for Mother, our father killing some poor scoundrel in an alley. No running water. No food. Every tree in the city taken down and burned for fuel and the smell of winter coming. No way to get out. Learning a foreign language on the fly while our parents had their lovers' tiff inside a post-apocalyptic city.

A place where names like Elvedina were part of the local landscape. Embedded into it. So much so that the very sound of her name in my mouth brought it all brimming back to the surface, all the blood running in the gutters of Sarajevo, and the smell of bodies decomposing on concrete roads where they lay. Their lovers and friends and family screamed for them because if they went to bury their dead, the snipers would fire.

"Who is Elvedina?" I whispered.

"You must believe me, I cannot answer that. I told you the rest of my mission at great risk to myself. Will you trust me at last?"

"You think I can be reformed?" I asked. "Because the thing you never elucidated was what you're supposed to do if I'm still a coldhearted monster on the inside."

"I haven't answered that," Lionel said, "because it's not going to happen."

I blinked.

"You may be very good at hiding from others, but your tears when I first came for you, at the sight of your father's letter— was the only proof I needed that you were in possession of a heart worth saving. As long as somewhere inside, you *feel*—you will recover. And I would point out that the many difficulties you've been experiencing up to now are all the effects of someone wrestling with his conscience. If you had not been, you would have shut this case down by now and killed the perpetrator of the crime, whether it's Highsmith or someone else undiscovered. But your feelings, Vitus—your emotional heart—muddies the waters of your logic. Fogs your reason.

"Now," Lionel sighed, and put his hand out, "now will you trust me?"

What choice did I have?

★

They brought Highsmith shuffling in his bright orange. Guards escorted him at either side. Clean shaven and bright-eyed as though they just woke him up to take him for a stroll around the country club. Comb tracks still in his damp hair. Staring with greedy curiosity and a sneer plucking at the corners of his lips. A strange familiarity swept in as though every dream up to now had forged our understanding of each other—the bravado and arrogance nothing more than a playact, an empty shell. Maybe the Highsmith I dreamt of had been the real man inside. But how could I know?

"I wondered when I would see you again. Dreaming well?"

A twinge of pain deep within my gutted abdomen. He looked well in contrast to my sullen and jaundiced figure—thinner than before.

Lionel played the consummate gentleman. He approached the table, set his cane to lean against it, and sat down wearily. With every motion he dragged out the seconds and the hours. Time moved at turtle speed. Lionel leveraged his condition to increase Highsmith's anxiety. Highsmith fidgeted as he waited for the old man to settle into place, carefully sliding his feet under the table, bracing his hands on the surface, and then at last looking up to stare at Highsmith.

"Pleased to meet you, Mr. Highsmith," Lionel said in an amiable tremolo. "I wish to you ask you a series of questions, which I hope you will answer honestly. We could so use your help, Mr. Highsmith."

Lionel's hands trembled as they always did. Was it me, or did it seem that their trembling increased, giving the impression of greater fragility?

Highsmith's shoulders relaxed and then eased as though he were a windup toy, his clock wound down. A revelation opened up within me—Highsmith *trusted* Lionel. He trusted Lionel because he thought him weak and ineffectual and of no consequence.

And Lionel was doing everything in his power to encourage it.

A long hiss unfolded from my Id. This was just Lionel doing his job, was it not? And doing it very well. What cared I if the old man was capable of subterfuge and obfuscation and disguise? Had that not encapsulated the whole of his career? And who could blame him for the deception when it was how he made his living?

You don't like to think that he could be doing the same to you, my Id pointed out.

I brushed it aside. The side effects of Atroxipine included paranoia. I chased shadows of my own making.

"Sure," Highsmith said, rendered docile before Lionel's performance. The predatory light in his eyes winked out and left nothing but a mild-mannered, bewildered man.

"You may call me Lionel. I understand you were associated for a time with a Dr. Adamson. Recently deceased. Did you know this man?"

Highsmith hesitated. His space of silence filled with debates and concerns that went unvoiced before he came to terms with himself and answered.

"I didn't kill him."

"We know. We're concerned for your well-being, Mr. Highsmith."

Lionel inserted a smile. Every wrinkle in his face expanded and turned him into a quintessential kindly grandfather before fading away once more. "We have been examining your case file. Just a part of our auditing process, closing out old paperwork. Very routine and all rather boring, I assure you. Perhaps you could tell us the nature of your relationship with Mr. Adamson. Our notes on that seem to be misplaced."

Highsmith opened his mouth and then closed it.

"I see," Lionel said. "We also wondered how *your* dreams have been, lately."

"They're nothing special."

"We think they might be special. Did you ever dream of killing your victims before they died?"

Highsmith reached up to lodge a set of fingers between his neck and his collar and loosen it. A ring of sweat around his throat, his forehead varnished in perspiration.

"I don't think my dreams have any bearing on that," Highsmith countered.

I rolled my eyes. Lionel was carefully constructing a trap but I'd lost patience. Sweat itched at my stitches in the damp room. Hungry, tired, and suffering, I hit the tipping point, putting me in mind of my halcyon zombie days when I'd miss my medication and crash out.

Was I in withdrawal? A quick dose could turn me around. Suppress the hunger and lift me out of the fog. I'd be whip-smart and lightning quick. No more of this wasted time, every hour dragging upon infinite, painful hour imagining the pills as they hit my tongue, the long swallow; those seconds between their disintegration and passing through into my bloodstream. That clearheaded euphoria married to invincibility.

I wanted it again and groped for the pill bottle.

Lionel teased answers out of Highsmith with the aplomb of a master hunter. If I waited, we could be here for hours in this claustrophobic room where the ceiling dropped down and the sweat continued to run and itch down every corner of my crawling skin.

Unless the interview came to an end.

"Highsmith," I cut in.

Lionel turned with a feeble head shake to look at me. Highsmith roused as though hypnotized, eyes glassy. I panted like a summer dog.

"Kill him. Now. With your mind bullets."

Highsmith blinked. "What?"

"You heard me. We don't have time for your bullshit. You think it's just so great to be a fucking serial killer, right? Prove it. Because I think you're full of shit. You're a fraud. You didn't kill a single person. We know all about Jamie's extracurricular activities with you. What'd he do? Strap a cape on you and tell you to fly? And then you landed on your face?"

"I killed them!" Highsmith snarled. He lunged over the table with surprising force until he caught on his own chain like a junkyard dog, pressing the limits of it, his teeth bared. "It was real."

"Who are you trying to convince? What's the real reason for this song and dance? Who's pulling your strings?"

"Who's pulling *yours*?" Highsmith snarled. His fingers clawed the air inches above the table.

"All talk. All bluff. You want to keep up with this tired old lie, then let's see it through. Prove it to me. Kill the old man. Shouldn't be that hard. His ticker probably doesn't have that many punches left, does it?"

"Vitus," Lionel whispered. His voice pressed the limits of concern and real fear. Lionel flinched and trembled and took up his cane with both hands. In another lifetime, it would have been a rifle, a bayonet; time takes everything from us. He shuffled along the concrete, making his slow and methodical way to the door, as though in fear Highsmith would indeed strike him dead.

"Go ahead," I said and gestured to Lionel. "Have at it. Someone with some real fucking skill could probably take care of him in the time it takes to have a power nap. Come on, Highsmith, what's stopping you?"

Highsmith swallowed and his Adam's apple bobbed. His entire body crooked and tensed and every muscle convulsed upon itself. He closed his eyes. As the minutes passed, his effort to strike Lionel dead with the immense power of his psychic abilities only became more pathetic and sad.

"That's what I thought," I hissed. "Let's get the fuck out of here."

I needed my pills. I tasted their memory in my gathering saliva.

Nothing could be more clear: Highsmith was a fraud. If he truly possessed the power to commit murder through some psychic channel, he would have done it by now; and when called on the spot to show evidence of his abilities, he could not demonstrate it for the simplest of reasons: because he couldn't do it, period.

Highsmith was not our killer.

This opened up new possibilities and sent my logical train of thought expanding outward to understand how this changed everything and altered the course of the investigation. *So we hit a snag*, I admitted, *but we drum up suspects and go on until we find the one that fits.* Except—

My Id, ever in the background, grinning. *You sure it's all as it appears?*

Inside, I felt the familiar sting of anxiety, the creeping realization that the entire hunt for a killer—this investigation, and all the other monsters I was meant to investigate after this, one by one—served one purpose: keep me busy. Keep me from—

From what?

Now, my Id purred, *that's the thing that should keep you up at night.*

★

We left Highsmith at the prison, but for myself, I carried the prison inside, around me. Different rooms in my own house brought my convict experience crashing back. Like the bathroom, for instance.

It nested inside the bleached walls and the tiles with moldy grouting. Lafferty's wheel tracks striped the door jamb, and the mirror was peppered with black spots like coffee stains, rendering my reflection mottled, a texture reminiscent of my pre-deceased past life. A thin and vanishing memory of my nephew stared back. The young man I knew as Amos Owen Adamson arrived in my life on the cusp of his twenties, hale and hearty.

Now, my burning corruption consumed this new body from the inside out. My failure to care for myself, or care what I do to myself, evident in the pale lines of my hollowing cheeks. Forgetting to eat, skipping meals, drinking more than I should. Puffy and heroin-chic eyes red rimmed, veined. My hair in need of a cut and all the other grooming that comes with cells that regenerate and die on a regular basis.

Now, in the privacy of the bathroom back at the house, I was about to make it all so much worse.

Lionel's cane tapped out his progress across the living room floor, to the kitchen, and then back down the long hall. We'd returned hoping to discover Lafferty waiting for us and arrived at an empty house instead. I'd ducked into the bathroom and sat on the toilet lid with my head in my hands before I finally brought out the pill bottle.

I held it up to the light. Pills like insects caught in amber. Deep down, I still hoped I would find Niko here. Niko, who seemed to bring with her all the promise of transformation and change. This titilating bravery. What lady would I ever know who wasn't afraid to touch a corpse or a falling-apart man, if not Niko?

And finding neither friend nor lover here meant only never. Never Niko, never again.

I licked the back of my teeth, ran my tongue over and over. I uncapped the bottle. The pills rested cool in my hand.

It's different this time, the Id conceded. *Before, your addiction was predicated by your condition. Now you're healthy. There's no reason to do this to yourself.*

But I could feel the mental processes reducing back to normal speed. The synapses slower than before. Sluggish to make connections. Being on Atroxipine opened up a kaleidoscope of hyper-speed thinking. Sharper. Faster. Atroxipine amplified everything into a dizzy euphoria.

My hand moved to my mouth before I could stop. Licked the pills out of my palm with a mewl and swallowed.

"Vitus!" the old man called.

I stuffed the bottle into my pocket, raked the hair back from my forehead, and attempted to look coordinated, aware. Not a man anticipating a supernova high.

Satisfied, I left the confines of the bathroom. With each step I grew lighter, my anxiety fading to be replaced by the pleasant hum of my beating heart. Down the hall, Lionel stood in the center of my bedroom.

Once, this bedroom had been a crime scene. It used to house the king-sized mattress my wife and I had conceived our child on. Later, it would be filled with blood. All gone. Replaced with new things, furnishings Niko had brought and given me to make my transition to human easier, without the crime-scene trappings of my old life.

And now, Lionel stood in the center of it. His cane in one hand. Covers on the bed pulled back, as though someone were readying to sleep there. The shades and the windows pulled shut. The vulture roosted on the headboard, his beak shoved into a wingful of black and dusty feathers. One rheumy eye peeked above, opening to regard me as though we held a secret congress with each other before closing like the seam of a scab and returning to his slumber.

"What's this?" I asked. "We should be heading out to find Lafferty at the funeral home."

Lionel turned to face me. Whirls of dust drew patterns in the dimness, fractured his face before he resolved out of it, the same old and tottering man.

"Indeed, we could do that," Lionel said and set the cane against the wall. "Or you could go. Just you."

He gestured at the bed with the covers pulled back, the vulture sleeping overhead as though this were not a bed at all but a grave, breathing in grave dust.

"From here, Vitus. Go to see him from here."

I laughed, and then saw he was serious.

"Lay down. Sleep. And leave your body."

"This is ridiculous."

"Could you not discover the truth on another plane of existence, in an alternate reality, if you would just give it a chance? Could you, Vitus? Will you?"

The entire thing still struck me as a fantasy designed for the gullible.

I could not wring the memories of the past from my mind. In the wasted landscape of my life, many fell to hopes and illusions that had never been real to begin with. Out-of-body experiences. Horoscopes. Alien abductions. Tabloid headlines. Was I to sweep all these penny dreadfuls into a rubric of possibility and chase the tail of conspiracy forever? Where did it end? If I believed in this fiction, would I have to think about all the other mythologies, heaven and hell, God and the devil?

Lionel remained upright. Lost in these ever-winding thoughts, under the influence of Atroxipine, churning my mind ever faster into every philosophical and occult direction. I culled fragments of evidence out of the air. Lionel approached with his frail gait, touched my arm. With a gentle push, he sent me to the bed.

I sat heavily and realized I had made my entire interior monologue into a public diatribe —talking aloud. Lionel nodded and laid the back of his hand to my blistering forehead. He tugged at one side of my shirt and lifted it, and before I could protest, pulled it over my head.

"What—"

"It works better with less barrier between you and the flesh," Lionel said.

He dropped my shirt to the ground. He planted one rough and age-calloused hand into the center of my chest and pushed me down onto the mattress. Another version of me without Atroxipine would have protested and cursed but I fell back onto the mattress, compliant and acquiescent.

The picture I'd found in my father's study resurfaced. The naked man on the cot, and the shadow hovering above him with the silver cord connected like a line of frosting in a layer cake.

"Listen to my voice, Vitus."

Everything in me bubbled up from my prone chest, my fingers spread on the rumpled sheet. Thoughts flitted through my mind, broke coherency to ramp up speed again until all of this became extraneous and silly. Highsmith never killed anyone. Wasn't that obvious? Case closed. Everyone can go back home.

"That's not good enough, Vitus," Lionel said. I'd spoken aloud again. "We need to know what Jamie did. Maybe Highsmith didn't kill anyone, that's well enough. But if not him, who did? We need to know. We need to find this culprit."

Atroxipine lit every section of my brain and my body. I could levitate. I didn't need to leave my body. I was everywhere. Living in every mote and molecule. I needed to either smoke this stuff or mainline it. I wondered if Jamie had ever taken it by himself. The bastard never shared.

"For what purpose? What's the point?" I asked.

"Don't be trivial, Vitus, this is serious, I need you to concentrate."

The euphoria shifted into a lightning crack of rage; the fury summoned up from a thousand steeping memories. I catapulted off the bed, bare feet gripping the floor as if I would be thrown up into space if I didn't, my hands balled into fists and my spine one rigid exclamation mark.

"Why do you need to find them? What will you do when you find him, whoever he is? Huh? You get commission on this kind of thing?"

"No," Lionel said. But his eyes were wide, his brows marked northward, wrinkles deepening. He licked his lips with one dry tongue, so dry it was gray instead of pink. "No, Vitus, I don't make commission, and it gives me no pleasure to bring these rogue criminals to heel."

"That's not much of an answer. You bring dogs to heel. Not people. So what does that mean, exactly? You kill them?"

"No, don't be silly."

"Don't they go to trial?"

"That's even more ridiculous," Lionel scoffed. "There's no court in this land in which we can air what Jamie did to the public."

"Because it's criminal. So if you can't bring them to trial and you don't kill them, what do you do with them?"

"Vitus," Lionel sighed.

"Answer me! Why are we doing this in the first place? Isn't this my splendid conscience at work? Your fucking humanitarian mission to 'humanize' me? Well, now you have to answer for it. I want to know."

Lionel lifted one hand. It pawed the air, shook an invisible maraca—and then I realized he was trying to direct my vision to an object behind me.

"Look, Vitus. Look."

I spun in place and staggered, catching myself with one hand on the edge of the mattress.

Looking back on the bed, I saw myself—lying there and snoring with my head tilted back and my mouth open. My hands beside me with the fingers lazy and relaxed. The starved rack of ribs fading into my belly and then my hips. I could make out the line where the belt of my pants had dug into the flesh and left a red line of pressure. Above it, the nest of stitches in the single sideways slice where Elvedina opened me up and disemboweled me with the edge of a knife.

And out from my belly, a long shimmering line surrounded by a hot white corona, glowing with St. Elmo's fire, twisting through the air and fading into a place I could not see, a place behind the back of my head and into the stem of my brain.

★

"Look closer, Vitus, and understand that with a great deal of time to study the mysteries of the universe, one day you too will be an old man. An old man, watching people turn themselves into ghosts."

"You can see me?"

"Not quite. But I can hear you," and Lionel tapped his temple, his faded eyes examining the room when I realized he was looking through me, at undefinable space beyond where I believed I was standing. "And there are . . . shimmers. Disturbances in the atmosphere where you are moving. With the right application of skill and medicine, a great panoply of experiences are at your disposal. But that is for masters, not fledglings, such as you are. You can go anywhere. All of the world is your domain now, Vitus. Nothing limits you but your imagination alone. Now, you can ascertain those things so much more difficult for us in life. You want to know if Lafferty found Niko, and if they are safe? You need only close your eyes, and imagine it, and you will be there. Want to know where Highsmith is at this very moment?"

"That's it? It's as easy as that?"

"Let's not talk about when it stops being easy," Lionel said.

The vulture looked upon us, his head cocked. He stared at my prone and sleeping body and flicked back to me where I stood before Lionel. The bird, puzzled and bored by it. He opted for sleep once more, stuffing his head back into his feathers.

"Can I be killed?"

"If another engages with you on this level, yes—but no one knows you are here, doing this, and what are the chances of you running into another? Let's be reasonable. What happened to your bravado and your devil-may-care, anything-to-get-the-job-done attitude?"

"If you want to manipulate me, you'll have to do better than that."

Lionel laughed. "The rules of this game are easy, as long as you keep them easy. Don't over think it. In this space between worlds, you need only think a thing for it to become real."

"Aren't there other things out there? People, like me?"

"Like I said—don't over think it. Don't pay them any mind. Most of them are fathoms away, asleep in their beds. They're dreamers. They'll wake tomorrow and all they'll remember is a fantastical dream in which they were flying, free falling, or riding an ice cream truck. Whatever it is people dream of. Just think of it like this—you've been doing this all your life, Vitus. It's as natural to you as breathing. You've just never remembered it before. Now you can. Now, the world is at your feet to be explored and penetrated."

Lionel leaned forward with his hand on one knee, eye cocked to me so I could see every white hair forming his lashes, note the scaly pattern of skin pulling across his scalp.

"Are you really waiting for me to tell you what to do?"

I drew in one long and shuddering breath and closed my eyes.

No more than a second, and in that space of darkness, my stomach became hinged on an elastic band and was hurtling through an elevator shaft, down and down with the flow of gravity until I opened them again, and when I did, Lionel was gone.

The room and the house and all its contents vanished.

★

I stood in Pleasant Hills Funeral Home.

It was as though I'd entered a secret door within myself and it led me here; returned me to the lobby where guests at the funeral home pass on their way to the final service of a loved one. Beside me into the opening hall was the old and ancient armor I'd once stolen and used for my own purposes. It looked to have been restored. Someone had cleaned the blood and gore from it.

New dings and scratches revealed the fresh gleam of restored metal in the familiar patina. The ominous helmet with its hungry slit. I nodded to it as though he and I were friends of old, and passed on through, refusing to think too hard about the mechanics of walking, if this were real or imagined. If I thought too hard about it, I feared it would fall apart, and the entire world around me would disintegrate and wobble and—*No, don't think about it.*

Through a window, the cement lot expanded in shades of blue and gray, dotted with grave stones beyond. Parked up against the building, the shape of Lafferty's motorcycle, resplendent in flames and chrome. How he had gotten from machine to door was a mystery, but I was beginning to realize there were depths and levels of independence to my friend that I had never thought possible.

The pungent fungicides. The mentholated air as delicious to me as any perfume. Formaldehyde. All of these were inseparable from Niko as I passed into the mortuary room. I heard her, making sounds as she put down surgical tools, moved jars of fluid like an alchemist. Her voice echoed subdued laughter and the scene appeared in full as I turned the corner and hovered in the threshold.

A body of an elderly woman arranged on a gurney, covered with a sheet and shrouded, a lock of silver hair escaping. Curiosity compelled me to stand over her and search for signs of a hovering spirit, if such a thing existed, but she remained inanimate and bereft of vitality. On impulse, I reached out to touch her and found my fingers made contact with nothing, slipping through her cheek and into the unseen confines of her skull. I registered a sensation of cotton candy against my fingers but nothing moved—she did not move, unaffected by my presence—and I realized all things I dared to touch felt like this, insubstantial and dissolving under pressure. I could affect nothing while I was set loose here, but that did not allay the desire to grab and hold, to open closed doors or move aside objects in my way. Instead, I must become malleable and work around everything else.

Niko stood with her back to the deceased elderly woman. Beside her, several feet shorter, Lafferty smiling with his hands loose around the arms of a borrowed wheelchair with the name of Pleasant Hills Funeral Home along the back, his hands reaching down to play along the spokes like a nervous boy and staring up at her with envious eyes. His vapor cigarette in her hands. I made out each fingernail she painted a blue-black to match the color of her hair. She inhaled off the end of it.

My own vision faltered and stuttered as I realized that was where Lafferty's mouth had been, where she so elegantly curled her lips and let unfold a cloud of flavored air until she began to choke with laughter. And there was Lafferty, laughing with her.

There was a flush to Lafferty's cheeks.

You don't want to be here, my Id suggested. *You've seen that smile on her face before.*

She made a face, cinched her mouth and her nose into a button of amusement, to hand the vapor cigarette back to Lafferty, and when she did and he reached to take it from her, she did not let go, and instead they were frozen there, linked hand to hand.

"You should have told me sooner," she said. She leaned in, touched his arm. I struggled to remain where I was and watch this final indignity play out, but whose fault was it but my own?

We have other matters to attend to, my Id whispered and now it seemed so much closer, that voice of my shadow self, of my deepest repressions and all my hungry desires unfulfilled.

Without the baggage of my physical body, it was easy to fall back at my Id's suggestion, as though I could feel the press of his rotten hand pulling me away from the fluorescent lighting. I closed my eyes to collapse into the ether, traveling through a whirlwind at the speed of light to see where I would come out on the other side.

★

I had no reason to feel betrayed. Yet, the recesses of the heart plumb deep. We cannot always predict what we find there. Mine seemed brand new with ever deepening complications, matters of conscience and feeling. My Id knew what was best for me and folded away that chamber of my heart as one might a book. Put it back on the shelf. Let it fade, let it dim. Think no longer on Niko and Lafferty, that man taking the place you once owned in her life.

Focus on the real. The case. The facts. Logic. Bury your heart, lest it bury you.

Before I had a sense of the direction I wanted to go in, the center of my chest expanded like a twister, lifting me up and depositing me; to think it, and then be there, as Lionel had said.

But my internal compass was muddied and uncertain; I did not know my destination, only my goal. Did Highsmith really believe he killed those people? He seemed certain of it. Was he covering for someone? Had he been coerced to lie? Had there been an agreement between he and Jamie? The questions and motives compounded.

A clue, a direction, anything, I prayed into the darkness inside myself. *Highsmith.*

I spun away into void and darkness until I opened my eyes on the other side.

★

I was standing in the Highsmith living room.

The contrast to my brother's house was stark. Both were McMansions worthy of the high-powered hedge fund set, with an eye quirked to the day they would sell their house to someone else at a profit in a neighborhood with good schools and low crime. But their good taste ended there. Polly Highsmith's house stood cold and empty, all of her belongings neatly in place. Everything clean and considered, every object appointed as though by museum curate.

Polly read a hardcover book with the dust jacket missing. A thumbprint in blue on one side as though this were a volume she returned to over and over again. An empty bottle of Stolichnaya on the table. Her figure small and demure on the oceanic couch. Everything matched in neutrals and beige hues. A world without blemish or color, as though a vampire had sucked the walls and the curtains dry of color.

If she suffered, she kept it concealed behind her melancholy expression, her somber eyes. Each turn of the page in her small-fingered hand made a whisper until a ring tone broke the silence. Her cell phone, a simple and uncomplicated older model. She set the book down to pick it up with a sigh.

"Yes?"

I glided through her living room. A large television on the wall. A stack of past due bills on a shelf. Some had stamps like URGENT across them and I craned my neck to peer at the one beneath, whose letter jutted free of the stack. In a salad of words, I read FORECLOSURE.

I thought about my sad and forlorn ranch. This mansion house made it look like a shack, and I did not feel so poorly about the unpaid telephone bill and the property taxes. What could she do to keep this house? I suspected very little. Who knows how much money they owed in court cases.

"I'll accept the charges."

I swung around. If you call from prison and you don't have money on hand for a phone card, you charge it to the person you're calling. A blink later and I was beside her, leaning down to match my ear to hers, listening.

"He visited you? No, I haven't seen them."

The lilt of Blake Highsmith's voice hummed on the line. A dull roar, fading out to a whining I could not decipher.

"Stop it," she whispered and rubbed her forehead. "Stop it, there's nothing we can do!"

Blake's voice again, and her shoulders began to shake.

"Don't go to sleep. He can't find you if you stay awake, you know that."

A pause.

"You shouldn't have called," she said. "They're waiting to see what move you'll make next."

A longer silence followed. Tears ran off her lashes, glanced down her cheeks and soaked the expensive upholstery.

"I love you," she whispered into the phone and closed her eyes. "I know. I love you, too. You're safer where you are. I'll come see you as soon as I can."

She pushed the button and ended the call, set the phone beside her on the couch and stared into the distance. Her lips thinned. I stared at her as though I could divine her thoughts through her eyes. Know her from the language of her face. The curl of her hair by her temple, glossy and brushed out, and her clothes simple and drab as the day I met her.

"What will they do to you?" I whispered. "What are you afraid of, that you think prison is safer?"

In my head, Lionel's voice insinuated its way into my mind: *It gives me no pleasure to bring these rogue criminals to heel.*

If our killer was this rogue criminal, what did that make me, exactly?

The walls around us began to collapse and fade. Polly's figure becoming diaphanous and intangible, everything bleeding into gray. Like a Polaroid photo, gaining coherency until Polly's palatial and chilly home disassembled. I stood in the county prison, the institution I had been held at under McSneer's belligerent watch, the institution also known as the main residence of Blake Highsmith.

I turned from the cinder block wall and recognized the room itself. Solitary confinement. A single mattress pad covering a hard bench, a tankless toilet in the corner. Endless cracks and fissures in the mortar with which to pass your miserable and unfortunate time.

Blake Highsmith sat on the edge of the mattress with his head in his hands. He tapped his bare foot against the floor and hummed, toneless and without tune. Without our usual setting, the stainless table bolted into the floor and his wrists and ankles in chains, he appeared smaller. Vulnerable. A man stripped of any reason to act the part of a vain and contemptuous serial killer.

He looked human. A human being with a heart, a husband to Polly. A man trying to survive and navigate dire circumstances. A surge of compassion swept through me and I was stunned by the impact. Only six months ago, I would have felt nothing, sneered and stepped over him on my way to my goal. But the rules of the game had changed. The eddies here ran swift and deep; and it was not enough to be heartless anymore.

I approached the man. He could not see or hear me, but I crouched down across from him to my knees, so we could be eye to eye. I stared at him and studied his features, the deep set of his eyes in purpled skin, and he slapped himself. The sound echoed and resounded and red-eyed, he swayed and stilled. His breathing deepened.

He was trying to keep himself awake.

"What is it?" I whispered. But I was lost in some unknowable realm without sound now; he could not hear me.

He struggled with himself, opening his eyes wide, yawning and pinching himself. He did it too hard and wiped blood away on his sleeve with a sigh, reclining back. Surrendering. Tears welled up under his closed eyes as they began to move and jitter beneath the folds of his eyelids, calculating movements like marbles beneath a chamois, and then, they circled and stopped dead center.

At me.

"Blake?" I whispered.

He screamed, leaping to his feet to stand atop his flimsy mattress and stare in the place I crouched, one hand on the wall, the other splayed and held up before me, in a universal gesture of calm.

"You have to leave!" he cried. "You can't be here when the Inspector comes, do you understand? He can't find you here with me. Get out of here, now. You find my Polly and you protect her, dammit—"

"Can you hear me? Blake, tell me—"

"Do not wait for the Inspector," Blake hissed, his eyes rolling in his head to their whites. Blind, he reached forward, planted his hand in my chest, and sent me flying back into the ether. "Get out of here, Vitus! It's not too late for you!"

★

The feeling then was akin to being lost in some unknown and inexhaustible, roiling ocean. Stuttering through space like a comet through frozen void; a penny caroming off the edge of a well and into vast deeps. Blake disappeared from my consciousness, something to puzzle over later when the dust settled. I twisted and turned in blackness to find my bearings.

Without meaning to, my meandering thought must have tapped into an invisible, supernatural river, lost and swirling within, because I was carried off by the current to stand, swaying, in a new environment.

The winds shifted directions, swept salty and hot off a fermenting ocean. The swelling air, the shifting pressure, and how the leaves of the trees flipped to bare their undersides, hinted at a coming storm.

What had brought me here to this grove of shadows? The street beyond trapped the sounds of traffic and tourists on vacation. The chain link fence and the barking dog all struck me as familiar. I stood in this dark and derelict corner of property and looked up to identify squares of light coming from the house before me.

I know this place. Lamplight and shadow undulated and rippled through strengthening moonlight beside me. A form appeared like swirls and eddies in a deep river.

Elvedina.

She stared at the house. Everything about her, frozen, her stillness unearthly. I studied her as though I could figure out the mechanics that dictated her intentions and intelligence. Understand if her violence was programmed or original. If she was designed for killing or for something more. Was she sentient? Did she comprehend what a special monster she was?

Had I, when I had been one?

Elvedina took a step forward out of the safety of the grove. The barking dog in the distance fell silent and I surveyed the backyard until my gaze returned to the house. Yellow lit windows. I was looking through a bedroom. In that bedroom, a tottering older man rose up from a narrow, hard-backed chair. His mouth open in a dry and chapped circle of lips.

White hair like the fuzzy end of a Q-tip. His wiry and many-knuckled hands gripping his cane in a worrisome tic he could not control.

That's Lionel, I realized.

I jolted upright. Elvedina's long shadow angled up the incline, tracking her way doggedly to the square of light, which was *my* house, *my* window, *my* bedroom, *my* sleeping form on the bed with the silver cord spiraling from my head.

As she went, Elvedina withdrew a gun from her side holster and a silencer from her pocket.

★

Any illusion of self-control broke. I became taffy gripped from both ends, stretching and disappearing into the throat of a black hole. My hold on the present space interrupted and I could not fix myself beside Elvedina. The world blinked out like a television kill switch. I burst from the other end of the void into the hot confines of the bedroom.

I deciphered my shape, tinged blue with moonlight and breathing shallow, as though I were drinking and drowning in the air. My eyes half-lidded and seeing nothing, the glazed irises focused on a distant point in the ceiling. Looking at myself sent a tide of disorientation washing over me as though I could disperse and disappear at the barest suggestion, and I looked away. Stitches worming through my center, a topographic map of bruises and ribs.

My other self faced Lionel. The silver line bound me to my physical self like a kinked water hose, swinging in a brand new direction as I tried to think of anything but the mechanics of this delirious and feverish world I'd entered. Lionel dropped the cane to the floor. Beyond, through the window, Elvedina lingered invisible, leaving her mark with every crushed blade of grass and high topped weed, seed heads dispersing in her path. Could almost hear the machinery moving within her, a toothy lawnmower chewing up every living thing. Relentless. Unstoppable. Eyes glazed in ice. Beyond my vision, I imagined her screwing on the silencing barrel that would muffle the blast.

Lionel did not see me. He could not hear me. He lurched over to the bed where I slept, my arms flung out and my mouth open to exude sighs and snores. He moved the back of his hand over my face, feeling for my breath.

Time to return. Elvedina was coming. I had to warn Lionel and brace ourselves for the assault. I ticked off escape paths and routes as I considered how to return. Did I lay down where I was? Or think it?

With every passing second, our lives hung in the balance. Lionel slid the pillow out from under my head and fluffed it.

His shaking frame was not shaking any longer. His hands steady when before they tottered and groped and stuttered with the frailty of age. When he moved, latent muscles in his arms flexed with more strength than he had ever revealed.

He laid the pillow over my sleeping face.

"Lionel," I whispered.

In the many moments at the table, in the prison, back and forth from one room or another, I pictured his slow and agonized gait. Had sympathized with the fragility of age. Wondered if I would assume such a role in a distant future. Deferred to him. Respected him. Handed over a portion of trust, believing we entered into a contract together.

I stood confronted with a different man. The hunch in his spine disappeared. His eyes, gone from rheumy and jaundiced yellow to livid and atavistic. He planted his hands into the surface of the pillow and pressed his weight down over my face with both.

He did not tremble now.

"Lionel!" I cried.

Lionel did not hear me.

The world turned upside down.

★

I split apart into two places at once.

One of me stood in the bedroom with my hands at my head, screaming as though to summon wind to swallow Lionel and pluck him up, toss him away to the jet stream. In reality, I was nothing but motes of stardust and air, ineffectual. His white and tonsured hair ruffled and fell still.

The constricting pull of the silver line snaked me back through an infinite vacuum, through planets and cosmos and bending time as I passed through a layer of infinity and out the other side, back into my own body. My mouth and nose filled with pillow, my lungs burning and my legs kicking. The old man like concrete. The bone in my nose crunched.

I would die like this. This time, for keeps. No last minute heroes to save me. No feats of science or medicine. No miracles and no prayers. You know how they tell you it was quick, they didn't feel a thing, they went in their sleep, smothering is pleasant? Bullshit. My chest and lungs ignited with fire, with a thousand megatons of dynamite and dying stars.

I bucked and thrashed. The weight of my lungs collapsed under an inconceivable suction.

Dying. My open eyes pressed into the pillow. Everything turned gray. Lights out. First thing that goes in asphyxiation. The brain fades and dies without oxygen. No hand gun. No handy lampshade to pluck off the end table and smash into Lionel's head. No knife or key or pen, nor anything at all.

That's how I die. People do it all the time. It's ordinary. It's easy, predictable. Just. Like. That.

A mental ripcord, jerked from me. I'd become an empty parachute floating on the wind, and I plummeted, plummeted to the bottom until I hit the floor . . .

The pillow ripped away.

I jerked upright, hauling in a ragged and screaming breath. Another scream echoed in harmony with me. Heard the rapturous thunder of the vulture, painting the walls black with the shadows of his massive wings, outstretched and flapping. He held Lionel's wrist clamped so tightly in his talons, fat drops of blood splatted on the floor like bugs hitting a windshield along an empty stretch of superhighway. Darkness turned the scavenger into a medieval harpy, a gargoyle with his beak open and his eyes a set of crystal balls. Black feathers shook loose and floated in the air. Every bone in my body gone nerveless as I struggled to restore air.

An inch beside Lionel, a hole punched into the wall the size of a quarter. Followed by another. And another.

At the window, Elvedina's face reflected like a mirror. Her jaw jutted out as though the hinge of it were optional, planning to undo it later and swallow us like a snake. Her hand around the gun in a velociraptor claw. The vulture flew into the center of the room, sending each of us moving and falling out of her line of fire. The damn bird had not figured into Elvedina's calculations and she stared at the screaming mayhem in the bedroom with a blank expression as though all of her algorithms were recalculating and folding in on each other.

Her eyes met mine through the pane of glass. Her stare sent a trident of lightning through me, grounded through my feet and fathoms deep into the earth. Froze and paralyzed me. Killed the meager breath in my lungs so I was left with nothing but cold and abject fear turning my saliva into ash. Lionel cursing until the vulture relented, flapping down the hall.

And then she was gone. Fading into the black with her gun at her side.

PART 4

CONTRAINDICATIONS

A storm came and lashed the coast with jagged spikes of lightning and sent thunder rolling over the pines. I watched it from the police department complex with my back against the concrete. The rain pattered a line beside my boots, leaving the rest of me dry.

Before I arrived at the station, I'd locked myself in the bathroom. I had broken a pill of Atroxipine apart and ground it down to a powder. Lionel called my name outside, *Boy, are you hurt, boy*. He cajoled in his gentle, old man's voice. I had flexed my hand, grinding, grinding as though I were grinding Lionel's bones.

"Talk to me, boy. Tell me what you saw."

I had inhaled enough Atroxipine that even a zombie would have been concerned. I leaned back, a wet line of crimson painted down my face, to my chin. I laughed while it dripped on the tiles and bled into the grout.

"The drug can warp your perception. Things don't appear as they seem. Will you not be reasonable? Let me in, Vitus."

I looked at the pill bottle in my hand. Lionel's voice reduced to a dim babbling in the background while Atroxipine entered

my bloodstream, coating my brain stem in its delicious powder.
It wasn't pleasure, but a pleasant uptick in consciousness. Every
thought coming faster now. I wasn't sitting on a toilet seat, but
levitating several inches above it. I was Christ. I was Buddha.
Enlightenment from the drug store.

Even when I reached the station, I hung onto the euphoria
of that initial hit as though I could ride the wave indefinitely.
I was treading unknown territory, chasing an addiction to
a drug whose contraindications were untested, untried, and
unknown.

What would I do when the refill ran out?

Like a junkie, I chose not to think about that too hard.

Instead, I thought about Elvedina. I pictured her monolithic
and immovable in the rain, letting the storm lash her. Lightning
kissing and ferning her before she rebooted and came to life
again. Her concrete and mercury eyes. I replayed the memory of
last night like footage from a home movie, the way some people
remember birthdays and anniversaries and weddings. Over and
over. Saw her arm with the weapon in one hand, the flat matte of
the silencer extending the gun into black space.

I drew the bead in my mind's eye. Who had she been aiming
for?

Lionel? Or me?

I should have realized from the beginning—none of this was
about Jamie's black projects. All that was ancillary. That's what
made it the perfect cover, because it was true, and they needed to
tie up their loose ends.

And I was a loose end.

But Elvedina hadn't been sent to kill me. Investigate me,
perhaps. Kill me? No.

I dug back farther. Atroxipine charged every sense, resurrected
memories in haunting detail. Every recollection awaiting my
perusal like a massive library contained within the space of
my mind. My Id stood in the doorway and opened the door. In
my mind's eye, he wore a crumbling and dusty smoking jacket
and brandished a highball filled with gasoline, beckoning me in
with a greasy, decayed smile. Lips furry with mold.

Good to see you're finally back on top again, he said. *What'd you want to know?*

I want to look at the footage from the night I got stabbed. We got any of that?

Hmmm, my Id said, sipping at his glass. He offered it to me. Maggots writhed in the muscle of his forearm. *Want one?*

I politely declined.

Suit yourself, and then he was trudging past racks over to big movie reels, old spools, and microfiche and, with a rousing clatter, set one unfurling on the floor. The room went dark. A projector powered up into a low hum. In the wall of my mind, I saw the memory back-lit with the power of a thousand suns. All of it sponsored by Atroxipine.

The projector cast an image of the prescription bottle, as fast as I'd thought it. Then the camera lens retreated, showing me the table, my kitchen table. Elvedina, Lafferty, Lionel and I, all of us gathered around it. I recognized the memory from the beginning. I had complained of a headache. Lionel had opened his briefcase and shuffled through a handful of medications and pills . . .

The projector hummed and showed me Lionel's shaking hands. Showed me Lionel, artfully pushing the prescription bottle of Atroxipine over the edge of his suitcase, with enough force to send it rolling to the edge, where I caught it. So proud of my new, human reflexes. How I quietly pocketed it.

My Id used a long wooden pointer like a college professor, smacking it against the screen so I jumped.

Right there, you see it?

His pointer terminated at the center of Lionel's eye, where the frame froze, and made a line directly to me, where I held the bottle in my lap the moment before I stuffed it into my pockets, thinking no one had seen me and no would know.

But someone did know, my Id whispered. *Someone did see.*

I stalled, unable to accept the truth.

Do you think a drunk is still a drunk when someone else is holding his mouth open and pouring the bottle down his throat? my Id said and laughed.

It's not the same thing; it's my own fault, I whispered. *I chose to take it.*

And he put it in front of you. Where he knew you would see it. And where he knew you would take it. Like the clever little thief you are.

He set me up, I said.

The screen flashed and went into motion again. My Id receded. A single image of the grinning Inspector filled the wall. A silhouette and a bare suggestion of that figure whom I'd dreamed of in passing and then never again. And beneath his picture, in block letters:

EVIDENCE

A sign beside it flashed a brilliant red: APPLAUSE. Like a family sitcom from the fifties, I heard Highsmith, my Id, the Inspector, and my father, laughing in one chorus.

★

Which led me here, to the evidence room at the police station.

Lafferty never came back to the house last night. His absence begged the obvious question, and I didn't need to replay that footage to see where it led. If any of what I had dreamed was real, if any of the delirious and fevered out-of-body experience was genuine and not conjured and ushered along by the drug itself, then Lafferty had spent his night with Niko.

It would have been easy to hate him for having the privilege to share in Niko's world. To shelter in her feminine vulnerability and steal her youthful passion for his own. It burned and ate in spaces within me. I'd thought myself one bad motherfucker, but the path of feeling opens to riven every wound and scar until your heart is a bigger target than you thought. All your hard shell, a facade that blew away at the first sign of a storm.

Atroxipine lingered under my tongue. I was a strung out junkie with blood on the belly of his shirt and his face hollowed out with too little sleep and too many drugs.

But I couldn't bring myself to hate Lafferty. The gray morning hours passed when I saw the van arrive. A fellow officer who'd once been Lafferty's partner in better days opened up Lafferty's wheelchair like a collapsible skeleton and wheeled it to the passenger door. Lafferty's sun-starved and muscular arm opened the door and he held out his hand. The partner steadied him. Lafferty hefted himself with a grunt, legs dangling without feeling or sensation as he collapsed into the metal beast. Too much rain for the motorcycle.

A dark shape circled the building and descended from the sky. Talons pulled at my shirt. I let him settle on my shoulder, shaking free of rain, the buzz and hum of his wings like an engine.

I often thought of Lafferty and his chair. Not in the way observers might pity or feel sorry for him, which was possibly the worst and most condescending of sympathies, but fascinated and curious by the mechanics of his universe. How the world must be realigned and reconsidered from his new height and all the details it contained.

I wallowed in the shadow beneath the overhang of the building until I was one with the concrete. Lafferty wheeled to the door and disappeared inside. I corralled my racing thoughts but Atroxipine drove them now, drove them into superhero limits and gave my brain horsepower beyond reason.

What you waiting for? my Id breathed.

I entered through the back door, made the trip down the familiar steps to the basement where the police department evidence room for the whole of the municipality resides.

★

I'd been a soldier, a private detective, and I now boasted the dubious accomplishment of being an ex-convict. For that last reason, the evidence room made my ex-convict's skin crawl. It's in the construction and the architecture of the place, a malaise— the same gray institutional concrete composes prison walls and public schools everywhere. The room terminated in a black cage enclosing the front, drawing a strict partition from any casual passerby and the oddments hidden behind the wall. Replace the bare industrial bulbs with candles and torches and one might imagine a large and angry dragon sitting atop a pile of gold in an underground lair.

But there was only Lafferty; wizened and older than I was now that I had cheated time and bought myself a body ten years younger. Lafferty would beat me to the grave, no small miracle he had evaded the Reaper thus far. I leaned over the counter.

"Wondered when you'd trouble your ugly mug," Lafferty said.

He did not look up from his paperwork. His writing was neat and orderly as though he were making up for the reckless youth in another past. A muscle in my forearm flexed and then relaxed. Stirrings of jealousy, want and possession, all wrapped within the name of Niko.

"You got something to say to me?" Lafferty asked when I did not speak.

This was my opportunity to crack a joke. Fill out familiar roles of quasi-friends the way we always had in the past. Hide our wounded egos behind machismo and posturing and continue to not talk about things that mattered to us.

Every time I opened my mouth to do so, nothing emerged but my hurt and pulsing silence.

Lafferty slammed down the pen. The paperwork flew to the floor. I withdrew from the counter. Wheels squealed as he jerked it through a tight turn and I listened to the subtle tracking of his chair as he came around the corner.

His face looked mean beneath the harsh lighting. Boxing ring bulbs. They spared us nothing. He let go of his wheels, set both fists on the arms of the chair, and leaned forward to look up at me.

"You wanna take a shot at me?" he whispered.

"What?"

"Go ahead," Lafferty said, moving his wheelchair closer. I moved back, step after step, keeping an equal distance between us until I hit the wall and I could go no farther. Lafferty put on the brakes at five feet from me.

"You think that because I'm in a fucking chair, I can't take a hit?"

"What the fuck do you want from me, man? You want me to punch you, is that what you're saying?"

"I can take a lot of shit in this life. Waking up in a wheelchair is one of them. But what I ain't gonna tolerate is another person condescending to me and pulling his punches just because he thinks I can't take it. 'Cause I'm down here, and you're up there, right? You've got that look on your face like I went and slashed your tires and poured sugar in your gas tank. You should just come out and fucking say what you're gonna say to me. Since you got back, you've been full of nothing but vitriol and bad attitude, and I got news: nobody gives a flying fuck."

Tired. Exhausted. Stitches stretched thin and my guts used up, shredded and trampled like confetti after New Year's Eve in Times Square. I wanted to lie down and sleep my way into oblivion. But Lafferty and I had business. Our nights spent reconnecting and defining the terms of our new lives, thrown together in unexpected and unforeseen circumstances, did not put paid to our underlying problems, our very human problems—how familiarity breeds resentment, how misunderstandings develop and grow, how even those we are most loyal to possess desires and wants that do not necessarily align with our own, and they all must be contended with in the end. Overtures of friendship must be followed through and demonstrated with something more than promises, and now Lafferty was forcing me to ask myself the question: all told, was I walking the walk? Was I being a flesh-and-blood human, with all the responsibilities of one, including recognizing and respecting others? Or was I a shitty example of a human, too self-absorbed to know when I was crossing the line?

A few parts shitty, I decided.

"Is she happy?" I asked.

Lafferty's face was a piece of hammered steel. His eyes glinted with flame, defiant. Daring me to say more, go further. Give him a reason to explode and lash out.

"What makes her happy ain't no business of yours," he said.

My Id cackled in the background of me. I reached into my pocket. My hand trembled and, at the last second, Lafferty's eyes tracked it and I couldn't stop. It wasn't in my control. Atroxipine had me now and I pulled out the cigarette, eager to give myself a distraction, to lace the Atroxipine with a nicotine high.

"I'll keep that in mind after she's done using you up," I said. I breathed in smoke with a sigh.

"Like hell you will," Lafferty said and wheeled forth.

I high-stepped but he clipped my shins. His wheelchair squealed and I careened into the counter with a groan, struggled to find my footing, and then lost it again. The cigarette skittered across the counter in a spark that sputtered onto the floor and hissed out. Lafferty's hands found the edge of my shirt and dragged me down so I fell to my knees on the hard concrete. I kicked my feet and turned in a circle. A thousand teeth bit into my burning belly. By the time he had his wheelchair turned back around, I was at his height.

"This what you want?" I asked. I gestured at my face and turned my cheek toward him, into the light.

Lafferty said nothing.

"I'm not gonna fight you, Lafferty."

"You better get it out of your system now," Lafferty said. "Or get the fuck out of my evidence room. I've done enough for you."

"I came here to ask about Elvedina," I said.

"What about her? You gonna throw her away like you did Niko? That a thing with you?"

I blinked. "Is that what Niko said?"

"You think she didn't have a heart? That you didn't hurt her?" Lafferty snorted in disgust. "You're the sort of asshole born with so much good luck, you don't even know what's in front of your own nose."

"You're right," I said. "That's why I need you to tell me what happened right under my fucking nose, the night I was stabbed. You came out into the hall with the rifle. What did you see?"

Lafferty's eyes changed in the hard yellow light. His jaw set as though there was still a discussion we'd be having later, like we were a fucking married couple instead of two guys having trouble figuring out that Niko was no one's possession and she would be with whoever she wanted. If that turned out to be someone else later on down the line, we'd still be fighting this same stupid fight.

He leaned down to pick up my cigarette butt with agility borrowed from a lynx and rolled up to me. I slumped back to the floor, back against the wall, and held out my hand. He gave me the cigarette. I relit it while he leaned over me and I looked up at him, our perspectives reversed.

"Strange night," he said. "I was sleeping out front on the pull-out, you remember. It's got this suck-ass metal bar that likes to dig up into your back."

"I know. It's a piece of shit. Jessica used to make me sleep on it when I snored."

I held out the cigarette to him. He took it and dragged before releasing a puff. Smoke crisscrossed over his well-used face, pocked and marked like the surface of the moon.

"Too bad it's not a joint," he said. Smoke uncoiled from his nostrils and passed it back to me.

"It's a fucking evidence room," I said. "I know you got shit back there."

"I ain't sharing. That's what they call 'fringe benefits.'"

"When did you wake up that night? When I started screaming?"

"No. I kept drifting in and out. That goddamned metal bar in my back. A man can't sleep well like that."

"Uh huh," I said, thinking he probably slept better last night. But I didn't want to drag in our troubles. I needed to stay on track, unravel this mess. "You must have seen something. Heard something."

"Yeah, well," and he scratched the back of his neck as he cast his glance inward, pacing himself back through the hours and the days. A mountain climber wearing cleats walked across my stomach, back and forth, back and forth over my stitches while I waited for his response and took another drag. "Sometimes I'd hear things. Like Lionel getting up in the middle of the night. And that Elvedina was always walking from one end to the other. Sometimes she'd spend an hour in one place, out front on the porch or out in the backyard."

"I woke up with her hands in my guts," I said.

"Yeah, but were you awake when you were screaming?"

I opened my mouth to answer yes when instead I heard the voice of my grinning Id: *Ah, ah, ah. Not so fast. Were you?*

And I didn't know.

"Maybe not," I said. Maybe I was screaming *before* I woke up.

Lafferty leaned forward. I could hear his chair creak, the tilt of his wheels and our eyes met, strung out along a line of gravity so strong I could not open my mouth against its force.

"I know after a car accident, 'twas a couple nights I was screaming and sleeping at the same time. And you gonna tell me, military man, you ain't never done the same?"

I said nothing. Some things, you just don't talk about.

"Okay," I said. "So I'm dreaming about being stabbed. And I start screaming—while I'm under, still. Then what?"

"What I know for sure is that I heard footsteps a little while before. But Elvedina was the first one running when the screaming started. You telling me you were stabbed before you started screaming? Because that'd be a key point before you start pointing fingers at Elvedina."

"You were the one who said she was the hired killer."

He shrugged. "Bitch is cold as stone. But that doesn't make me right, now does it?"

I cursed when I realized I'd let the cigarette burn down into the filter and dropped it, crushed it with my heel.

Lionel's name hung between us, but neither of us spoke it. I looked up at Lafferty with my hands dangling over my knees.

"So what about Highsmith and his mind bullets?"

"You know how a pickpocket gets away with all your cash, right? Or how the magician pulls the rabbit out of the hat?"

"Distracts you with something else. That's what the whole Highsmith thing is about? A fucking sham? A distraction? Jesus Christ," Lafferty said, running his hands through his hair and pressing them to the sides of his head. "Do you know how much that freaked me out? Thinking a guy could walk out of his body and play the invisible man and kill me?"

I said nothing about the out-of-body experience or Atroxipine. We were floating in a whole new conspiracy world of half-truths, things Lafferty didn't need to know.

"What was the fucking point of all that? What's the rabbit in all this?"

"I think it's to kill me," I said.

"You're so fucking important, eh?"

"My father's scared. It's a testament to his fear that he wasn't satisfied to let me languish in prison."

"So they're letting Highsmith languish in prison instead."

"Do you know what happens to them? To people like Highsmith, who were brought into black missions like out-of-body stuff? Did you ever talk to Lionel about that? What happened to the rogues?"

"Who cares? They're criminals. Highsmith said himself he killed those people. They can rot in hell."

"What if it's not Highsmith, though? Look, Highsmith got a court case, was judged by his peers. It was all on the level. Even if the case was flimsy, don't you think every suspect deserves the same? Don't you think they should have his fair treatment like every other citizen, instead of being locked in a cell and having the key thrown away after his own government uses him up? Isn't that really what they did to Highsmith?"

"Edmond Dantès," Lafferty blurted.

I hadn't thought about that book in years. Long ago and far away when we'd been in the same classes, that had been our summer reading project and we had taken turns slogging through Alexandre Dumas's *The Count of Monte Cristo* between bouts of sneaking off to swim in the next door neighbor's pool after dark. I recalled Jamie, sourpussed and sullen while he bent over his medical texts and dissected frogs. As far as he'd been concerned, Lafferty was too low class to hang in our end of the neighborhood. The few good moments in a cesspool of childhood memories.

"You think that's what they're doing?" he asked. "You think they're taking people they used up, hired as tools, and are locking them in and throwing away the key?"

"Lionel seemed to evade the question when I asked," I said.

"Lying by omission. Sweeping up anyone who can implicate the government in wrongdoing and vanishing them."

"How very Soviet of them," I said.

"You know who killed them, if not Highsmith?"

"Not sure. Just a hunch."

Lafferty nodded.

"You gonna turn him in, when you find him? Just turn him over to Lionel and hope for the best while they figure out new ways to kill you better?"

I said nothing. I had no answer. The trust and loyalty I had assigned to Lionel had broken beyond repair. Yet, the terms of my freedom were reliant on carrying out this job to the end, and all the other monsters awaiting investigation once I finished with the current monster at large. Handing the killer over was out of the question, but I had no clearer idea of what I would do when the time came to make the decision.

To be, or not to be, I thought, reflecting on the interminable hours when my father drummed political science into my head via Shakespeare. Faced with the choice between duty and conscience, Hamlet was no help to me now. Even my Id was quiet and contemplative until I spoke once more.

"You still have my evidence from my brother's case?" I asked.

Lafferty grinned.

"So. You want the gun back?"

Lafferty leaned down to pop open a box and withdrew a plastic bag. Through the transparent material, the matte black of the semiautomatic carved a silhouette I knew of old. My fingers quivered to touch it, and Lafferty made an amusing ceremony of pulling it out of the plastic and holding it out for me as though his next move would be to knight me with it. Done with the frivolity, our expressions set as it passed into my possession. The metal seemed to jump into my grasp, fitting into the flesh as though it, too, had missed me, longed for me, yearned for me during our long absence. Having her was like returning home at last.

"Look," Lafferty said as I pulled the slide off the Glock and took out the barrel, staring through it and frowning at the buildup. "I ain't gonna tell you what to do with your weaponry, but now that you're not a hell-bent for leather zombie, maybe you wanna try a little harder not to rack up the body count?"

"I killed my brother, Lafferty. What does it matter now?"

"Don't talk that shit. You know it matters. Try this."

He slapped a taser on the countertop.

I lifted an eyebrow and set the frame of the gun down to pick up the taser.

"Fewer dead people. Maybe you can avoid a second murder charge in your life. You're not dead anymore. No gray area loopholes for you now."

He had a point. I pressed a button on the side of the object and, between two metal fangs, a brilliant line of blue electricity appeared and then zipped out of existence.

"Where'd you get this?" I asked.

He grinned and said nothing.

Meanwhile, somewhere on an evidence shelf, a taser goes missing from a lapsed case.

"Let me rephrase that—what did the previous owner do with it?"

"Some kid was going around and shocking vending machines with it. Can you believe it?"

I smiled, remembered Lincoln Tanner, my one-time bunk mate in the prison. "You don't say."

"Shorts out the circuit. Machine spits out food, or quarters."

"Really," I said, and thought of Elvedina.

What would she spit out?

"I'll take it."

★

I came back into the rain from the evidence room basement. The vulture circled above the roof, and I surrendered my shoulder to him. He took up the space beside my head while I stoppered my mouth with another cigarette of tightly packed death, stared at the oil stains casting rainbows in parking lot puddles. My Thunderbird was worse for the years, nicks and dents where I'd driven it through the garage door after Elvedina. I wondered where she was now. If she was out there in the rain like the Tin Man, frozen in place with her oil can discarded at her feet. Trade her ax out for a gun, frozen in space.

The idea chilled me. The vulture squawked and protested, flew away into a screeching black mark on the wind as I jerked open the car door and inhaled the stale exterior, then filled it with smoke. But thinking of Elvedina, I kept rerunning the image of her kissing Megan's forehead. How could a cold, hard machine summon up all the trappings of human feeling to kiss another?

I started the engine and turned out onto the main drag. I smelled the ocean in the air. Heard the cry of the vulture tracking me from above as the vehicle shot like a silver bullet through the town, through the boarded up and foreclosed homes lost to bad investments and personal tragedies; past the tent shelters of the homeless, the strangers hitchhiking up the route; past the old secret burial grounds where the mob buries bodies in the pines; until the landscape changed and the houses turned along more upscale tastes. The road leveling out into new paving afforded by the rich and the well-connected. No more heroin addicts drowning in the gutter here. Now, I drove in the perfumed avenues of the affluent.

The northeast storm winds brought more stinging rain. The vulture sulked and followed me as I drove and put my hand over the firearm. I made sure it was real and, satisfied with the comforting weight of it, I wound my way back out of the gated community and over to the next one, navigating through a warren of cul-de-sacs and well-groomed lawns.

I parked the car in the double driveway of Polly Highsmith's house. The events revolving around that ill-fated night when I left my body occupied my mind, and with it, Polly's conversation with her husband, and most of all, Blake's terror of the Inspector. This did not seem to me the cold-hearted killer I'd been led to believe I was hunting. I kept returning to her, this unremarkable women who appeared all but invisible, who grew smaller with the weight of her tragedies, until I perceived her in a different light, a different understanding. It put me in mind of Megan, it put me in mind of my mother, even Elvedina, who in her illimitable silence embodied some unspoken melancholy—this trio of women tied to disasters like latent Furies from a Greek Tragedy, giving shape and form to crimes others had wrought. It left the last possible conclusion, the most logical direction left to me: Polly.

The driving rain lashed thick and the first whip crack of angry thunder rent the air. The vulture soaked and shivered at the porch and stared at me as though I authored the foul weather.

I passed a row of shrunken and withered pansies, all the color sucked from them, except brown. As though the degradation I had cohabited with for so long as a zombie had evolved like a virus, insidious and invisible, to visit Polly. I carried the stain with me, destroying lives in my ominous wake. All my convictions and newfound conscience for naught.

I ducked into the shadow of the house and rang the bell. Rivulets chilled a line down the back of my neck, soaking my shirt. I imagined an alternate world in which I had not survived Virus X. I imagined Lafferty, tending his evidence room with no knowledge of Niko only three blocks away in the funeral home; Lionel would be tending grapes on some faraway South American spook foxhole. My father overlooking the Capitol with disgust and disdain, pinning a medal on my smiling brother's jacket. Beside Jamie, his intact and perfect family. Amos.

One virus turned it all upside down and led me here, to this very moment. It seemed to me that all that effort and monstrous fissuring in the universe should have singular meaning. A lightning strike, pivotal moment. A climax to punctuate the senselessness of life. Perhaps a choir of angels trumpeting a delightful chorus in answer. A deus ex machina to lift me from this inferno.

Instead, all I have is the shitty version of a poor man's parrot, a beat to shit body like a crumpled candy wrapper that'd seen the inside of a toilet bowl. One of these days, I promised myself, I need to get my ass to the beach, buy a houseboat. Take it out to the distant canyons. I would forget all the bullshit and bake in the sun, try not to think about Niko and—

Shattering glass.

The vulture curled his tongue into an S with his beak open and hissing. I tried the door knob. It turned, slick with rain water.

I withdrew the gun and threw the door open wide.

★

All the lights blacked out. Yellow-gray storm light churned through the diaphanous curtains. Polly Highsmith's home smelled like fresh lemon polish and whiskey. I surged forward with my arm out and steadied into an isosceles lock. Each wet step from the rain was muffled by the expensive carpeting. In a distant room, a *bang-crash!* as an object met its fate, shattering into pieces beyond my sight.

Through the living room. The couch littered with the remains of a newspaper. A cell phone turned face down on the end table. An empty glass rimmed in whiskey. Bland neutral walls tinted eerie and gray in the rain light, turning everything into a mist.

Around the corner and into the hall, I caught my breath and held it.

Elvedina and Polly stood in the center. Around them, the detritus and debris gave suggestion to the battle ranging through the kitchen. Polly's headlong flight, the place where Elvedina caught up with her. In seconds, I play-acted their recent past: I pictured Elvedina, a storming bull, reaching one hand out to catch Polly's streaming hair and yank her back with heartless machinery. Send her to the ground where Elvedina towered over her, straddling her with her face erased of emotion.

Like she was now, with her weapon drawn and the silencer making a long, black exclamation point to Polly's chest. Polly, a kitchen knife in her hand. The kind of knife you buy with a maxed out credit card at 1 a.m. because it can cut through uninvited cyborgs when the occasion calls for it. A big one-piece, steel pig-sticker. She rammed it up and thrust it into Elvedina.

They were too far in to care; too locked into each other. Faces drawn in the grimmest and bloodiest expressions that left no expression at all. Women hell-bent on killing one another. It drove the breath out of me. Turned me cold to my toes.

Elvedina stumbled back with the knife sticking out of her chest. The silencer wobbled in her grasp. Elvedina grunted and reached up like a wind-up toy, all fluidity gone as she negotiated this new turn of events to grip the blade handle and snap it from her. The hallway lengthened into a marathon mile. Too long to traverse in time. See-saw nausea rollicked in my belly as I dug in and ran anyway, dropping the gun to pull out the taser as I gained momentum. The knife crunched like metal cans in a compactor as she slicked it out of her. A line of dribbling, black blood. Motor oil permeated the air. She dropped the blade to the floor and readied herself to take aim at Polly, who huddled on her expensive carpeting with her hands above her head, her knees curled to her chest, screaming.

I skidded and slid into home base. The taser gleamed and crackled like handheld fire. I thrust it up into Elvedina's arm, to the meat of her ribs and her eyes, flying open wide to meet mine as we made impact. She felt light as aluminum as I reached out with my other hand to hold her, take her shirt by the fistful and rivet her there while her eyes dissected me, deconstructed me, viciously took me apart bone by bone with all her hate.

"I'm sorry," I told her.

Her eyes rolled back in her head and Elvedina collapsed.

Adrenaline pushed through my veins, made my mouth taste like I'd eaten a plateful of wet cigarettes for breakfast. I kicked her weapon away. It cartwheeled down the hall and disappeared into the space of a shadow as I came down to my haunches to reach for Polly.

She rose up and took my arm, leveraged it so we both came to our feet together. Her hair become a witch's mire of filaments, her eyes dazed and mouth turned into a permanent stain of bloodless shock.

"I can't," she whispered and then burst into tears.

"Polly," I said, and held her while she cried into my arms and whispered, *I'm sorry,* over and over again. *I'm sorry, I never wanted this. I never wanted to hurt anyone.*

★

I poured her a drink and gave her a box of tissues. Polly stared at the collapsed shape in the hallway.

"Is she dead?"

"I don't know," I answered while I turned the taser over in my hands. "I think it's a short circuit."

Polly didn't ask what that meant and I wouldn't have explained it to her if I could. I was exhausted. My stitches itched, fire ants lapping honey off my abdomen. I helped myself to her bottle of Laphroaig and sat on the opposite side.

"Do you know why I'm here, Polly?"

She looked down into the bottom of her glass where her reflection wavered. She looked about to cry again. This time around, she was wearing more than sweatpants—cargo pants and a dark shirt. Dim and neutral colors matched with luggage by the door. Her hair combed back into a ponytail and her eyes hollowed and rimmed with sleepless circles.

"Yes," she managed to choke out.

I gave her a minute longer to swallow her drink. I followed suit until I emptied my glass. I set it down on the coffee table and folded my hands.

"How did you do it, Polly?"

She didn't look at me.

"It's complicated," she whispered into her glass. She looked frail and breakable in the half-light. The rain tapped and drummed above us with ferocious purpose.

"Nothing came up on the tox screen," I said.

"It wouldn't," she said, putting her glass down. Then she laughed, jagged, running a hand through her hair. "What will my husband say? It will break his heart."

I blinked. All of this, all those dead people, and all she could think about . . . was her husband. And in the end, it seemed a human concern to have.

"Why don't you tell me how, and maybe we won't have to break his heart after all."

"It started," she began, "with the drug trials for Atroxipine."

Halting, stumbling over her words, she began to tell me.

PART 5

DRUG TRIALS

I *don't know what kind of business you're in, Mr. Adamson,*
but—oh, there it is! How on Earth did you get a prescription
for this? It's not on the market. Never mind. Doesn't matter
now.

But it mattered, once. My husband was the one who engineered
Atroxipine. I know you have not seen the best of me, Mr.
Adamson. You've seen me as the woman riding the downward
spiral into the nadir of life. But when I met him, I was on the
incoming wave. And maybe I was deluded by my own youth.
Your twenties become a mythical decade of invincibility. Ah, I
see in your eyes, you know something of what I say, though you
can't be barely into your twenties yourself, if you don't mind me
saying so, Mr. Adamson. A little too young for this line of work.

I was too young to be a bauble on the arm of a rich and
successful businessman. I thought I knew the world. Thought
I knew myself. I wanted a fabulous Mr. Darcy to enter my
life; and I know now I was not unusual in this desire. I was in
college and gaining my own degree in organic chemistry with an
interest in biology—do you know that cinnamon has the same
organic compounds found in hallucinogens? This was how Blake

and I met. Over drinks at a bar, arguing over the chemistry of wormwood in the casual glass of absinthe.

He was impressed with my acumen, my depth of memory. I could draw compounds on the bar napkin with my eyes closed and I won't lie—our interactions were kinetic. I knew there was a ring on his finger. In every way, we made no acknowledgment of the intensity building in the air around us. I think he was unwilling to admit that his marriage had already failed. He gazed at me when he thought I wasn't looking, turning his gold band around and around as though it was a time machine he could use to unwind the clock and meet me under better circumstances. But he needed a tech whose head wasn't halfway up their ass and I was more interested in hard experience than a paper degree. I had no carnal designs on him, at the time. It provided an amusing distraction, to be whisked away by this secure, intelligent, and intense individual to a place where some of the foremost drugs were being produced.

In retrospect, I can appreciate how little I understood of the nature of the drug lab. In all ways it seemed a private enterprise but I couldn't know it was funded by public money—military money. My first days were spent in the awkward overtures of a new and eager intern attempting to find her place in the company structure—listening to the break room gossip and hearing rumors. Non-disclosure forms. Black suited men with no identification. And once, the rumor of an "Echo Inspector"—oh, do you know him? No? You looked as though you recognized the name—and others besides.

All these things should have given me a thousand and one warnings and raised up all the red flags, but I was young. Hormones working overtime. For me, it was exciting and I'd always had something of the thrill-seeker in me. Spending time with this older man. A married older man. Possibly involved with government conspiracies. In my head, I was courting James Bond. I know—silly, right?

Blake Highsmith was the one who began mapping out Atroxipine for us. Drawing up the dry-erase boards with his left hand until every spare inch of white board was filled. All of us *discussing variants. I stood quiet and holding as much poise as I could manage as a newcomer, waiting for my chance to ask: what effect is this drug supposed to achieve?*

Atroxipine was designed to accomplish several goals: to reduce or even reverse the effects of aging; to excite and increase the frontal lobe activity; and lessen the symptoms similar to schizophrenia and other psychological disorders. What disease or affliction it was intended to treat was never revealed to us. Even Blake himself did not know.

He consulted a herbalist, a homeopath, fringe doctors, a veritable medicine cabinet of wonders. Blake was a maverick in this way; prior scientists were not risky enough to satisfy him, he said, and thus their work fell short of satisfaction. He wanted real results. He took us out to rainforests in Puerto Rico. For a whole month, he plied me with orchids and pretended not to know where they came from, that a secret admirer must be sending them to me. During business, he hired, and insisted we work with, elders of indigenous tribes. Several of the technicians left in disgust; they felt working with prehistoric natives was akin to superstition rather than science, and that next we'd be sacrificing goats over sacred stones to achieve results. They'd had enough when he suggested that we could make a drug for that too, and they walked out of the lab, leaving only myself and him to engineer the entire thing.

He moved the lab into his own kitchen. He owned a house big enough, and I didn't know just how big it was without a wife there to occupy it. I expected to meet her at last and was stunned to find she was not there; no second car parked beside his in the driveway. Bills with her name piled by the door. The pointed absence of a certain feminine touch—no flowers in vases, and if there had been window treatments, they'd been traded out for blinds. No woman's coat in the closet. The fridge had the usual earmarks of a bachelor's residence rather than a married man— all condiments and leftovers from take-out joints.

I didn't ask. I was afraid it would take us to an inappropriate place, and even with my dangerous longings, I was beginning to understand there was a difference between the anticipation of

*the object of desire and attaining the actual object itself. Blake
was a highly driven man. He never slept at first. That's not an
exaggeration. I spent nights in the house strictly as a professional
function—sleeping on the pull-out couch. As far as I knew, he
never made it upstairs to collapse on his own bed. He spent the
night "cooking" strange batches of witches' brew, searching for
that perfect alchemical mix of ingredients for the drug that was
supposed to cement his career, if only he could deliver it. While I
worried about contamination in the unsecure, and hardly sterile,
environment of his home, he laughed me off and told me to
pretend it was a field office. "How do you think people made
medicine a thousand years ago?" I said that maybe that's why
it took so long to come up with penicillin and he scoffed. Told
me witches were wrapping wounds in moldy bread long before
science put it into a pill.*

*He opened my eyes to a different way of medicine and science—
asked me to consider a world in which all of our conveniences
and gadgets were no longer available. He prized innovation and
experimentation over rigid protocol. When he wasn't working in
our makeshift lab over his expensive counters and stainless steel
cookery, he was reading a dog-eared copy of* The Serpent and
the Rainbow *by Wade Davis. If anyone had seen him doing that,
he would have been laughed out of any institution, much less the
pharmaceutical one.*

*But there was another man who came and went and he did
not laugh. And that man looked like you. His name was Jamie.
Imagine my surprise when I discovered he had been killed. You'll
have to tell me what that was all about. So I tell all this to you
with some reservation; but knowing you are the flesh of his flesh,
surely, you will keep my confidence? I fear the consequences if
those in positions of power discover I have spoken about things
I am not allowed to speak about.*

*It was Jamie and Blake, bent over the papers and the books,
comparing notes and talking in whispers back and forth until
I fell asleep and woke to their voices in alternate hours. Tested
compounds they put before me, cleaned glass beakers in the
massive stainless steel service sink. Another man would come,*

and they always called him the Inspector. He seemed as a shadow. Insubstantial. I was always leaving as he was arriving, catching glimpses of him as he blurred past. He never acknowledged me. At least Jamie was civil, but the Inspector deepened the coldness in the air by twenty degrees. Had his own gravitational pull like a magnetic planet. I was happiest when he was gone.

Jamie looked haggard, in those days. As though a deadline were ticking away in the background. Blake told me that Jamie was bringing in "heavy" stuff—pscyhotropic drugs. Ayahusca, mescaline. Making batches of mushrooms and feeding them to a team of rats we housed in the garage. Jamie ordered us a new batch and cleared out the old ones and sat us down at the kitchen counter.

We had a sit-rep, though no one called it so. It seemed to me more and more that Blake was keeping information in his head instead of writing it down. I discovered him in the hallways, or accidentally brushed past him to the bathroom, and found him, clenching his jaw as though he could turn his teeth to dust, muttering figures to himself to commit them to memory.

The white boards were erased—and disappeared. Months of work vital to our production, vanished. Even the pens and the paper began to disappear. I spent hours digging through junk drawers to find something, anything to write with. I asked him how the hell I was supposed to record my findings and he put a finger to his lips and shook his head and would say no more. I can't write anything down? I asked, and he only shook his head and that was the end of the discussion.

If I hadn't been so sleep deprived and focused on stretching the memory muscles in my brain to help me keep track of what experiments I'd done and what more I needed to do, I would have realized something was amiss. That we were being spied on. It's a slippery slope to the tin foil hats once the paranoia starts in. It didn't hit me until later that he didn't want us writing anything down in case we had to answer for it later. Answer for it, the way some must answer for wrongdoings at a Nuremberg trial.

You'd be surprised how far back into the land of memory you can travel. I know people would scoff, say that it's not possible to conduct work in the manner that we did and call it valid. That there's no way I could remember all that needed to be remembered.

It was the Inspector who taught us.

It was true that I never saw him for any length of time. I never studied with him directly; but there was a basement in the house. Blake followed the Inspector down there, sometimes with Jamie in tow—and I remember looking up to see Blake descending the stairs, back lit by bare bulbs in the engulfing darkness. He looked like a boy—a boy sinking into a quagmire of quicksand from which every desperate struggle only pushes him deeper in. They spent hours down there, in a frightening triumvirate of silence and secrecy.

Blake resurfaced to sleep. He would stumble through the basement door and scare me half to death. Who knows how many tests I destroyed from jumping two feet out of my chair at the kitchen counter and upsetting serums and test tubes. He would stagger out as though someone had yanked his spinal cord from his body and go so far as the couch before stumbling into the cushions and passing out. Jamie and the Inspector, with his collar turned up to render him eerily invisible, would troop out and leave. Blake would sleep for a day straight.

This happened over and over again across the course of a month. The three of them disappearing into the basement and reemerging in the midnight hours with the sun still transiting the other side of the world. My worry and concern for Blake's ability to weather this intensity and to keep it sustained increased.

I tried to wake him once, to take him up to his bedroom so he could be ensconced in some familiar territory. I even thought about finding his wife and reaching out to her for help, though I wasn't so naive as to consider how badly that encounter might go. That's how desperate I was over his worsening condition. His skin lost its healthy glow. His hair crept in gray at the edges and he was not what I would call an older man. Too young for that.

I tried to lift him up from under the arms. He dragged me down into the couch with him, taking my mouth in his, and I didn't stop him. I was as exhausted as he was. I smelled like an alchemist come from a graveyard, burned by the cauldron I slaved over. All my resistances and objections were null and void in that moment. It was the beginning of our relationship. I fell asleep beside him on the couch and we slept more deeply than we had since we began. When he woke up next, it was as though nothing had happened, as though Jamie and the Inspector had never been there.

This turning point came with unexpected revelations; Blake became confessional with me in ways he was not before. More willing to discuss the nature of the work while we watched workmen open up the garage and set up massive structures for rat cages. This is how he taught me to remember. To explore the power of memory recall. To begin with the earliest memory and then doggedly track my way backward through my senses and my mind, bringing every event back to life as though it were happening before me. To take snapshots with my mind and imprint what was most important there, so I could come back later and retrieve it. To create structures and architecture on the dreaming inside of me. I had not realized how impoverished my mental space was until he taught me how limitless my imagination could be. Blake didn't just change my view points on science— he demolished them.

Meanwhile, hired help stacked cages in the garage. When they finished, Jamie arrived with coffee and take-out food and we gathered around the kitchen counter while Blake ate nothing at all but sipped at his coffee and ground aspirin between his teeth to kill the headache; Jamie explained what the next stage was.

We are moving into trials, with rats, Blake told me.

We're going to infect those rats with a virus, Jamie explained over a box of lo mein that he picked at with his chopsticks. He eventually set them down to wipe his hands on a napkin and stare at both of us.

Take note of what happens when you test, he explained, but if the rats bite you, and you become infected, we will have to kill you.

Up until then, there'd been no commentary on all the erratic comings and goings of dark-suited people. No identification, *or the complete lack of professional structure. The entire thing must not even be real, because how could it be; when there wasn't even a paper trail to prove our work existed? I realized the house Blake and I had been living in was a bigger rat cage holding smaller rat cages. We'd built our own trap.*

The realization that Jamie would have us merely wiped out—all over the greasy armpit smell of Chinese food with this mild-mannered desk jockey eating with his chopsticks—struck me as surreal and part of a fever dream. I understood what he had said but could not absorb the import, its overriding implication. If I had my senses about me, I would have left at that instant and never come back, but instead I made my first priority not letting Jamie know how terrifying I found his statement, and covered my fear with a new question. As though, if he knew how afraid I was, he would cut me down.

What is the virus? I asked.

Virus X, he said, and he didn't eat after that. It's what you've been building the cure for. And all you need to know is this: Don't. Get. Bit.

We never did bring a single rat back to life during our endless testing of compounds and serums and tinctures. Blake and I moved deeper into our own relationship. In a way, the experiments fostered it. Gave us an environment so hectic and strenuous that we didn't have time to destroy the romance before it began. There was no time to talk about the conventional things most couples talk about, like what the rules of the relationship should be, where we were going with it, how serious it would be.

We were careful with the rats; though even after Jamie's special crew of soldiers came to dispose of them, I never forgot Jamie's casual, off-hand warning, as though murder was something he could tack on to a supply list for a Staples run. That was how little he thought of the act itself—and how little he thought of us.

I thought once the rats were exterminated and disposed of, Blake and I would get the chance to talk about what the nature of our dalliance was. Before we could, the Inspector and Jamie were whisking Blake away into the basement again, and this time, for much longer stretches of time.

I moved in. There were no more drugs to mix or experiment with, but Blake wanted me to stay. My only other option was returning to the cramped apartment with the unreliable roommates who liked to rifle through my purse and lift any extra cash I had. Blake's place was the better deal, but the truth was, if I wasn't intrigued and interested by the man himself, I would never have gone. I would have stayed in that shitty apartment.

Can you fault a woman for loving the wrong type of man, Mr. Adamson? I suppose they have our work stowed away in a secret laboratory somewhere. I always wondered what the treatment was designed for, and when I would see the fruits of our labor.

But now I think of my husband, and now I know what the fruits of our labor were. To destroy my love and sacrifice our marriage.

Jamie was some kind of spook and you're just another one of those, those things this government machine spits out. I guess it doesn't matter now. I'm not getting out clean from this, am I? And if this is the way it has to be, if you're gonna turn me in or bury me in a ditch . . . send me off to a black site. I don't care. You've taken away everything that matters now. My love, my husband, my self-respect. But I don't care what you try to take from me now, I'm not killing for you people anymore.

Things got deeper. I stayed upstairs on the second floor but I was awake and listening for when the ghoulish figure of the Inspector would leave, often with Jamie. And that was when Blake began to tell me that there was an interesting side effect to Atroxipine.

You're not taking it, are you? I was aghast. It wasn't as though Atroxipine was going through any committee I knew of. There were no approvals or safeguards in place.

Blake didn't answer. His silence, damning.

You're taking it, I said.

Don't be angry, he answered, rubbing away the lines in his forehead. Every night he fell asleep with a permanent scowl and the lines were etching into a V mark between his eyes. He was too young, I thought, to slowly destroy himself in this fashion.

You don't know what it's going to do to you, it's not designed—
He slammed down the coffee cup on the kitchen counter and it broke into porcelain halves, one rolling off the edge to the floor and the other shattering into the sink.
Don't you understand! I'm too far in. They want me to do things. They want me to test, they want me to . . .
He stopped and stared at the wall. The rings under his eyes formed a mottled horizon of purple and orange. A shell of the man I'd first met. Love has a way of warping your perception. You still see the man inside, even when the exterior is falling apart.
What do they want you to do, Blake? *I whispered.*
Remember the rats?
Of course.
They're done with rats. They've done all they can do with rats. We failed with Atroxipine and they want something more, something better. They want . . . people. They want certain people to test on. And if I can't do it, I'm done for. I'm finished.

★

I listened to Polly with the back of my hand pressed against my mouth. Elvedina was a crumpled outline in the dark and dim hallway, casting soft shadows on the Berber as though she had not fallen into a carpet but drowned in a river of white.
"Jamie looked so much like you, you know," Polly whispered.
I cleared my throat. My last mental image of Jamie was pointing the gun at his heart. The look on his face. He hadn't even been angry. Kept his hands open as though if he could hug me to him and we'd be restored to little boys cowering in our father's shadow. If we had ever stopped being them.
I wanted another drink but I feared to sink myself into a liquor stupor and slow my faculties. A tremor in my fingertips.
I wanted more Atroxipine.
I took out the bottle and rattled it once before setting it on the coffee table between us. The high polished glass reflected a double of the orange bottle. The gun, warm against my rib cage reassured me, sistered up my exhausted heart.

"Atroxipine," I said.

"It wasn't a cure," Polly sighed. "I still don't know what was wrong with the rats. But they were dead. We could never get them to come back but . . . they functioned much better with Atroxipine. But Atroxipine wasn't good enough. It was the Inspector who wanted to know what would happen if regular, healthy people took it."

"Side effects," I whispered.

She nodded, grim. "Most of all, all our hard work had been abandoned. They were exploring other 'cures.' That still left us with a useless drug that Sisemen Pharma, Inc. had sunk a lot of investment into. These investors were not going away until they had something to show for it."

"Finish it out, Polly. The hour grows late."

★

One of Atroxipine's active ingredients is nightshade. You ever hear stories about witches? I see you have. There's more than enough folklore out there. Nightshade, or wolf's bane. Can I tell you how many times I've gone to the movies or flipped on the television to watch something with werewolves or witches or creepy crawlies that go bump in the night, and suffered through a mangled dissertation on wolf's bane's "magical" properties? You'd think people would be smoking it through a glass pipe with a reputation like that. Now it's been living on as a myth in ancient recipes for "Flying Ointments"—turned into an ointment meant to be smeared into the skin. Sit back and enjoy the hallucinatory effect with broom in hand. Or so the rumor goes. In fact, nightshade would never have found its way into our own witch's brew if not for Blake's unconventional ideas. He gave permission to explore every wild avenue and urge—and nightshade was it.

I don't know who discovered that it could be put to use. Jamie and the Inspector came to Blake, whispering in his ear that there were limits to this drug that had not yet been plumbed. They were conducting trials on prisoners—prisoners! People they'd packed off to black sites. Who knows what their crimes were, if they had committed any wrong. They were experimenting with them and out-of-body experience.

Jamie, and the Inspector, insinuated that if Blake didn't want to end up beside all these nameless men and women that had been scooped out of their ordinary and banal lives and gone missing into unnameable spaces scattered all over the world, he'd better listen and do what they said.

You know how prisoners are. They're recalcitrant. They don't appreciate being held in a place against their will for no crime and then ask to be drafted into an experimental program, because that's what it amounts to, right? Paranormal phenomena. It's like the books I used to read from the supermarket shelf with the gutsy heroines and the alpha male heroes. Paranormal, as in things you didn't think were real and now you have to account for. Things like leaving your body while you sleep and directing yourself into limitless space.

They wanted Blake to demonstrate the drug's effectiveness. That with practice, he could do it invisibly with no one the wiser.

Blake couldn't say no; once they'd gotten us in deep with making Atroxipine, you couldn't just extricate yourself. We talked about leaving. Packing our stuff and disappearing into the wilderness. It was nice to dream about, but our hearts weren't in it. We weren't made for that lifestyle. What if we wanted children? What if we got hurt? The second we popped back up on the grid, that would be it. All life would be reduced to a waiting game in which Goliath need only shift his boot and crush us the second we ran out from the rock we chose to hide under.

We had to stay. But Blake was under pressure to perform. They wanted him to engage in the out-of-body program. The Inspector and Jamie would teach him the rudiments and monitor his sleep. When enough time elapsed and Blake passed out of the initial phase, they would give him targets—people they wanted him to "incapacitate" while out-of-body.

"Then what happens?" he'd asked them. "What do I do when I face them in this dream state?"

"Cut the cord," they said.

I had yet to know, to experience, or to see it for myself, but they were talking about the life line that connects the dreamer to the body.

"Won't that kill them?" Blake asked.

They answered in half-truths and vague statements. They passed it off as though nobody knew for certain what the outcome was and surely it would be no worse than momentary paralysis. The Inspector and Jamie were not the kind of people you probed with penetrating questions. There's something in their stare that refuses to give ground or even understand your concerns. Attempts to do so are tinged with fear and paranoia. If you question them, is that enough to be dismissed, to be marked for suspicion, for investigation?

We could not simply ask why they wanted it done. At this point, Sisemen Pharma, Inc. was the financial loser in the deal, and their last hope at recouping the loss was to work in tandem with the military for exclusive drug contracts. Or so we thought. Asking Jamie flat out if that were the case would have been overstepping our bounds, but it was clear if they could utilize Atroxipine for other purposes, there was a lot of money to be made. The government had been pouring money and effort into Remote Viewing operations for years with little success. This was the chance to turn it all around. Sisemen would produce the pills, the military would eat them up. But first, they needed to prove it out.

Why Blake was being asked to "incapacitate" specific people, though, that was another pickle entirely. They were young professionals. They weren't criminals or thugs or people on the FBI's Most Wanted list. And we were pretty sure that the consequences of "incapacitation," no matter Jamie's assurances, were dire.

They were really asking Blake to kill them.

You ever read Slaughterhouse Five? That Kurt Vonnegut book? My English professor made us read it. It was never my thing, books. But I remember very clearly reading about Vonnegut recall the bombing of Dresden in World War II, and how he researched the event afterward, trying to understand

what business the Allies had in obliterating a whole city, what
the reason was.

In the end, there was no reason. It was because they could.
Because they had all this firepower and wanted to see what would
happen if they used it. They leveled a whole city, and all the people
in it. You spend all this time asking big-picture questions about
the why of things, looking for sane and rational answers because
you're a sane and rational person that can't conceive of any other
answer but a sane and rational one. In the end, it doesn't matter.
There is no sane and rational answer. It's because they can.

They wanted Blake to go after these people, just because.

Blake began in earnest. He collapsed into bed after spending
most of the day sleeping in the basement under the gaze of the
Inspector and Jamie, taking doses of Atroxipine and increasing
them steadily. They believed Atroxipine was the key. We heard
they might still be able to use it to mitigate the effects of the disease
it had originally been intended for, even while not a complete
cure. For everyone else not afflicted by disease, the effects were
substantially different, radically changing the relationship of
the drug to the body. Most ordinary people would either need
a predisposition or endless training to achieve an out-of-body
state, but Atroxipine would halve the effort and allow immediate
results. The intense euphoria and increased sensation and activity
in the cerebral cortex and other areas—they indicated exciting
results. An unexpected side effect of the drug.

Blake even got me to try one. The experience was memorable.
Everything was clearer. My thoughts came organized and fast. I
felt like I could do quantum physics from the Marianas Trench,
refurbish the dining room and then maybe have time left over to
bake cookies. It was exhilarating.

Blake didn't want it. The effects were fascinating, but even
I could see the potential for Atroxipine to have an unexpected
domino effect. If this ever escaped into the public, the black
market would make it the new cocaine, but better and more
intense than any previous drug. And, it keeps you young. But
none of us knew what the long-term cost would be. Would
organs become stressed and inflamed and then ultimately fail?

They were toying with Blake's life and threatening to take it away if he didn't act on their orders. The threat was implied if Blake didn't kill these people: they would spirit him away. Jamie would wave his hand, like he had over his box of lo mein. Take him away. And he would be gone.

All that training, and Blake said he didn't know what the hell they were talking about. Sometimes he felt something bigger shaking on the inside of him and, a few times, he floated up and out before he said he felt snapped back in by his own terror. He was petrified of what would happen if he strayed too far. Could he lose himself? He told me a thin, silver cord unspooled out of him and connected back to the body, but what frightened him was the Inspector. He could picture him, scything through that cord just to see what would happen.

Haggard and wasted, they dragged him back down to that basement. While the boys played with their drugs and machines, I began to take Atroxipine. Not all the time. Just now and again. I'd be bored and time lost all structure and meaning with the blackout curtains over every window and Blake sleeping all hours of the day. I'd swallow a dose and fall asleep.

And then, my dreams, usually mundane and trivial stress dreams, morphed into another level of intensity. I should have understood then, great changes were at work within me and that innocuous-seeming pill lay at the heart of it. The dreams took me into a world that was the mirror image of the one I was already in. In fact, it ceased to be a dream at all. I blinked and I would be in my house but not awake. And the first time it happened, I was frightened and would not move, stayed on the couch where I fell asleep and waited until the world shifted and I was dreaming again. And then it was all at peace again. I could take another pill and forget about the whole ordeal.

It happened again, repeatedly. I remained fixed wherever I found myself, refusing to move. Until it came to pass that the next instant I opened my eyes, a man sat across from me in the deepest shadow against the wall. He drew the darkness to him, like a black hole swallowing light until all I could see were his glittering eyes. And he spoke to me.

Aren't you a surprising one, *he said.*

I wanted to answer, but above all I wanted to wake up. I could do neither, as though a grand piano sat on top of my chest and pinned me there, left me blinking at him, and I realized he was floating in the air, a foot above the floor where he should have feet.

Do you like to dream, Polly?

Not like this, *I thought, and he nodded. He'd heard me, even though I hadn't been able to speak.*

I suppose that makes this a nightmare, and that means you're trapped inside it. I know that feeling well, my dear. Of course, that's nothing compared to what your dear husband is going through.

What about Blake? Where is he?

Oh, he's trying very hard, but he doesn't have the knack for this kind of thing. In fact, I think he's about outlived his usefulness. That could be very bad for Blake, you know. You, on the other hand. You might be able to save him.

Why? What's wrong? Hasn't he done what's been asked of him?

Oh, it's really not his fault. He just seems to lack the talent, is all. But you, unexpectedly—quite pleasingly!—make up for all his flaws. Who would have realized? I'm afraid in our foolishness, we men overlooked you. That should not have happened. Let me correct my egregious error now and recognize you, Polly.

But I did not like being recognized by him at all. More than this, would prefer to have continued going on unnoticed by him forever. Having his glittering eyes fall upon me was like being dipped in grease, squirming on the end of a hook as a feral, snarling vermin sniffed me and licked its chops.

You see, Polly. If he can't be useful, then he will have to be disposed of.

He disappeared. I woke up in a fever-sweat. The place where the man had floated in the air was several shades darker than the rest of the atmosphere around it, as though he'd left a stain.

After that, this thing, this shadow, this shade, this—specter, visited me with greater ferocity than before. Every time I closed my eyes, I feared to open them again and find the shadow around every corner, staring and awaiting me with his glittering eyes and his grin curling a semi-circle out of the smoke. He wanted me to do what Blake would not, or Blake would be "expendable." I broke down. He told me if I agreed to take Blake's place instead, Blake might have a chance at survival.

The specter showed me how to leave my body. Under different circumstances, I might have found the experience wondrous, astonishing. Pressed the bounds of dreams and imagination alike. He showed me how to go through walls and come out on the other side, and then, he led me out into the world. It was exhilarating to be able to walk through the world and never have to fear it. Or so I thought. On the other side of dreaming, I was younger, somehow. Vital. Unburdened by my heavy body. But I wasn't ready for the emotional consequences later.

The specter gave me an artifact from Dietrich. He was the first subject—or target. The shadow stole a swatch of fabric from his suit, gave it to me and instructed me to hold it, imagine myself there and I would be. It's as simple as that. And when I reached the other side, to take the silver cord that bound his sleeping self and sever it.

Travel in this realm is ethereal, faster than the speed of light. Dietrich was just a young kid. I found him in his apartment in the middle of the night. He was sprawled out naked on his bed with a woman sleeping beside him and their figures were fuzzy—as though their souls were hovering just an inch above their bodies. Floating gently like buoys in an ocean current. I could see the compressed silver line and I reached in. I touched it. It purred and hummed like a cat, but I hadn't thought it through and the specter hadn't showed me what to do. How to split the line? So I made my fingers into a pair of scissors, as a young kid does when they play games, and I snipped!

The line fell apart.

Dietrich lurched out of bed immediately. Shot up out of the darkness with his eyes rolling, his mouth open, choking on the air. The cords in his neck like shoestrings held taut. Shocked, I looked on. While I looked on, the light in his eyes came apart. Like a line of Christmas light strings when you take one bulb out and the whole thing goes dark.

I heard they took him to the hospital and he died there. But there were inconsistencies in the reports. I don't think he died right away. I think he was paralyzed, in some fashion. During the investigation, the police tried to talk to the EMTs on the scene that night. They couldn't find any of them. There were no records of those emergency personnel who reported there. Somewhere between the ambulance and the hospital, Dietrich went missing for an hour, from the time the call was logged in with dispatch to the time the mystery ambulance arrived and then disappeared forever. When he finally arrived at his destination, he was dead.

In the end, missing hour or no, it ends the same: I killed him.

I took no pleasure in it. I didn't dare tell Blake. They kept testing him out and noting Blake's experiences. If they couldn't coerce him to successfully engage with the drug, then they would squeeze him for every drop of research and development they could get out of him. I cried for days. Everything came out of me and broke apart. I saw Dietrich's face in my mind. Carried him with me, in my heart. Saw it in the faces of his widowed wife and his forlorn children. And saw it all over again when the loathsome Inspector came trudging into our house with Jamie in his shadow and kidnapped my sick and strung-out husband to stretch him on the torture rack that doubled as his bed again.

PART 6

VITUS TAKES HIS MEDICINE

As a child, I used to study the stars. I camped in the backyard and opened myself to the endless void above me, stippled with distant points of light. It was Jamie, in his pretentious desire to show off his high-end education, who pointed out that if I stopped looking at each individual star and pulled back my limits of perception, I would perceive millions of stars even more distant, all together forming a light wash in the sky called the Milky Way. All that time, I'd been staring at the brightest stars and missed the galactic tide right in front of my face. But Jamie had been right in the end.

Listening to Polly, I had come full circle, pulling back to see the universe entire. I understood now, Atroxipine had allowed me to leave my own body under Lionel's tutelage, and I understood that Lionel, too, was taking the drug. Was it not his name on the prescription bottle when I had found it, the bottle he had dangled in front of me to hook me, to draw me in? To prime me for an out-of-body experience of my own?

To what purpose? But I needed no intense soul-searching to understand why. They wanted a tool, whether they sent me on investigations or decided to move me into assassinations, either way, they could hold me in reserve like a knife in their government arsenal.

Blake and Polly would have served that purpose; but some knives, if not formed well, shatter on impact. Blades break all the time.

Lionel had told me many things. But now all his words were suspect. His paternal confession that I was supposed to be terminated if I could not function like a normal human being with a heart no longer had value; if they were setting me up to commit heartless deeds and conduct dirty missions then, if anything, the possession of a conscience was a liability.

Lionel lied, I realized. Maybe it was the other way around. Maybe *he* was assigned to kill me if I didn't fall into step with their program, if I didn't have the nerve to do their bidding and conduct every dubious request thrown at me.

Now that had the ring of truth to it. If all Lionel had told me wasn't true, then it cast Elvedina in a different light. Could I be so sure her purpose was malevolent? Everything was thrown upside down once more and I looked down the hall to Elvedina's form, crumpled and curled in on itself. There would be a reckoning between us yet, as soon as I had laid Polly's case to rest.

"This entity fed you the targets," I whispered, "and you delivered them."

She laughed with her hand forming a claw over her mouth as though she could stopper it in.

"Passed it off as Blake's handiwork. They even promoted him. Said he was the best they'd ever seen."

"How did it end?"

"I refused to do it anymore. I thought I was saving Blake's life, but how many lives are worth one, even when that one is a beloved husband? I couldn't justify it any longer. All I could picture was an endless future where the targets got bigger and bigger and harder to kill. How many would they ask me to kill in secret? I was already at my breaking point. I envisioned that terrible future of endless killing. He confessed so easily, so readily. I don't know if he ever realized it was me. Sometimes, I think he did."

"And the prisoner who tussled with Blake in the prison? The prison guard who we hired to be an informant? Was that your handiwork as well?"

She looked away. "My husband wasn't made for prison. He doesn't have it in him to do the hard things. At least in prison, the violence is more honest. Before all that happened, when push came to shove, he wanted it all to end. He wanted out, and he figured a prison cell would be safer, where Jamie and the Echo Inspector couldn't get to him."

She laugheed, bitter. "Of course, if you plan on sleeping, nothing is guaranteed. In the end, he acquiesced with the authorities and our lives were destroyed. And isn't that what I deserve?"

I thought of my dead brother.

Isn't that what I deserve?

She let the plaintive question hang in the air the way people do when they want someone else to tell them it's going to be all right. That what they did wasn't so bad after all. That everything could go back to the beginning.

This human body with all its human complications had made of my emotions a miasma of conscience and recriminations. She'd killed many in cold blood, under an odd coercion of government influence. I'd killed my brother in the fit of passion. But elementally, the same crime. With the pressure of a larger force at work, making pawns of us.

The old gray fox, a voice sneered inside me. How like Jamie it sounded.

I stared at her as though I could cull the answer from her face. The deep etchings of her wrinkles. The heartbreak in the lines of her mouth, her forehead. She looked sad and crumpled in on herself as a woman might when everything has been taken from her. Did I look any better, like a junkie gone twitchy, heroin thin and with blood spattering the belly of my shirt?

"Are you going to take me in?" she whispered.

I reached into my hoodie and withdrew the Glock. Held it in my hands, the muzzle pointed at the ground. Her breath hitched.

"Or kill me?" she said. "Like you did Jamie?"

"Not like Jamie," I said, agitated and got up to pace the window. Elvedina, still unconscious—or whatever passed for unconsciousness if you had all the life functions of an Atari mounted on a bicycle frame.

"You're not in prison," she hissed. "How did you get out? And you want to send me there?"

This was not a direction in which I had anticipated our conversation going. I thought it would be easier, to apprehend her and turn her over to the government and not ask too many questions. My freedom was contingent on it, like any business contract, and failure to hold up my end of the bargain could end with me back in prison, serving time for Jamie's murder. But by the minute, with each violation of law and ethics, the terms of the contract itself appeared to be eroding and now she was interrogating me.

I still held the firearm in one hand. This gun had seen me through more extremities than I could name and now it seemed an empty symbol of a dead life I no longer owned.

"They say you killed him in cold blood," she continued, relentless. She knew it needled me and hit on the tectonic plates in my psyche, setting into motion quakes and shifts beyond my control. "They say you killed him—"

"I don't care what they say!" I roared and rounded on her. All the life in me fled and left behind the rotted carcass of my primal identity, my broken Id pushing through the surface before I subsided. Calmer. Rational. "I don't care what they say. They didn't know Jamie."

"I knew Jamie," she snapped.

"Oh did you? Did you know him like you knew Dietrich? Know him like you knew Kylie Stefano? Know him like you knew Anna Maison?"

"But I'm the only one who's gonna do time for it," she said and made a fist, slamming it on the coffee table. The glass crackled and spider webbed beneath and she did not notice or care. Blood oozed from the edge of her hand and she didn't feel it. Her jaw flexed and twitched with agitation. "They say you didn't remember what happened."

I glanced at her and looked away.

"You remember," she whispered.

"Be silent," I said. "I can't think with all this noise."

"You remember but you didn't want to talk. I might have killed people and that makes me no different than you, but they weren't my own blood, for God's sake. Why do you get special treatment? Why should you walk free after killing people, but my husband and I get sent to the cage when we didn't ask for this, we didn't ask to be coerced into this? You don't know what they'll do to us once we're inside. They'll take us away. They'll vanish us. And you, you can keep on killing people by the dozen like it doesn't matter—"

"You don't know anything," I said and came over the couch, stepping right into the cushion and over the arm rest. She leaped up before my relentless pursuit, but I'd had enough. I itched for another Atroxipine hit. Her endless revolving back to my own crime brought me full circle, past to the present. She wasn't Polly Highsmith anymore. She was Jamie when I burst through the door—

"Is this what you want to know?" I asked and pushed the muzzle over Polly's heart. "That this is how I did it? That I remember every detail, that I think about it when I fall asleep and when I wake up?"

Her lower lip trembled but her eyes were forged in steel and cast in iron. She lifted her chin and pressed into the muzzle, daring me to shoot.

"Go ahead," she said. "Why wait?"

An echo of the past, and I heard it resound in my brother's voice:

Why wait?

"Every time I dream, I forget that I killed him, and every time I dream, I forget I'm living a nightmare. I'll wake up and Jamie will be alive. I'll hate him with the same fever as before."

"When you do it," Polly said and closed her eyes, "take care of my husband. That's all I ask. Take care of him."

"Take care of her," Jamie said. "I love you, brother. Beware the echoes and specters."

"I'm not going to kill you, Polly," I said, and the gun fell to my side.

She screamed. Thrust her hands into her hair and screamed.

"I'm not going to kill you, Polly," I said again when silence filled the room. "It concerns me, that you'd rather die, than serve time. Because I gotta wonder, what it is they are doing to people and prisoners that is so horrifying you'd rather be shot by a villain like me than face what's waiting for you in secret rooms where no one will know where you disappeared to, and no one will know you're screaming and dying in the deepest dungeon, as fodder for the same experiments you put those rats through. You'll never see a day in court. Your husband got off easy compared to what they'll do to you. Is that about right?"

She put her hands over her eyes and would not look at me.

I cursed. I wondered what my father would want me to do. If he was counting on me to do anything at all. I groaned and rubbed my hands over my face and closed my eyes. I squeezed my head in my hands.

Get up and arrest her, my father's voice commanded.

You know, sometimes, a pawn can just walk off the board, my Id chuckled as though he sat beside me on the couch, plucking the whiskey glass out of my hand and staring down into it with disappointment. *There's another way. And won't that burn the old man's ass hairs.*

More than that, Polly was right. I killed my brother in cold blood. I should, by rights, be sitting in a jail cell. I deserved no mercy. Polly and Blake had been coerced and corrupted and threatened. They did not deserve this. She did not deserve this.

This new body, with ready-made chemistry and fizzing cells, brought with it a conscience I never had as a pre-deceased corpse. I had been beyond the law because laws were made for living citizens, not the dead. I didn't have to care because nothing mattered.

Living now, everything mattered. My human condition was literal, and membership to the ranks came with a terrible choice—which would I choose? Acknowledge that I had no right to be her judge when I belonged in a prison cell? Turn her over to the authorities, and do the right thing and turn myself in as well? Or hand her over to Lionel and sleep at night on a nice mattress in a spacious room and never think on Blake and Polly again?

My duty? Or my conscience?

To be, or not to be.

My fist spasmed around the gun, and I realized that I had the chance to do the thing I hadn't the courage to do for Jamie: let her go.

"You were never here."

Polly startled. Her mental state flipped on a switch. Tears drying as she lurched to her feet. Eyes becoming hard and cold and small in her face.

She grabbed her duffel with a grunt. She'd been ready for this and was making good on it. I rose up to my feet with a glance down the long dark hallway where Elvedina still lay, shorted out and useless as an Energizer Bunny that ran down its battery.

Polly turned with her bag in one hand and her other on the door to look at me.

Thank you, she mouthed.

The lines in her face from worry and nights killing persisted; they would always be there. They would never fade. I found solace in the fact that Polly would provide a punishment for her crimes of a different sort; and it was the best I could hope for in this new and uncertain warped world I had entered where courts were perverted and laws rendered meaningless.

I approached and stopped short, waiting for her to open the door.

"One day, if things should change, I may have to find you. Do you understand?"

She nodded, tight.

"Tell Blake I love him," she whispered, swallowing down a sob, and then jerked open the door.

It had stopped raining. The sky overcast, bled gray in a weepy half-light. The vulture scowled over us from the roof of the porch as Polly made her way down the stairs and I closed the door behind me.

I thought about going with her. I was surrounded by too much intrigue and a leave of absence could reduce the heat and give me time to convalesce. The thought balanced on the tip of my tongue and I had decided to open my mouth and tell her, *Wait, I'm coming with you* when the putter of old exhaust, a heaving engine like a rough beast slouching in our direction, turned the corner. A panel van, pulling across the driveway, blocking the exit.

I lifted my hand to shade my eyes and saw a man I did not recognize behind the wheel. The kind of meaty, heavy-duty weightlifter who would have beaten the shit out of me at the prison.

Polly dropped her bag outside the car door and stared.

The passenger door opened.

Lionel stepped out.

✱

His silver cane sent a slash of light across my face as I rushed down the porch. The vulture stared, erect, his eyes black volcanic glass as I stood beside Polly, my boots sinking into the long grass.

The driver of the van turned the key and the ignition died, spoiled exhaust fume evaporating across the pavement. In the silence, a distant hum subsumed the outlying traffic, the sound of our breathing, until a familiar motorcycle painted in flame careened into view.

Lafferty's modified motorcycle painted a line of heat down the road surface to the shadow of the van. The machine sputtered to a stop and he leaned with one hand set against the panel van, black glove mapping the numerous dents of bad driving decisions past. His face grim with a bandanna over his mouth, eyes unreadable behind his sunglasses.

"You bastard," Polly whispered. She quavered in and out of my periphery. If she thought I had betrayed her, I didn't disavow her of the notion.

Lionel shuffled up the driveway, past the withered pansies sitting in muffin-topped red mulch gone faded with decomposition. Lionel looked as though he were merely a man on holiday as he navigated the driveway, slow, slow. But now I calculated him anew. Wondered how much of his pace was a show for my benefit to make him appear more fragile than he actually was. I pictured how he had concentrated and steadied the trembling of his hands. How much of that was made up? His pocket bulged out with the weight of the grenade, if that story had ever been true. From here, he looked like a harmless man, making any act of aggression on my part unwarranted and criminal. I could only stand there and wait to see what he would do when he finally finished his long and drawn out approach. The hint of a smile on his face, knowing that he drew out the tension with every step as Lafferty coaxed the bike up over the curb and eased it, inch by inch.

Lionel came to a stop, tapped his cane on the ground, and looked at the house with his expression still fixed as that of a kindly old man. Your dear sainted grandfather, out on a country walk.

"Oh, excellent, Vitus. You've apprehended the suspect."

I said nothing.

"Your father will be pleased."

Polly opened her mouth. "I want an attorney—"

"Shut your mouth," I hissed, and Polly said no more.

"What happens to her?" I asked him.

Lionel raised one eyebrow.

"I thought we already talked about this, my boy. We have our own way of meting out justice."

"How about the constitutional way? You got room for that in your playbook?"

He laughed, generous and gusty.

"What's gotten into you, Vitus? You know we have our own guidelines. She'll be treated very well."

"But she won't see the inside of a court room."

"Well—"

"Say it," I cut him off. "Answer me, instead of obfuscating. You capable of a direct answer?"

"Boy, I thought we'd been through enough now that you would trust me. I've already given you the answer, why would it matter now?"

Lionel's last ditch efforts to wheedle into my good graces had all the greasy charm of a desperate carpetbagger waving cash in front of my face. I could not be bought so cheaply, not anymore. No doubt his years among politicians and criminals could not prevent him from trying. For some, duplicity comes embedded in their bones. Lionel would, until the bitter end, lie even when it made no sense to do so, lie because his tongue only moves in one direction and no other, making him the most hideous monster of all.

Polly's eyes flicked to me. Everything about her, frozen like a deer crossing a super highway, dazzled by the stream of endless lights crashing down upon her.

"Run," I said.

She looked at her duffel bag, looked at Lionel and Lafferty. The man in the motorcycle balanced atop the thrumming machine, gripping the handles tight.

I grabbed her by the arm and pushed her past Lionel. She stumbled across the driveway.

"Run!" I yelled.

"Look here," Lionel said, "that's rather ridiculous, you can't let her do that—"

Polly ran. Her shoes hit the pavement and her breath picked up. The cul-de-sac amplified the sound like an echo chamber and she glanced backward and I screamed at her to run again. The man driving the van tracked her through the windshield with nothing to say and no reaction. Hired thug or just a hired driver? Lionel's lips and face imitated a twisted rag, a sudden flash of the real man inside. Angry and deadened. Stony and heartless eyes behind the glitter of his false compassion. The old gray fox was better at this than Lionel; he never would have shown that much of himself, not even in extremity.

"Lafferty!" Lionel barked. "Shoot her."

Lafferty blinked and did nothing.

"Dammit, you'll do as I say!" Lionel hissed and reached up to strike Lafferty with the cane. Even I had not seen that coming. Lafferty flinched and his motorcycle took the impact with a faint listing; with the second strike, he snatched at Lionel's cane and tore it out of his grasp, his face reddening. The old man stumbled, hissing like a snake to stand on his own two feet with energetic aplomb.

He lunged for his weapon, yanking it out of the shoulder holster beneath his suit jacket. An old 1911. *The sort my father likes to use*, I thought with disgust. He leveled it to take a shot at Polly, who fell to her knees and put her hands over her head without a sound, waiting for the bullet to descend.

I reached out and jerked his arm up into the air. The round discharged. Lionel gave a frustrated cry, showing the row of his yellow teeth like the edge of a paper. He surrendered the weapon to my grasp. Pants of his furious breath and his muttered curses. He reached into his pocket to withdraw the grenade.

"Oh, shit on me," Lafferty cried and wheeled backward out of Lionel's path. He jerked the handle bars and hurtled into fresh speed and away from the incendiary device. He carved a path to Polly, who stood, stunned and confused, to commence her run in the aftermath of the gun blast, her mouth open and her eyes wide as she watched Lionel withdraw the iron ball in one hand and pull the pin.

I want to tell you the vulture swooped down from his perch and plucked the grenade out of his hand and carried it away where it exploded into mid air, harming no one.

I want to tell you it was too old to be viable and the dynamite buried deep in the heart of the grenade was null and void and all it did was give an ineffectual puff and become nothing more than harmless dust.

But we don't deal in happy endings here.

I saw everything in hyper motion. Was my intensity fueled by Atroxipine? I'd remember the elapsing seconds forever. Seeing how his gnarled fingers twined 'round the ring in rows of bone and then yanked and the pin worked free. Committing to memory the yellow paint on top of the grenade, marking it as a wartime munition. Thinking that my very own father had held that grenade in his hand and if he hadn't saved Lionel's life all those years ago, we wouldn't be here with that grenade in Lionel's hand today.

I had only several seconds with which to decide all of our fates.

Atroxipine sped up everything, Atroxipine sent my mind racing through every possibility. Made me see all the timelines stretching out from me in a thousand directions. Made me imagine and perceive with terrible clarity every detail of Polly's agony as the grenade landed near her and then blew a hole at her feet, taking her legs with it. The pavement streaming blood into the gutter that would leach out into the mighty and terrible Atlantic Ocean. Blood and sand. I pictured if Lionel missed. I saw myself try to shoot him. I saw myself try to save Polly and fail. I saw myself, ducking and taking cover. Saw Lafferty, his motorcycle upturned and new parts of him missing. The wheels of his bike, spinning in empty space.

This was what my own father had faced when the man had pulled the pin and thrown the grenade. Like him, I had only several seconds. On the surface, you believe time is the problem. If only you had more time. But that wasn't it; the problem was no outcome could be favorable.

Except for one.

Lionel stretched back his hand to lob the grenade.

And in that second, I reached out and put my hand over his.

"What are you doing, boy!" Lionel roared. His entire body shifted so he could stare at me, his mouth pulled down into a clenching jaw transformed by rage and frustration. "Let go!"

"No," I said. I heard myself speak from fathoms of distance. Heard Lafferty yelling as he pushed his velocity to the limit, heard the steady *slap slap* of Polly's shoes on the ground as she ran. *Fly*, I thought. *Fly, Polly, fly.* And Lafferty, leaning for her with one open arm, to take her with him and sling shot them far away from here.

Lionel struggled as I counted down in my head. His grip was iron and his entire body tried to shake me out of his grip, but I held it there, tighter, tighter through my sweat until I thought his hand was a sheet of tissue paper through which I could feel every ridge of the grenade beneath. Squeezed his knuckles until the cartilage cracked beneath the burden. Could feel the expanding metal as the final second counted down and the explosion began.

Everything disappeared into a white-out blast and rendered me deaf. A buzzing drummed through my ears. One second, I'd been standing with Lionel's hand clutched in mine; and then I was jolted into the air and on my back. The sky above spat intermittent rain into my face. The trailing silhouette of a huge black bird drew lazy circles through the clouds. A vulture. Distant screaming. The belching of the motorcycle exhaust arrowing away from me and Polly with it. Unharmed. Sound whinnied and warped through the air and I realized that it was Lionel and me. We were screaming and the screaming stopped when I shut my mouth.

Well, that wasn't so bad, I thought and sat up as though the entire lawn I found myself in was my bedroom and I'd awoken from a terrible dream. I looked around the driveway where Lionel and I had been standing, but now there was only Lionel on his back, spread eagled on the lawn some distance from me. He, screaming and holding aloft his obliterated arm that had been mashed and splintered into an unrecognizable limb. Like a tree branch shoved through a wood chipper and then yanked out.

That looks pretty bad, I thought. *I guess I just got lucky.*

I climbed to my feet and my vision swam. Nausea simmered through my belly and I hiccuped once before I kneeled to vomit into the grass. I reached up to wipe the scrim of bile from my lips but I missed. I tried again.

And again.

Each time I missed.

I looked down.

There was no hand to wipe it away. Blood spattered out from the termination point where I could see each particular tendon and ligament and vein, blood spray casting a weak rainbow in the half-light. Mesmerized.

My arm stopped midway between wrist and elbow.

"Oh, fuck," I whispered and fell back to my knees.

This is bad, I decided. *I think I'm just going to stay here for awhile. Maybe take a dirt nap.*

Good idea, my Id agreed.

Lionel kept screaming. The door to the house burst open and a huge shadow dominated the threshold, then down the steps. Each step an earth-shaking lurch. Light slanted over her shoulders, crosshatched her rigid and expressionless face, the place in her chest where she'd been stabbed with a carving knife.

The gun gleamed in her hand. Lionel rolled and rollicked on the grass, spurting blood into a red arc like a garden hose. He reached his good hand out to her, his mouth open, supplicating.

She looked past Lionel. Her eyes tracked the blood and then tracked it all the way to me. I could not guess what dark things lurked inside of her. What wires and microchips. What secret programming. How much of her was human and how much of her was machine.

I held my stump out into the air. It did not seem like mine. It belonged to someone else, someone else on their knees in this ragged lawn holding up this destroyed version of myself.

She lifted the gun. Lionel screamed and screamed and then she shot him once, twice.

His screaming silenced and his body fell back onto the lawn.

She stepped over him. Grasshoppers whirred out of her path as she stopped before me and her half-shadow fell over my face, drowning her in black.

"Gonna kill me now," I whispered.

Didn't I deserve it?

The gun in her hand seemed a part of her as though she was polycarbonate plastic down to her bones. Her fingers tightened around the grip and her face sent me careening back to childhood memories of my mother, of my father reading *Oedipus Rex* to us and then, the statue of Mother Mary on his desk. A nonsensical stream of images. Lady Liberty, raising her lamp over Ellis Island. The terror of this steel giant.

"Do it," I whispered, and I was quaking. Shaking through and through. The shock reeled through me. I craved Atroxipine. Wanted it shot straight into my blood stream to dull the scathing pain. Pain I could not yet feel but only sense the edges of.

"I killed Jamie. Isn't that what you're here for? Do it!"

But she did not do it.

Instead, she reached out with her free hand and snatched at the chain around my neck. She pulled, the chain cut into my neck, and then it snapped off. Stared at the skeleton key in the palm of her hand and her mouth parted with visible animation, eyes wide in the imitation of human surprise. Could she feel? Did she have that capacity?

She wound the chain around her wrist and held the gun with it.

"You're *her*," I whispered.

That's what Jamie had meant. *Take care of her.*

The key had been for Elvedina.

She reached out with her free hand and grabbed my stump. I made a noise with no language. She cut off the spurting arc of blood with her grip and squeezed.

A sun flare of agony drove through me, from spine to crown; crucified me with raw nerves.

I screamed and writhed and flailed. She anchored me in place with a vise pushing unmeasured pounds of pressure on my wretched and crippled wound. She grinned and squeezed harder until the blood spurt became a thin trickle and then even the trickle stopped—saving my life.

I howled and then whimpered into silence when I could scream no more, pinioned in her grip. I could smell motor oil on her. I gasped and wheezed and prayed to stop the pain. And in those seconds before the pain and shock sent me skyrocketing into unconsciousness, I heard her voice.

"Oh, Vitus. *Look at what a mess you've made.*"

PART 7

REDACTED

The man, from here, looked as though he were dead.

The room's layout contained in a four by six-foot prison cell. The dim outline of a prisoner slept in the top bunk and another on the bottom: Blake Highsmith. I'd think he was dead, but his chest rose and fell in steady rhythm. His mouth pouted out puffs of air, snored on the inhale, and swallowed and smacked his lips. Blake Highsmith slept like the dead, slept like . . . well, like he's innocent.

A dark fog collected through the bars of the prison door. Seeped in, like tendrils, smoke curling and uncoiling along the floor to gather in harmony in the center of the room. As the smoke intensified, it deepened and took on an identifiable shape. A man in a suit who collected the darkness to him in a teneberous corona, sucking the ambient light as a black hole in space. The figure rose up out of folds of darkness to occupy his full height, eyes aglitter, sunken in the space where his head should be.

He took a step forward, approached the sleeping man with one hand outstretched. Desecrated the air between them and the stone underfoot, and then, a second figure, knocked away his hand, pushed him backward into the stone.

Vitus, the Echo Inspector said.

"Not yours," I answered.

His employment is ended. This is not your department.

"If you think you're going to be able to get your way, you've got another thing coming. Kill me if that's what gets your rocks off, but I'm from a new department. The Department of Go Fuck Yourself."

The figure shook, heaved with laughter.

Kill you, Vitus? Oh, why on Earth would we kill our most valuable employee?

"I don't work for you."

In the silence, I thought about it. Blake turned in sleep, scratched his chest and hugged himself with a whimper, before subsiding.

"Okay, I guess I kinda sorta work for the government, if that's what you mean, but I don't take orders from you."

Oh, you don't understand. You've misunderstood this whole time. You, of all of them, remain our favorite monster. Of course you don't take orders from us. We take orders from you, Vitus.

"But you'd kill me with no problems, right? Is that supposed to make sense to me?"

Not kill you. Grow you. Change you. Test you. Transform you. But never kill you, King of the Flesh Eaters, Master of Monsters.

And then, he was gone. Left me alone to grow cold with the sound of the Inspector's voice in my ear, an insidious terror buried in his reverent naming of me. Blake's snores beat out time and awoke me to myself. He, at least, would be safe.

★

"Gimme the arm."

I opened my eyes.

I'm laid out on the kitchen table and I detected her shadow, serpentine, with lips sealed as a sphinx, a mythological and forgotten idol. She could kill me without a second thought, without reservations or conscience.

Instead, she pulled up a chair and pretended to be human by sitting down. I opened one eye to look at her.

She set the needle aside and helped me into a new shirt. She folded my sleeve down over the gutter tracks on my arm. The nice side effect of Atroxipine is how it dulls the pain of one's healing amputation.

She didn't give the arm to me so much as she strapped it on herself, with one hand on my chest, as though I were an unruly animal that would go charging into the wilderness without her pinning me in place, and I let her. Her dead fingers pushed in the tender spots and I wondered what they were made of. Rubber? Plastic? Did they make her skin at a fucking toy factory? Beneath the layer of skin, was it metal? Or poly resin?

All these months of convalescence later, and I still didn't know; feared to look her in the eyes and ask. Afraid of how she'd answer, and what I would say.

She fitted it snug against the nub of me. I closed my eyes and let her. Can she intuit comfort, pleasure? The moment should remind me of Niko when she once did the same, insinuate the heartbreak of our severed union—but it did not.

"What now?" I croaked.

But I knew what it was she wanted, wanted me to do. It was time to get a move on. Time to see where we stand on my father's chessboard.

She gripped me by my false hand and forced me to sit up. A blood rush carried Atroxipine away from me and thudded through my heart where it recycled and pumped back through me. Clear and intense. Every sense collaborating in controlled fire and tingling. The distilled essence of all I'd known and seen and done, perfected and mastered.

My fake hand held her robot hand, her fingers tickling at the sensitive and still healing meat of me where it strapped into the prosthetic.

Everything about her made my skin crawl.

I loved her for it.

★

Elvedina drove the car.

The vulture followed the car from above and now and again his shadow swung over us. I was getting tired of having talon tracks in my shoulder to match the gutter marks on my arms. In a couple hours, I'd crave another hit of Atroxipine as my mind slowed, but that was part of the fun. The ritual of addiction was as important as the addiction itself.

She wound through these destroyed streets. The landscape like the abandoned set of a dystopian movie, but it was not a movie. All the players had left. Houses blown out from the center and collapsing from the inside. Cars forgotten and raised on concrete blocks. Old gas pumps from a station that stopped being functional in the seventies. Classic cars, piled up in junk yards.

She turned down the side roads and skirted the edges of the town. I smoked with my good hand, and finally the car came to a stop on the parking lot. We remained in the car, listening to the engine cool and the scavenger at my side, shifting his wings and preening before I finally flicked the butt and stepped out.

Elvedina rose beside me, my living shadow.

"I'll meet you inside," I told her. "I'm going to make a phone call first."

She nodded and headed there with her determined and steady gait. Automated and exact. I stared at her and thought she looked different to me now than she did before, when I thought she was trying to kill me. Now that I knew and understood other forces between Lionel, the Inspector, and my father had been at work trying to snuff me out and the only thing standing between them and me had been Elvedina—everything about her was changed.

I brought out the brand new cell phone. I thumbed over the screen. I was tempted to turn it on until I decided to hell with it and tossed it into the brush beside the parking lot. It hit the curb and bounced into the air and landed in a dense thicket of weeds. The vulture, ever present, squawked once and subsided into silence. Like my false appendage, the bird had become a part of me now.

Uncomfortable and not quite seamless, but getting there. Learning to acclimate. I'd been dead once before. This would be a cinch.

I headed into the police station. Several of the officers working the desk already knew who I was. I'd been in and out since the accident and they all knew I was friends with Lafferty, the evidence room troll. I made my greetings with a stiff nod of my head and some even made it over the counter to shake my good hand like they weren't ever going to see me again. They had no idea that not that long ago, I'd been the misanthrope called Vitus with the bad skin condition. Now I was Amos to them, protected from on high by a mystical and unseen hand, a murderer walking free—oddly familiar, but if they suspected, they kept it to themselves.

I picked up the pay phone by the desk and dialed the number without dropping change in. This was a number that worked for anyone who had it. I listened to dispatch try to calm down a woman who'd been in a collision while the phone clicked and rang on the other end. A television behind the desk stayed on CNN. The news ticker flashed by in a word salad while a nice-looking man with a fake plastic haircut conveyed a serious message about deaths in the Middle East.

After a minute of ringing, the line picked up.

There was no sound on the other end. There wouldn't be. It wasn't that kind of line.

He guessed who it was, just the same.

"Vitus," the old gray fox said.

"You don't send another errand boy to kill me, and I might just forgive you," I said. I nodded and smiled to a passing police officer dragging a juvenile delinquent behind her and kept my voice light and conversational, my smile tacked in place.

"We know Lionel is dead. Your handiwork?"

"Something to do with a grenade," I answered. "But I'm sure a certain muscle-bound weight lifter who left the scene must have kept you informed. I wonder how he's doing. Maybe I'll see his face on a milk carton soon."

He fell silent. I wondered if he remembered all those times he and Lionel had been close, had been shoved into quarters and sleeping in barracks. Running missions on the sly and being mercenaries. Heads bent over school books as they studied political science together and memorized administrations, doctrines, and atrocities. Read aloud the ancient Greek classics and studied Latin.

"You should come to the capital and visit me soon, son. I was always fair with you. I always rewarded good work when I saw it. And you always were a hard worker. You just never showed an interest in those games that prized discipline and intellect."

"I'm not a child anymore," I said. "You remember *Oedipus Rex*."

"He lost his eyes, Vitus. You'll have to give up more than a partial limb to take my place. Have you visited your mother lately?"

"I've been meaning to."

"Tell her I love her. And do visit me sometime, Vitus. I have to be going now. I'll be late for the State of the Union address." *Click.*

I held the phone a moment longer before I hung it up. Past me and beyond the desk where a policeman filled out paperwork and a police woman trained him, I could see the television relaying an endless stream of news and propaganda. The program cut away to the House Chamber with Congress spread out before the central hub. A man stood up to take the lectern with the flag and the presidential seal behind him. An older gentleman smiling wide for the cameras and the news networks, his hair gray. His face, a wily fox's.

"You sure do look at lot like him," the younger cop said, pointing his pen at the television.

"I get that all the time," I said.

Elvedina touched my sleeve; it was time to get going. We went in tandem while Fluffy hung on for the ride. Officers and staff spared the spectacle of a vulture being escorted into a police station a wayward glance or two, but they had seen stranger occurrences. If no one was bleeding, they weren't interested, and all their paperwork wasn't going to do itself.

Down the hall to the last door. Down a series of steps and into the cellar lit by industrial bulbs. Lafferty moved from shelf to shelf down below in his wheelchair. When I got to the bottom, I heard his voice, booming and jovial as he turned to greet me. Elvedina leaned against concrete blocks before the first row of shelving, so still she seemed a part of the structure itself, immovable and anchored in place. Seeing her resolute and unbreathing invested in me a sense of rightness in the universe. I knew nothing about her, but I knew her machinery and algorithms were absolute. Incorruptible. She could not be seduced, persuaded, coerced. She could be tortured, beaten with rubber hoses, and never betray.

"Look who it is," Lafferty smiled and wheeled to me.

His time spent with Niko did him well. Bright and glowing like a teenager with his first steady. He might even have gained a pound or two in this happy bloom of romance. I wondered who would break their hearts first, him or her. In the end, it didn't matter.

"Vitus."

Niko.

I turned. When I'd been dead, it had been nothing to control the urges of the flesh. Seeing her alive set my belly on fire, the blood pounding through my veins and my heartbeat, tenderizing the underside of my chest. I remembered she and I together. The kitchen counter. Soap and foam.

"He told you," I said.

She came from between the crooked shelving, out of the darkness and into the light. Tapping over concrete with her black pumps. She painted her cat's eyes on today, hands thrust into the pockets of an indigo hooded shirt.

I hesitated. "I meant to tell you—"

"Bullshit you did. But rest easy. It's not as though you owe me anything, and I've given up having expectations. Throw a pretty woman into the world," she laughed, her teeth white like a crescent moon beneath her blood red lips, "and you all scramble over yourselves like lost children. Now, if that's not power, I don't know what is."

Self-conscious and confused and embarrassed, I'd forgotten I could blush now. Blood tingling the cheeks. I turned to Lafferty.

"I'm here for the evidence from my woe begone murder trial."

"I gave you the gun—"

"The *other* evidence," I said quietly. I looked pointedly at Niko and back at him.

He was silent. Elvedina absorbed it as though she were a black hole sucking in all the light around her, adding to her gravity. Niko stood with her hands on her hips, waiting.

"I wondered when you'd ask," he said. He wheeled back to a stack of shelves and opened a drawer beneath. He rooted through it with one hand and found it, dug it out, the brass key stuffed in his fist, and held it out.

I took it from him and stared at it in my hand. So small. This was all that stood between the world and what it kept locked away. I cleared my throat and looked at Niko and no one moved. As though we occupied a stage filled with props from old plays, waiting for the next narrative to play out.

"Maybe we should give him a moment alone," Lafferty said and gestured to Elvedina, but I reached out with my false hand without meaning to, restraining Elvedina.

"Stay with me," I asked her. I didn't want to beg or to plead but all my art fell away and I was naked as a newborn and raw with feeling, the Atroxipine reducing as much as it gave. Niko's eyes on me added a brand new, uncomfortable pressure. "Don't let me do this alone."

Elvedina nodded.

"I'll hang back," Lafferty offered. "Just shout if things get out of hand."

"Thanks."

Lafferty rolled to the counter with one determined spin of his wheels and shifted papers from one envelope to another. Niko did not move and though Elvedina remained close by, she no longer seemed beholden to all the rules and privations of human life—transhuman, and like myself, occupying a station in life to which normal laws did not apply.

"So now you know," I whispered to Niko.

I could see no trace of anger or betrayal in her any longer, leaving behind her smooth, unsmiling face, as serious as a tragedy mask. I cursed myself and wondered if this is what happened farther along down the Atroxipine spiral—those moments between one dose and another when the brain speed lags, or thoughts twitch and jump with too much power. Leading the way to confusion, missed signals, false flags.

"He loved Selina, very much. He was heartbroken to lose her. Not all men are like you, saving up their man-pain for a rainy day drunk. Why couldn't you have told me, Vitus?" Niko asked.

"Would it have mattered?"

She drew closer and I didn't move until her breath was at my ear, her hand on my shoulder. Both of us warm. The memory of our brief coupling, buried in that thrumming tension in the skin.

"If you were the type of man who didn't hesitate to ask questions like that, yeah, it would have. It would have mattered a lot."

I caught my breath and let it go. And when I did, I let her go with it.

"I'm sorry, Vitus. You don't need me. You've never needed me. Someone else needs me, now."

I closed my eyes.

"You're taking care of *him*, aren't you? After everything he's done."

"I take care of the dead. It's what I do, Vitus."

I looked at Elvedina but her gaze was faraway, scanning with ruthless efficiency the darkness and the concrete all around her.

"Yeah," I said. Unbothered and absorbed in the new mystery before me. I didn't know what it meant; I didn't know if I was changing for better or worse or Elvedina was insinuating her way into my every thought now. But you find with the advent of time and experience, letting things go becomes easier, not more difficult. Until every grudge and resentment burns off like impurities from a forge, leaving behind gleaming cold steel.

"Go on now," Lafferty said, and I realized then they were all waiting for me. Waiting for me to do what I knew I had to. The vulture snuffed at my hair and I jerked my head away and he resettled. I held the key out.

"Let's do this."

★

Through the heart of the evidence room, endless lines of shelves laid out like dominoes. A library of objects used in crime scenes proliferate toward the back. The bigger and more awkward the object, the more buried it becomes in the no man's land past the files and the rolls of money and the heaps of drugs.

But beyond all this is a door to the basement beneath this basement.

I punched the key in and once more looked at Elvedina. I doubted she had any sensation or capacity to feel. She intuited with her unearthly intelligence that I needed something more than silence to push me on.

"Get it done," she hissed.

I bore down on the lock. The tumblers clicked and the door swung wide into dark.

A single bulb on a bare chain swung from the center. A circle of light gave hint to bare and sweating walls where the room temperature was a steady sixty four degrees without the aid of air conditioning, the temperature of deep earth.

I stepped forward, every sense seeking the light. Elvedina spilled out behind me, our steps amplified in the balmy dark. The vulture on guard beside me. I made my way to the center of the room and wondered if I had taken a wrong turn. If there were more rooms and basements hidden away and I had stumbled into the wrong one.

Elvedina grabbed my collar in her fist and drew me back several inches. The vulture furiously flapping as a creature leaped from the shadows, grunting and rasping into the center. The figure snapped back at the end of his chain and drew it taut as he leaned to get at me. A straightjacket kept his arms pinned in the most terrible self-hug man can devise. His eyes bugged from their decaying sockets and his mouth opened, sucking in anaerobic air like a septic system. His skin peeling and rotting off his bone structure.

Elvedina released me. If she had not pulled me back, I would be standing where his jaws snapped and bit the air.

"Thanks," I swallowed.

I could not look away, but continued to stare at him before I jerked the bottle out from my pocket. I shook out two pills onto the palm of my false hand, balancing them there, and looked at Elvedina.

"Just . . . keep an eye on things, will you?"

Her silence was reassuring, when before it had been sinister. She nodded, once.

I leaned forward into the circle with the zombie, his eyes slowly turning sour, filming over with fungus and decay. I thrust my prosthetic forward and gripped him by the shoulder. He snapped and snarled and yowled but went in the direction of the hand like a carrot dangling from a stick. I guided him to it while he gnawed on the old plastic, tipping the pills into his mouth. He choked and swallowed. Red foam formed at his lips in a pink circle as I stepped away until I was back beside Elvedina.

She lifted her hand into the light and bared a wrist watch. The hand raced around the numerals as we counted down the minutes, the seconds. In increments, the pre-deceased individual began to quiet, his salivary glands shutting down. His eyes refocusing and his face gaining the familiar range of expression.

Had I looked like this, all those years? Walking backwards from death to life?

I shuddered.

At last, he lifted his head and stood erect.

"Vitus? Is that you?"

"Hi, Jamie."

He jerked his head back and forth in the darkness to assess the area and understand his situation. He blinked several times and then retreated within himself, becoming still as though he could summon dignity out of his situation and retain some portion of control out of his own personal catastrophe.

"I came here today to ask you," I said, "about the Echo Inspector."

Jamie blinked.

And he began to laugh. And laugh. And laugh.

Epilogue

FROM THE DEPARTMENT OF H.E.A.

"Take it off," she said in a whisper.

I unbuttoned my shirt with one hand. It's a skill I acquired during my convalescence, the art of being one-handed. I shrugged out of the shirt and let it drop to the floor. I unbuckled my belt and my clumsy fingers slipped; I cursed until she came forward and took it in hand. I searched her eyes for an emotion and wondered if she felt anything at all behind cogs and clockworks. I pretended her hands were somewhere else, that this was cold and impersonal. Just business.

The belt slipped away from me and snapped tight in her fists.

"Like this?"

"Yeah. Just like that," I whispered.

"Lower?"

"Mmmm, lower. Go lower. Yeah, just like that, right there—"

"Here?"

"Ye-ess, put it in . . ."

"You want this? You can stop, any time."

"I can't, do it, do it now."

A network of interlaced veins ran like rivers beneath the skin of my one good arm; my hand made into a fist, the belt held taut by Elvedina's reliable hands around my upper arm. Blood swelled with no place to go and the syringe balanced her hand, bending light and space through the glass. She set the needle against my arm. The skin formed a divot, and then punctured.

Five minutes before this, I was cooking Atroxipine with a Bunsen burner that used to be Jamie's. The lab beaker foamed up with a satisfying, yellow tint. I held it with my good hand, the only one I have that's real.

The other jutted out from my arm and stopped inches from where a wrist should be. When I'd been a zombie—or pre-deceased—losing pieces of myself was a condition I'd gotten used to, though it unnerved me regardless of how much I steeled myself for the inevitable decay. I took solace from the fact my body was so rotten that a butcher wouldn't keep it around to sell as shark chum, but here I'd been wearing a brand new one, and I had a head start on righteously fucking it up.

Chemical stench filled the confines of the ranch. While Elvedina depressed the needle and sent pure Atroxipine sky rocketing through my hungry blood stream, I paced back through a landmine of memories: Jessica and I had been married here and my son had learned how to walk here. And then afterward, I remembered, the tragedy. When I was dead and could not be coaxed back to life and every day was one long funeral in which no one came to bury me. The ensuing troubles when Jessica came back from the grave. Meeting Amos, who went by his alias and pulled me deeper into the conspiracy. The maggots that consumed me. And Jamie, stitching me into Amos's skin so I could live in the body of my dead nephew.

Falling back onto the mattress and trusting myself to the steadfast arms of a heartless, beautiful machine, feeding me this illicit honey through the vein. When I wanted to leave my body, I could, whenever I chose, as long as my refills on Atroxipine were endless. For now, I was satisfied to let it take me to a place where I could forget the past and metamorphose without pain;

to curl up like a child in a place beyond sleep, where no Echo Inspector could follow me into the abyss, where I could be safe in my private inferno, and awaken on the other side, truly human as if for the first time. Cast away the psychopathy of my zombie years, leaving me hollow. Leaving life meaningless without something to numb it, to fill it, to control it.

Atroxipine. Let's ride out into the sunset together.

Forget everything, long enough to recover and start over again. This white out, this raw heat, enough to sustain me while I gather my strength.

Because in the shadows, the Inspector waits. My father waits. Medals on his chest, his ring on his finger that scratched my face a thousand times. And the monsters my brother made, forming an invisible army. Polly far away from here in a South American country. I wished her well. Hoped her nights were dreamless.

The only thought I have, as I fell back onto the table with Elvedina holding my belt in her hands, is this is as good as life gets.

I white out, riding an Atroxipine haze.

This is my happily ever after.